Skeletons in the closet . . .

"You know about the skeleton on the boat they raised?"

"Yes . . . How dreadful for the divers, to find something like that."

Shelly nodded. "We're involved again."

"Who is?"

"The shop, Crewel World."

"I don't understand."

"They've left a big clue in our shop, and people are being asked to look at it and see if they can identify it."

"What is it?"

"It's a piece of silk with lace edging, or rather a picture of it. It was found on the boat, which means it went down with it in 1949. No one has come up with anything yet, but you just watch. Of course, Betsy won't suspect you or me, because we weren't around in 1949."

FRAMED IN LACE

Monica Ferris

BERKLEY PRIME CRIME, NEW YORK

This is a work of fiction. Names, characters, places, and incidents
either are the product of the author's imagination or are used
fictitiously, and any resemblance to actual persons, living or dead,
business establishments, events, or locales is entirely coincidental.

FRAMED IN LACE

A Berkley Prime Crime Book / published by arrangement with
the author

PRINTING HISTORY
Berkley Prime Crime edition / October 1999

Visit our website at
www.penguinputnam.com

ISBN: 0-425-17149-3

Berkley Prime Crime Books are published
by The Berkley Publishing Group,
a division of Penguin Putnam Inc.,
375 Hudson Street, New York, New York 10014.
The name BERKLEY PRIME CRIME and the BERKLEY PRIME CRIME
design are trademarks belonging to Penguin Putnam Inc.

PRINTED IN THE UNITED STATES OF AMERICA

10 9 8 7 6 5 4

FRAMED IN LACE

1

It wasn't even Halloween, but autumn was over. Betsy sat at the little round table in the dining nook of her apartment and gazed out the back window. There was a small parking lot, with the ground beyond rising steeply through mature trees. Only yesterday the trees were ablaze with orange, red, and yellow leaves. She had planned to drive around Lake Minnetonka this weekend and take in the colors. But there had been a hard freeze last night, and now, in a light breeze, there was a Technicolor blizzard on the slope that would leave the branches bare by nightfall. Already she could see a gas station and a white clapboard house that had been hidden by foliage yesterday. The sky was clear, the sun was bright, but the weatherman on the radio had said that perhaps the temperature would break fifty by early afternoon.

Betsy, fresh from San Diego, didn't have much of a winter wardrobe. She had planned to buy winter woolens locally—Minnesota was heavily Scandinavian, and

Betsy just loved their sweaters—but hadn't realized she'd need them so soon. Today she was wearing her warmest work outfit: a federal-blue cotton skirt, a bell-sleeved white blouse, and a brown felt vest with carved wooden buttons.

She looked at her watch and hastily drank the last of her tea. She put the empty cup and the plate that had held a fried egg sandwich into the sink. Sophie was already at the door of the apartment, ready to accompany her to work. The cat had a better sense of time than she did—not surprising, really. Sophie had been her sister's cat, and therefore in the business longer than Betsy had.

Like the Queen of England, Betsy "lived above the shop." She went out the door, down the stairs, and to the obscure door into a back hallway that led to the back door of Crewel World. Sophie trundled along beside her.

It was just nine-forty, and the store opened at ten, but the back door was unlocked. Betsy froze with her hand on the knob, key in the lock. The last time she had gone through a door that should have been locked, she had found her sister's body.

Sophie made an inquiring noise, and Betsy waved a shushing hand at her while she leaned forward to listen at the door. Faint conversation. One voice, a light tenor, rose to understandability: "And I'm just *so* fond of magenta, it's a warm, clear color without being *quite* so simple as red."

There was a murmur as another voice replied; but Betsy couldn't understand the words.

"That's *right!* You know, it's just *great* dealing with a customer who has a decent sense of color."

While Betsy hadn't understood the reply, she heard the pleased note in the voice, and she smiled as she opened the door into the back room. Sophie scooted through, and she closed it behind her firmly enough to be heard in the shop.

"Oh, good, now I won't have to make change out of my own pocket," said the tenor. "*Good* morning, Betsy!"

"Good morning, Godwin," replied Betsy, coming into the shop and pausing automatically. Sunlight poured between the front-window displays of counted cross-stitch patterns and needlepoint projects. It lit up the counters and tables with their baskets of wool, cotton, and silk. On one wall, the big swinging doors that held painted canvases stood open just enough to call attention to themselves. Near the front door was an old dresser painted white, its dim mirror holding advertisements for conventions and classes on knitting and needlepoint. All looked in perfect order.

The customer was a medium-sized woman in a long tweed coat, and in her hands hung a sky blue drawstring plastic bag. It had Crewel World printed on it in little *X*s, as if worked in cross-stitch.

"Good morning, Mrs. Schuster," said Betsy.

"Good morning, Betsy. I was on my way to the Waterfront Café for breakfast when I saw lights on in your shop and stopped to see if I could pick up my order of magenta silk, and Godwin was kind enough to unlock the door."

"How's the project coming?" asked Betsy, going behind the big desk that served as a checkout counter.

"Very, very well," said Mrs. Schuster. Encouraged by the question and still pleased at Godwin's compliments, she pulled a needlepoint canvas from the bag. It was a square canvas of grapes and grape leaves, not quite abstract. The stitching was an appropriate and very competent basket weave. When finished and framed, it would hang in the office of a friend of Mrs. Schuster's, who vinted wines as a hobby. The grapes were being done in silk, the leaves were already stitched in various green wools.

"Oh, I like how it's turning out," said Godwin, coming to look. "You were so clever to do the grapes in silk to make them shimmer." He cocked his head. "Chalk-white wool for the background, of course."

"Yes—of course," said Mrs. Schuster, and Betsy shot him a grateful look. Mrs. Schuster had taken up a lot of Betsy's time discussing colors and fibers for this project and had changed her mind three times about the background.

But Betsy wasn't surprised that Mrs. Schuster was quick to take Godwin's suggestion. The young man had developed a serious talent for needlework during the two years he'd worked for Betsy's sister and now for Betsy. That he was gay only added to his reputation for selecting the right color and texture for any project.

Betsy was new in town, and not knowledgeable about needlework or about running a shop. Crewel World had been her sister's, and for her sister's sake its customers were giving her every chance to climb the steep learning curve into the intricate world of needlework.

Mrs. Schuster left with her magenta silk and enough white wool to do the background of her project. As she went up Lake Street, her breath streamed out behind her. *Brrr*, thought Betsy. *And it's not even Halloween yet*.

She looked around again. The track lights were on, the front door unlocked, the needlepoint sign turned so that Open faced the street. When Mrs. Schuster had paid her bill, Betsy had put the forty dollars of startup money in the old-fashioned cash register. The hot-dust smell in the air meant Godwin had turned up the heat. Even as she turned to remind him, he was stooping to turn on the Bose radio, tuned to a classical music station. Sophie clambered up onto "her" chair, the one with a powder blue cushion that set off her white fur with the tan and gray patches perfectly. They were ready for business.

"What brought you in early?" asked Betsy.

"Oh, John was being a pissant last night, so I just went to bed early; and so I got up early, and so here I am." John was the wealthy lawyer Godwin lived with, whose support enabled Godwin to work for slave wages at Crewel World.

"Trouble?" asked Betsy.

"Oh, nothing we haven't had before. He's so *jealous*, and really, right now I'm not giving him the least *reason* to be jealous." Godwin tossed his head. He was a slender man, a little under medium height, and his wardrobe tended toward Calvin Klein Slim Fit jeans and silk knit shirts, though today, in honor of the season's change, he was wearing a brown-plaid shirt under a fine-woven Perry Ellis sweater with textured pinstripes. His short hair was an enhanced blond color, his eyes a guileless blue, his nose almost too perfect. He looked eighteen, though Betsy knew he would be twenty-six in December.

Betsy smiled at him even as she hoped there wasn't a breakup in Godwin's future. He was her best employee: knowledgeable, loyal, and reliable. He could be charming, gossipy, witty, and sympathetic in turn with customers, all in an exaggerated, self-deprecating way designed to make them remember him, talk about him, and come back for more. Betsy sometimes wondered if there was a deeper, more reflective Godwin—though she had no intention of doing an archaeological dig on his personality. He suited her, and the shop, just fine as he was.

He smiled back, and they moved with one accord to the library table in the middle of the floor. They sat down opposite one another. Betsy reached into the basket under the table, he unzipped his canvas sport-club bag, and each pulled out a project. Godwin was knitting a pair of white cotton socks. Betsy was trying to learn knitting in the round by making a pair of mittens.

Betsy found where she'd left off and, after a brief struggle, got her needles under control. Knitting with alpaca wool onto three double-pointed needles is a definite step up from stretchy polyester yarn on two single-point needles. She glanced across at Godwin who was knitting with tiny, swift gestures while looking out the window. He had turned the heel of his sock and was heading for the toe.

"Why do you knit your own socks when they're so cheap to buy?" asked Betsy after a few minutes. "And why white? I should think you'd be into argyle or at least magenta."

He laughed. "I'd *love* to wear magenta socks! But my feet are so *sensitive*, they break out in *ugly red welts* when I put colors or anything but one hundred percent *cotton* socks on them. And advertisers will say *anything* to get you to buy their products."

"Uh-huh," said Betsy, who had never been plagued with allergies.

"The weatherman says snow flurries tomorrow, did you hear?" said Godwin. "Say, did I ever tell you about our Halloween blizzard?"

"Yes, you did, at the same time you told me that I really should get going on my mittens." She had thought the famous Halloween blizzard a serious anomaly in the Minnesota weather until she, too, had heard the forecast. Snow flurries in October were apparently standard: the weatherman had been blasé about his prediction. Minnesota children must wear snowsuits under their costumes when they go trick or treating, thought Betsy.

She had been raised in Milwaukee and thought she had a good grasp of winter weather in the upper midwest, but she couldn't remember snow of any sort in October in Milwaukee. Good thing she was going to the Mall of America tomorrow on her day off. She would buy sweaters. And a winter coat and hat. And mittens. She was only halfway up the cuff of her first mitten, and at the rate she was going, she wouldn't have this pair finished until January. The only thing she didn't need by way of winter wear was a scarf. She had learned to knit by making herself a beautiful bright red scarf.

Betsy had come to Excelsior from San Diego at the end of August for an extended visit, planning to work her way through a midlife crisis. She'd been here barely a week when her sister was murdered. The police had thought Margot had interrupted a burglar in her shop, but Betsy had been convinced there was a more sinister connection between the shop and her sister's murder. She was proved right, and because of her efforts a murderer was in jail awaiting trial.

Shortly before her death, Margot had incorporated Crewel World, naming Betsy as vice-president. Now, as sole surviving officer, Betsy could do as she liked with the shop. She had thought to close or sell it, but since she had to remain in town anyway until her sister's estate was settled, and because Crewel World's customers were both friendly and insistent she not do anything hasty, Betsy was still here and Crewel World was still open. And, perhaps, dealing every day with people who had known Margot well was a way of holding onto her just a little while longer.

Betsy Devonshire was fifty-five, with graying brown hair and big blue eyes surrounded by lots of laugh lines, plump but not unattractively so. The loss of her sister was too recent to do other than weigh heavily on her heart, and the midlife crisis that had brought her to Minnesota had been triggered by an angry divorce, so the fact that at times she could smile and even laugh was proof of a resilient soul.

There was something else that helped. Margot had been the childless widow of a self-made millionaire. Since Betsy was Margot's only sibling, the estate would come entirely to her. The prospect of wealth made Betsy more of a gambler than she might otherwise have been.

At ten-thirty, the knitting became an aggravation and she put it away. "Coffee?" she asked Godwin.

"Thanks," he said. "You know, you can work on more than one thing at a time."

"I know. I'm going to try one of those little Christmas ornaments I ordered. I hope counted cross-stitch isn't as confusing to learn as needlepoint was." Betsy had long ago mastered embroidery, but only recently picked up the basics of needlepoint. To round out her understanding of her customers, she needed to venture into counted cross-stitch.

She paused on her way to the back room to stroke Sophie, who, after a hard morning of getting Betsy out of bed, wolfing down her pittance of Iams Less Active cat food, and making the long, difficult journey down the stairs and along to the back entrance, was ready for her morning nap. Perhaps it really was a difficult journey; Sophie had broken her hind leg a few weeks ago and still wore the cast, which she now arranged in what Betsy was sure was an obvious display. Sophie had quickly learned that seeing the cast excited customers to sympathy and even small treats.

I believe she'll be sorry when that leg heals, thought Betsy, bending to search in the tiny refrigerator for a bottle of V8 Extra Spicy for herself before pouring Godwin's coffee into a pretty porcelain cup.

She had barely brought them back to the table when a shadow darkened the doorway. There was an electronic *bing* as the door opened to admit police officer Jill Cross. An expert needlepointer, she was a tall woman who looked even bigger in her dark uniform jacket, hat, and utility belt. But her face below the cap was the sweet oval of a Gibson girl, and her figure, while sturdily built, was definitely female.

"Hi, Jill," said Godwin, getting to his feet. "How may I help you?"

"Trade jobs with me," said Jill in her best deadpan.

"Not bloody likely," Godwin said sincerely, then added, "Tough day already?"

"No worse than usual," she sighed, then brightened. "But I think things are improving. Betsy, can I offer you a change in plans? They're raising the *Hopkins* this morning; Lars and I are assigned to boat duty. Want to come along?"

Betsy hesitated. She didn't want to change plans; she really wanted to go to the Mall of America, where Shop Till You Drop was an actual possibility.

Godwin said, "How about you take off the morning today, Betsy, and tomorrow afternoon? I'll be okay here by myself; it's shaping up to be a slow day."

Jill said, "It must be something to watch; there's been a crowd gathering since daylight."

Betsy weakened. "Is it okay to take me along in a police boat?"

"Sure. It'll be a kind of ride-along. Except it isn't a police boat; Lars is using his own."

Jill had twice asked Betsy if she wanted to go for a ride-along in her squad car for a shift, to get a look at police work on a street level. But Betsy, needing all the time she could get hold of to learn how to run a small business, hadn't found a big enough block of time to go.

She asked, "What's the *Hopkins*, that they want to raise it?"

"You saw the *Minnehaha* before they pulled her out of the water for the winter?"

Betsy nodded. The old steam-powered boat had been raised from the bottom of the lake and restored by a local group of volunteers. It retraced part of its old route on weekends for tourists. Its shape was reminiscent of a streetcar—which was deliberate, as it had originally been one of six boats owned by Minneapolis Rapid Transit and used to take passengers to the Twin Cities streetcar terminus in Wayzata.

Besides being a wreck on the bottom of the lake, how did the *Hopkins* relate to the *Minnehaha*? "Oh, the *Hopkins* is another one of those streetcar boats!"

"Yep," said Jill. "The *Minnehaha* is doing so well that the people who restored her want to do the same with the *Hopkins*. They thought they'd have the money by next spring, but an important grant came through, and now they'll have all winter to work on her restoration."

"I hear the Queen of Excelsior Excursions are so pleased they're going to have more competition they could just spit," said Godwin. Queen of Excelsior Excursions sailed along without volunteers or grants and made a profit besides.

"They'll manage," said Jill, and to Betsy, "Want to come?"

"How long will it take?"

"They only asked for police patrol till noon, so Godwin's right that you could go with us this morning and still go shopping tomorrow afternoon."

"Then I think I'd like to see it. When do we leave?"

"I'm supposed to meet Lars down at the wharf in fifteen minutes. Better go change into slacks and a sweater. And bring your jacket, it's chilly, though not as cold as it could be. Say, did I ever tell you about the Halloween blizzard?''

"Yes, you did, but why don't you compare notes with Godwin while I go upstairs and change?"

Betsy reappeared six minutes later in an old pair of jeans and her heaviest sweater. She had a long-sleeved T-shirt on under that, and her only jacket over one arm. She hoped the boat wasn't fishy.

It wasn't. It was an immaculate flat-bottomed, flat-topped, four-seater, fiberglass, with a windshield and a steering wheel. It reminded Betsy of a '70s compact car; it was even two-toned, raspberry and cream, and its motor was hidden under a hood at the back. It being Lars's boat, he got to drive.

Lars was Jill's boyfriend, a big blond Norwegian who looked like a poster telling schoolchildren The Police-man is Your Friend. His huge hands were callused, which surprised Betsy when she shook hands until she remembered Jill had told her he was buying a five-acre hobby farm. The notion that someone might take on the labor of farming as a hobby amazed Betsy, but Lars had done it, and he worked as hard on it as he did at being a policeman.

The boat's motor burbled deeply as they pulled away from the dock, then Lars pushed a lever and it roared, stood up on its stern, and went flying over the blue water.

Betsy shouted to Jill, "Where are we going?"

Jill shouted back, "Other side of the Big Island!" She pointed to what looked like part of the shoreline on the north side of Excelsior Bay. But as the boat went by it, Betsy saw that it was indeed an island.

As they came around to the other side, Betsy could see two barges sitting broadside to one another, each with a crane on it. Near the barges were eight or ten motorboats and a couple of sailboats, their sails furled. Lars slowed as they approached, and when the roar of his motors fell to a guttural murmur, Jill picked up a small bullhorn.

"Move back from the barges!" she ordered. "You are in danger of being struck from below! Move back from the barges!"

Heads swiveled, but nobody moved.

"Is that true?" asked Betsy. "Being struck from below?"

"There's a seventy-foot boat down there," Jill replied. "It's gonna need some room when it comes up." She spoke into the bullhorn again. "This is the police! Move back from the cranes!"

That worked. Boats started moving. Betsy looked at the slowly widening area around the barges. She could see cables running from the cranes into the water, which was otherwise undisturbed. Huge engines in the cranes whined deeply. "Is it happening now?"

"Beats me," Jill shrugged. "Our job is to keep the gawkers away until after it does."

"And then to keep them from bumping into the thing, or climbing on it, or trying to steal hunks of it for souvenirs," added Lars.

Betsy chuckled uncertainly. "People wouldn't actually do that, would they?"

Lars said over his shoulder, "Civilians do things you wouldn't believe. I was sitting in a Shop and Go parking lot so near the door the guy in the ski mask had to walk around me to get in and hold up the place. I actually sat there and watched him do it. I couldn't believe it. And guess what he said when I busted him?"

When Betsy shrugged, Jill said, "What they always say." She and Lars drawled in unison, " 'I didn't dooo nuthin'!' '' Then she and Lars laughed wicked, evil laughs.

The whining of the cranes went on long enough that Betsy began to realize that was the sound of their engines in neutral. Lars and Jill realized it, too, and, once they had established a perimeter, they relaxed and took turns telling Betsy stupid-crook stories. The stories were so hilarious Betsy forgot this was taking a lot longer than she thought it would.

The sun shone, the water rocked the boat. Lars and Jill removed their jackets. A couple of the motorboats went away, a new one joined the watchers. Several of the boats standing watch were of a size that looked capable of going to sea. Betsy wondered what kind of job it took to afford a cabin cruiser and yet have time to come out on a Tuesday morning to watch volunteers raise an old boat.

Jill identified some of the boats, gossiped a little about their owners. ''I thought Billy'd left for Florida by now,'' she noted about one called *The Waterhole*.

''What, is there a river out of Lake Minnetonka that connects to the Mississippi?'' asked Betsy.

''Yes, but it's not deep enough for that boat,'' said Jill.

''Not to mention the sudden forty-foot drop going over Minnehaha Falls,'' added Lars with a grin.

''Then how does he get that boat down to Florida?'' asked Betsy.

''He doesn't,'' said Jill. ''He has an even bigger boat down there.''

''Is it called *The Waterhole Two*? And why *Waterhole*?''

Lars said, ''Anyone with a boat will tell you that it is a hole in the water into which you pour money.''

Jill added, ''And a water hole is a place where animals

come to drink, which is why taverns are sometimes called water holes. Billy's a party animal, and you'd be surprised how many people he can haul in that boat.''

''You know something about just about every boat owner out here,'' said Betsy. ''Is that because you're a police officer, or do you have a boat, too?''

Lars laughed. ''Neither; it's because she's from Excelsior, gossip capital of the state.''

''Have you lived here long, Jill?'' asked Betsy.

''Third generation,'' nodded Jill. ''My grandfather used to run the ferris wheel at the Excelsior Amusement Park, and my mother put herself through nursing school by working at the Blue Ribbon Café at the Park.''

Betsy said, ''That's right, I've heard that there used to be an amusement park in Excelsior. This is a sweet little town; it doesn't seem like the kind of town for that. I mean especially years ago, when amusement parks weren't the high-class operations they are today.''

''Oh, it was pretty high class,'' said Jill with something in her voice Betsy couldn't read.

''Did your father work in it, too?''

''He was a highway patrolman. His uncle was a deputy sheriff, and my mother's brother was an investigator on the Saint Paul cops.''

''So you kind of went into the family business,'' said Betsy with a smile.

''It does run in families,'' agreed Jill. ''What did your father do?''

''He worked in the engineering department of Poland and Harnischfeger in Milwaukee. They build cranes. I still catch myself looking for the P&H logo whenever I see a crane. It never occurred to me to follow in his footsteps, but when I was small I used to wish there were still cattle drives, because *his* dad was a cowboy in Utah, and I thought that was one of the great, romantic jobs.

My dad used to tell some great stories about him."

"Can you ride?"

"I used to be good at it. You?"

"Oh, I don't fall off half as much as I used to." Jill looked out toward a boat drifting close to the perimeter she and Lars had established, but it stopped before crossing it. "You know what I've always wanted to do?" she asked.

"What?"

"Go on one of those cattle drives. They still have them in some places, and they allow paying guests to take part. You get your own horse to take care of and you help keep the steers in line."

Betsy stared at her. "Really? Where does this happen, in Texas?"

"They run one in South Dakota, less than a day's drive from here. Lars won't go with me."

"Gosh." Betsy's eyes became distant. The lowing of cattle, the dust of the trail, the campfire at night, sleeping under the stars . . .

"Want me to find out the details? We can go next year, maybe."

Betsy tried to make her acceptance as casual as the offer. "I'd like that very much. Thanks."

They fell silent for awhile. The sun warmed the air, the boat rocked, the motor burbled and gave off noxious fumes. Betsy began to feel a curious combination of sick and sleepy. She regretted the fried-egg sandwich she'd had for breakfast, then the seafood salad she'd had for supper last night. She was beginning to be concerned about the lo mein noodles she'd had for lunch yesterday when Lars said suddenly, "I think we're gonna see some action now. And look over there!" He pushed a lever that stirred up the motor and steered the boat toward the nearer barge.

Jill shouted through the bullhorn, "You in the blue boat, you're in danger! Move back, away from the barge!" The passengers, a man and two women, turned to look at Jill. One woman waved to show she wasn't concerned. "Move . . . away . . . from the . . . barge!" repeated Jill. "Now!"

The man shouted something at whoever was steering, and the boat began to shift around. The woman stopped waving and instead made a rude gesture.

Uh-oh, thought Betsy, and was surprised when Lars didn't go after them but only moved back himself. Then she heard a serious change in the sound of the cranes' big engines, and her attention came back to the space between the cranes. The water roiled, as if about to boil. Smoothly, as if in time-lapse film, enormous black mushrooms bloomed onto the surface. They were floats, balloons, in three clusters of three. The cranes' engines were straining now, and big drops of water drooled off the cables. Betsy realized belatedly the cables were moving.

Then, gently as dawn, a long, sleek object appeared under and then just on the surface. As it rose, water sluiced away, and Betsy could see the lines of curved boards appear, gleaming in the sun. More of the object appeared, and still more, until it was a boat about seventy feet long, canted to one side, held in place by wrappings of cable. It didn't look much like the restored streetcar boat; there were no railings, no cabin, no upper deck, just this long, narrow wooden boat.

Air horns saluted the arrival of the *Hopkins*, and only when they stopped could Betsy hear the people cheering.

Waterfalls of various sizes cascaded off the boat, and the crane operators did something so that it mostly righted itself. Three men in black diver's wet suits appeared at the edge of the far barge and dived in. They swam to the boat and helped one another aboard. They began a quick, running inspection. One picked up a large rock and threw it over the side. Then he threw a hunk of what looked like concrete, and then another rock.

"They weighed the boat down with rubble before they sank it," said Jill to Betsy. "The divers threw a lot of it overboard before it was raised, but I guess there's more still in there."

Betsy could see the divers to their waists as they moved along the boat and she deduced the presence of a deck, because otherwise they'd be out of sight. As soon as she realized that, the rubble-tossing diver went out of sight. Betsy was deducing a ladder when he straightened—he'd only bent over. He shouted and gestured to the other two divers. They came running, and more rubble was tossed. Then one leaned against the side of the boat to shout, "Police! Police!"

Lars glanced at Jill, who nodded, and Lars ran his boat alongside the big boat.

"Got something here you should look at!" the diver shouted.

"You stay here," Jill said to both Lars and Betsy. She raised her arms and was lifted over the side of the raised boat, which Betsy could now see had once been painted white. But there was lots of slime on the boards, and Jill had to scrabble for a foothold. Her light blue shirt and dark trousers were smeared by the time she vanished over the gunwales.

She reappeared less than a minute later. "Lars, there's a human skeleton under the floorboards of this thing. Looks to be adult size. Call it in." She went away again.

"Be damned," said Lars, and he reached for the radio microphone on the shoulder flap of his jacket.

Betsy rose to her feet, not sure if she did or did not want Jill to pick up the skull so she could see it. Wow,

a skeleton! Had a diver from years ago been exploring
the wreck and gotten trapped? Or was it a murder victim,
the knife still stuck between the ribs? The boat had been
filled with rubble, so the murderer must also have been
a diver. Betsy had a sudden image of a man in a wet
suit hauling a motionless victim down, down into the
depths of the lake, finding the boat, moving hundreds of
pounds of rubble—no, that was silly.

What it probably was, was a diver who found a hatch
he could open and went in exploring. Then something
in there ripped his air hose, and he panicked and
couldn't find the hatch to get out again. Poor fellow.

She sat down, the image shifting to what the skeleton
might look like now. Sprawled and shining white, the
ruins of his wet suit crumpled around him. Were there
clues to his identity? A wedding ring perhaps, one with
initials engraved inside it? Or an ID bracelet? She could
imagine the metal, at first dimmed by algae, which
would slowly yield to rubbing, and the letters would
appear. And an old mystery of a disappearance would
be solved at last. How exceedingly interesting!

2

Detective Mike Malloy watched the medical examiner cover the bones laid out on a metal table. Malloy had been present during the examination—it could hardly be called an autopsy—and had taken notes. Now he consulted his notes and read the important parts back to make sure he hadn't missed or misunderstood anything.

"You say the skeleton is about ninety-five percent complete," he began. "That it is a white female older than eighteen but younger than thirty-five at her time of death." He stopped to glance at the medical examiner.

"That's right," nodded Dr. Pascuzzi, a darkly handsome man.

Malloy consulted his notes again. He was a redhead with a thickly freckled face, light blue eyes, and a thin mouth. His suit was conservative, his shoes freshly but not highly polished, and he tended to think before he said anything. His career goal was to be sheriff of some rural Minnesota county, one with a really good bass lake in it; so his criminal investigations, like everything else about him, tended to be by-the-book and not splashy. He didn't like this case because it was odd and was already drawing inquiries from the media. Investigators who got known for notorious cases didn't get asked to run for out-state sheriff.

"I noticed the skull was badly damaged when I saw it on the boat, the *Hopkins*," Malloy continued. "But I thought it might've got that way banging against things under the water." He raised a pale, inquiring eyebrow at the ME.

"No, I'm sure the injuries to the face and skull happened shortly before or very soon after death. The same for the broken radius." He saw a lack of comprehension in the police investigator and said, "The smaller of the two bones in the forearm."

"Oh, yeah." Malloy searched through his notes and found the place.

"Like the other injuries," said Dr. Pascuzzi, "it happened right about the time of death."

"How can you tell that?"

"Because it happened to living bone, but there is no evidence of healing. My opinion is that it was a defense wound."

"Sure, I get it." People under attack would raise a hand or arm and it would get injured; Malloy had seen examples of that. Weird that there might be such specific evidence of something so momentary in a crime this old.

But finding it meant this was a homicide, all right; there was no other way to explain the injuries. And then, of course, there was the hiding of the body on the boat.

He continued to recite, "You say she was about five feet, two inches tall, not skin and bones or a fatso." What Dr. Pascuzzi had said was that she had been neither emaciated nor obese, but Malloy liked his English plain. He went on, "You said that when a woman has a baby, it leaves marks on her skeleton, but you don't find those marks on this one. I suppose if she was pregnant at the time of death, we could tell that?"

"Not necessarily. If she were in the first trimester, there would be no way to know."

Malloy nodded and added a little note. "You said her front teeth were broken?"

"Yes, and probably also at the time of death. I also noticed some problems with decay that might indicate she wasn't fond of the dentist. Or, perhaps, was too poor to afford proper dental care."

"So a lower-class woman who maybe had been beat up some."

"Well . . ." Pascuzzi rocked his hand to indicate doubt. "Women who are abused regularly show other signs of it, healed broken ribs or fingers. I saw no signs of that. I do think her nose might have been broken, probably while she was in her early teens, but that's all."

Still, this last severe battering to the face indicated rage or deep-seated hatred. A husband, maybe. Or a boyfriend. In either case, Malloy thought, what we probably have is an old-fashioned domestic that got out of hand. The *Hopkins* was sunk in 1949; it was possible the perp was still around. And that would for sure be a lead story on the evening news, with a camera shot of the cops rolling up to the nursing home to take him away.

Dr. Pascuzzi asked, "Want more?"

"Is there more?"

"By the look of the wear on the shoulders, elbows, and wrists she did a lot of hard labor. On the other hand, there aren't the changes to ankle and knee joints that mean prolonged squatting or kneeling. Not a char lady then, hauling water-filled buckets and kneeling to scrub floors. She might have been a farmer's wife who helped out in the dairy barn. Or a waitress, staggering under heavy trays of food. When was the boat she was found on sunk?''

"About fifty years ago."

"Not long after World War II, then. So perhaps she worked in a factory or drove a truck during the war. There are some small signs of malnutrition, not uncommon on the skeletons of people who grew up during the Depression. Apart from the nose, I find no sign of injuries or any illness that would leave its mark on bone."

Malloy grunted. That, plus the lack of dental work, was going to make positive identification difficult.

"Enough?" asked Pascuzzi again.

"For now. You'll send me a copy of your report when?"

"Couple of days. I may be able to come closer in my estimate of her age, weight, and height."

"Thanks," said Malloy and left him to it.

Malloy was right; the story of the skeleton received heavy play in the media. Small wonder that the following Monday, seven days after the discovery, the Monday Bunch gathered eagerly for its weekly meeting at Crewel World. Betsy, they knew, had been out on Lake Minnetonka watching when the *Hopkins* had come to the surface with its grisly surprise. Betsy had taken a major role in solving her sister's murder, so they were sure she had come to some marvelous conclusions about this new crime and knew things that had not yet turned up in print or on television. Thrilled to have an opportunity to hear from her in person, the women turned out in force.

The Monday Bunch was an informal group of women who loved needlework and were free at two on Monday afternoons. Some were retired, some were homemakers, some worked part-time or nights, one even arranged for a very late lunch hour. The numbers varied from week to week, rarely rising above four or five. Today, every current member was present, all eleven. Betsy had to bring folding chairs from the back.

"Did you see it?" asked Alice Skoglund, a large woman, not just plump but tall and big-boned. She had faded yellow hair well mixed with gray and a lot of jaw. Her plastic-framed eyeglasses caught the light as she looked toward Betsy. Her fingers moved mechanically, crocheting afghan squares in bright-colored polyester yarn, dropping them as they were finished into a plastic bag already bulging with them. "The skeleton, I mean."

Eyes looked everywhere but at Betsy, most at the needlework in hand. They all wanted details, too, but were embarrassed that one of their number was so open in her inquiry.

"No," said Betsy. She sat at the head of the table, where she could see the front door in case a customer came in. A cordless phone stood handy in case a customer wanted to call in an order from home. She was still working on that first mitten. Last night's flurries had melted, but under a gray sky the temperature struggled to reach forty.

"It must have been exciting out there," said Martha Winters, a pleasant-faced woman who at seventy-four worked only part-time in her dry cleaning shop, but whose eyes were still sharp enough for her to do counted cross-stitch on twenty-four-count evenweave. Flick, flick went her needle, and a chickadee had a beak.

"Oh, not so much," said Betsy "Well, it was exciting to see the boat actually come up, but we waited a long time for that to happen."

"And when it did come up, who found the skeleton?" asked Martha's bosom companion, Jessica Turnquist.

Jessica was three inches taller but twenty pounds lighter than Martha. She had a long face with large, slightly bulgy eyes, and a patrician nose over a mouth pressed thin by years of firm opinions. Jessica was crocheting a white baby blanket in swift popcorn stitch; it looked as if a cloud were forming on the table in front of her.

"Some divers. They swam over and climbed on the boat, and suddenly one of them shouted to Jill and Lars that they'd found a skeleton. Jill went aboard for a look, then told Lars to radio for help." Betsy looked at her incipient mitten, made a noise, and undid two stitches.

"Is the skeleton a man or a woman?" asked Godwin, who was working on a magnificent needlepoint Christmas stocking.

"I heard it was a woman," said Alice, the woman with the manly jaw.

"That's right," said Betsy. "Jill told me the medical examiner said that. I think I saw him out on the boat, but there were so many investigators and police and all, I couldn't say for sure. I didn't realize finding a skeleton would create such a fuss. He may even have arrived after Jill arranged for someone to bring me back to the dock, a nice man with a perfectly enormous boat."

"Any idea who?" asked Jessica, who could crochet without looking.

"I think his name was Dayton. Luke? Matt? Something like that. Very handsome and polite."

Several of the women coughed as if to cover chuckles, and Jessica said, "No, I mean who the skeleton is."

"No, there weren't any clothes or a purse or anything. Just the bones."

"How could they even tell it was a woman?" asked a very pregnant young woman named Emily, new to the Bunch. She was knitting a crib-size afghan in blue, pink, and white. "I mean, a skeleton is a skeleton is a skeleton, right?"

"Not at all," said Martha the dry cleaner. "Don't you watch The Discovery Channel? They have a wonderful show about autopsies and things. They can tell all sorts of things just from a leg bone, the age and sex and everything; and here they have the whole skeleton." Martha had curly white hair around a sweet face; that she was interested in forensic anthropology was surprising.

"Was she murdered?" asked Alice.

"Oh, no," said Godwin in his most faux-dulcet voice—for which he must hold several international records, thought Betsy, amused—"it's a suicide, obviously. She crawled under the floor boards and waited for the boat to sink so she could drown."

"Tsk," went several women, but the rest giggled. Godwin's sarcasm was part of his fame.

"When did the *Hopkins* sink?" asked Emily. "Maybe she was a leftover from the accident."

"It wasn't an accident," said Godwin. "The streetcar steamboats were sunk *deliberately.*" When Emily tried an uncertain giggle, he continued, "I'm *not* joking. They didn't need them anymore, so the company *sank* them. Happened during the roaring twenties."

"Not the *Hopkins*," said Patricia Fairland, a handsome woman in her thirties with dark hair held back by a headband. She was crocheting a lacy edging on an embroidered table runner, using a number-ten steel hook and yarn thin as sewing thread, her long, delicate fingers darting swiftly.

"Sure the *Hopkins*," disagreed Godwin, glancing up from his Christmas stocking. "They sank them all about the same time, 1920-something, when roads were tarred and everyone could afford a car, and public transportation wasn't absolutely necessary anymore.''

"The other five, yes, but not the *Hopkins*,'' insisted Patricia. "It was sold to the Blue Ribbon Café, and they renamed it the *Minnetonka III*, painted it white, and used it to give rides to tourists until 1949. I'm a member of the Minnesota Transportation Museum, Steamboat Branch. It's in several books, about the *Hopkins*.''

Betsy said, "When it came up out of the water, I could see it used to be white, not that mustard color the *Minnehaha* was restored to.''

"You can tell she's new to this business,'' remarked Jessica with a smile, "because the rest of us would have tried to decide whether the color is closer to DMC 437 or 8325.''

"Oh, DMC 437, definitely,'' said Martha. "You know, I remember the Blue Line buying the *Hopkins*. They painted it white after they converted the engine to run on oil instead of coal. My Aunt Esther and Uncle Swan celebrated their golden wedding anniversary with a ride on it in 1938. I'd forgotten they renamed it. I think everyone from around here still called it the *Hopkins* most of the time. My Carl used to love to watch it out on the lake. He said it was the prettiest boat he'd ever seen. It's a pity he didn't live to see it brought up again.''

"Maybe he isn't dead,'' said Alice. "Nobody knows, right?'' Blinking behind the lenses, she looked at Martha, and there was a little stir in the group; it wasn't polite to bring up old scandals when the scandalee was present.

Jessica said, "She doesn't like to talk about it.''

But Martha said, "It's all right, Jess.'' She said to Betsy, with an air of making a statement for the record, "My husband left our house for work one summer morning in 1948 and never came home. *Some* people think he ran off with another woman, but I think he was mugged and the robber killed him and pushed his body in the lake or buried it somewhere or threw it in an empty boxcar so it got taken away. Because no trace of him was ever found. His disappearance was a great shock to me, but it happened a long time ago, and I'm pretty much over it.''

"But he never knew they sank it," persisted Alice, frowning over her afghan square, "if he disappeared before it was sunk.''

"I don't remember them sinking the *Hopkins*," said Martha, pausing to consider. "Maybe because it was just an old wreck they finally got rid of, not a news story. But I definitely remember Carl disappeared in July of 1948, and if the *Hopkins* was sunk in 1949, then of course he never knew." She looked around with uneasy defiance. "And yes, a woman who worked at the Blue Ribbon Café disappeared at the same time. *Some people* assumed they ran off together.''

Jessica gave a sniff of support without looking up from her crocheting.

Patricia said, "There was all kinds of talk, I suppose, about Carl disappearing.''

Kindly shifting the focus from Martha, Godwin said, "I hear the boat was very hard to sink. They had to fill it with stones and concrete to make it go down.''

Betsy said, "That's right. Jill told me the divers said it was a real job to remove that rubble before they raised her, and I saw them throwing the last of it overboard just before they found the skeleton.''

Martha, who had stopped work to think, said, "You know, it's a funny thing my not remembering them sinking that boat. I remember all kinds of other unimportant things. Like it being damaged by ice two or three years earlier. It sat against the shore over by the dredging company not far from our house. My neighbor's little boys used to fish off the back of it." She smiled at Betsy. "The younger one grew up to be mayor of Excelsior." She frowned. "But I don't remember anything about them sinking the *Hopkins*."

Patricia said, "It's interesting how everyone still calls it the *Hopkins*. Because it sailed the lake from 1926 to 1949 under the name *Minnetonka III*."

Betsy said, "I understand how you know these things, Pat, being one of the volunteers who run the boats, but how do you know so much, Godwin?"

"Because *I* am not from here and therefore am interested in local history," said Godwin loftily. Then he grinned. "Besides, John is a member of the museum, and he puts their monthly magazine in the little stack of reading material in the bathroom. They did a long article on the *Hopkins* in the last issue."

Martha chuckled. "My husband used to call the bathroom the reading room."

In the middle of the nods and laughter that remark drew, Emily began to look funny and once the ladies found she'd been having these kind of cramplike pains every twenty minutes or so, a part joyous, part worried fuss began of notifying her husband and her doctor and arranging for her to get to the hospital—all despite her protest, "But when the cramp lets up I feel just fine!" And by the time Emily was safely on her way, the Monday Bunch meeting was over.

"Godwin," Betsy said when the last woman was out the door, "why do you keep building me up so those ladies can put me down? You keep telling me how well I'm doing—"

"You are, you're doing beautifully!" insisted Godwin.

"Sure I am. Did you see how they laughed when Jessica pointed out I don't use DMC numbers to identify colors? I'm sure they all saw how I had to keep going back and picking up dropped stitches in that mitten. Thank God they don't yet realize how bad it really is; how little I know about all sorts of needlework—or running a needlework business, for that matter."

"Oh, pish-tush; I repeat, you're doing *just fine.*"

"I wish I could believe that. Especially late at night, when I'm trying to fall asleep after suffering through Quicken and the checkbooks and withholding, and could just cry. But the little failures hurt, too. I thought Shelly was going to have a stroke trying not to laugh out loud when a customer asked if I thought she should do the background of her project in oriental or gobelin." Shelly was a part-time employee.

"What did you tell the customer?"

"I got out my book of stitches and looked up both stitches and said I thought the oriental would be better."

"And what was wrong with that?"

Betsy hesitated, then smiled. "Nothing. In fact, when I saw the finished project last Saturday, it was beautiful."

"See? And honey, if Shelly does something like that when I'm around, I'll remind her of the time *she* forgot to figure sales tax on a five hundred dollar order. Who cares if you *haven't* mastered every needlepoint stitch? You can do this. You *are* doing it. You *have* to do it. If you put this shop on the market, Irene Potter will buy it, and the first person she'll fire is *me.*" He reached out a slender hand to touch her shoulder. "Think of it as a memorial to your murdered sister."

Betsy twitched away from his hand, not sure if he was being melodramatic. It was still too soon for her to endure casual reference to her sister's death.

"No, listen to me!" said Godwin. "I'm *serious.* You

solved her murder, you are a heroine *and* a sleuth *and* a role model. You are the *happy-ever-after person;* you *can't* quit."

Betsy smiled; she couldn't help it. Godwin's charm was as warm as it was silly. She went behind the big old desk/checkout counter. "Have we got enough Madeira silks on hand?" she asked. "I see here you sold an awful lot of them to Amy yesterday."

"I wrote you a note about that. No, we don't. We should order some more right away. By the way, Shelly says we're also low on DMC pinks and blues. There should be a note from her on that desk somewhere."

"We're going to have to find a better way to keep up with inventory," grumbled Betsy, shuffling through papers to look for Shelly's note. "This business of waiting till someone notices we're running low seems awfully chancy. What if no one notices? We'll find ourselves totally out of something and screw up a big sale one of these days."

"Hasn't happened yet." Godwin was smiling again, but this time she frowned at him.

"Come on, how can we tell ahead of time what we'll run out of next?" he asked reasonably. "We notice we're running low, and we order more of it. We could increase our inventory, but that ties up money you need to pay rent and our salaries. The system we have is a good system."

"Yeah," said Betsy sarcastically, "invented by someone with nine whole weeks' experience in the retail business."

"You didn't invent this system, you inherited it," said Godwin. "Your sister used the same method. We all know to write a note when we sell enough of a product to create a shortage. The problem happens when someone forgets to write a note. Which we didn't. So, do you want me to call the order in, or will you?''

"I'll do it.'' She opened the center drawer and pulled out the spiral-bound address book. But before dialing, she put her hands on the open book and said, ''Goddy, the Monday Bunch doesn't think I'm going to get involved in this skeleton business, do they?''

"Not once they think about it. I mean, you aren't a policeman, so it's not your job, and I didn't notice anyone coming in trying to hire you as a private eye to solve it. The last one was up-close and personal. This one has nothing to do with us, so why should we get involved?'' Betsy was to remember those words in the days to come.

3

It was Halloween eve. Detective Mike Malloy was proud to know Halloween means All Hallows Eve (though he could not for twenty dollars have told anyone what All Hallows was). Therefore, he considered, the term *Halloween eve* redundant, so he corrected it in his head to *the day before Halloween*.

Appropriate to the season, he was about to meet a scientist in his laboratory, which he pictured with stone walls, gurgling test tubes, spirals of glass filled with colored liquids, and a couple of those things like old-fashioned TV antennas making thin crackles of lightning between their rods.

He knew it wouldn't be like that, not really, but it was kind of disappointing to find it was a kitchen-size room, very clean, with microscopes and a personal computer. It did smell funny, which was something, but the scientist wasn't there.

Malloy was directed by a student in a stained lab coat to an upper floor and a small, cluttered office. It wasn't a cubicle, but a real office, with walls that went to the ceiling, and a door that shut. Which Malloy did.

The man behind the desk wasn't a disappointment to Malloy's Halloween-colored imagination. Dr. Ambling had the fluffy gray hair and thick glasses of every mad scientist from every movie the detective had seen as a kid. "Ah have examined the fabric you-all sent to me," Dr. Ambling drawled—not in a thick German accent. Texas, thought Malloy, amused.

Ambling picked up two sheets of glass held together by strips of gray tape on the corners. Between the glass were four pieces of thin green fabric, three very small, the fourth roughly triangular in shape, about two and a half inches on a side. All the pieces were frayed, and there were fine threads knotted and tangled along two sides of the triangle. "The material is silk, partially edged with silk threads that may have been lace. The lace, if it is lace, was probably made by hand, and it was attached to the rest of the fabric after it was finished." He put the glass down on a low stack of books and consulted a sheet of paper occupying a cleared space on his desk just large enough to hold it.

Mike had found a tiny, flattish, filthy, slimy thing during a search of the raised boat. A forensics expert from the state crime lab had identified it as fabric and recommended Dr. Ambling as the person to further identify it. Mike still wasn't sure if it was important, but the first thing a detective learns is not to assume something is unimportant just because it doesn't fit a theory you've been too quick to form.

"Ah," said Ambling, finding his place. "It is impossible to tell what color the fabric was originally," he continued. "The green color is from being pressed under something made of copper or a copper alloy." He looked up at Malloy through thick lenses. "Did you find it under a piece of pipe?"

"No, it was in a puddle of muddy water. But they cleared away a lot of rubble before they raised the boat and more after they got it to the surface, before they found the skeleton. We don't know where on the boat it was hidden originally."

"It was under a piece of rubble that was, or contained, some copper or brass or bronze—copper and its alloys are a good preservative of fibers. But they turn things green." He went back to the report. "Judging by the shape of the surviving pieces, the fabric was wadded rather than folded and only partly covered by the metal. The biggest piece is the only one with the edging on it."

"So what do you think, was it a dress? Or was it something smaller?" asked Malloy.

The man shrugged. "The fabric seems thin for a dress, but I don't know much about clothing from the forties. A handkerchief seems more likely, but I wouldn't testify to that as fact. It could be a fragment of sleeve, though you should check to see if lace edging was fashionable on sleeves in 1949. On the other hand, my mother used to crochet lace edgings onto her hand-kerchiefs. Very fine, very delicate work. That's what this made me think of. But it's only a guess; the fibers have been so stretched and pulled from the pressure of what-ever was holding it down all those years, I can't see what the pattern might have been."

"Could it just be string from the fabric? Maybe it frayed a lot, from the motion of the water or some-thing." Malloy bent over the glass for a closer look.

Ambling reached for a pencil, which he used as a pointer. "No, the fibers here and here are thicker and coarser than the rest of the fabric. And here and here and here, see? These look like knots. So not fraying, and not fringe, but trim of some sort, of a thicker fiber than the fabric, and attached to it—see, here and here. I'm quite sure these strands were formed into a pattern with deliberation. Could be crochet, but that's only a guess.''

"So a woman's handkerchief, right?'' said Malloy. "I mean, a man wouldn't have a silk handkerchief, would he?''

"My grandfather carried a silk handkerchief every day of his adult life. But not with lace edging, of course. For that, you'd have to go back to the eighteenth century.''

"Hmmm. So a woman's handkerchief, or part of a dress. The sleeve you say? Why not the collar? That would be more likely to have lace trim.''

"A collar would be doubled over, and this was hemmed, not doubled.''

"Okay, I get that. This lace edging, is it silk, too?''
Ambling nodded. "Yes.''

"So this was an expensive article, right?''

"Possibly, but not necessarily. You have to consider the era. Handmade at this time meant homemade, and in the forties and fifties, only poor people wore homemade clothes. Of course, silk is another matter, as is lace. Poor people didn't make their clothes of silk.''

Mike picked up the glass and held it to the ceiling light. "No initials or anything,'' he said. "So I guess even if we identify her, we'll never know for sure if the skeleton was the person who owned this.''

"Jill, you crochet and do stuff like that, don't you?''

Jill, coming out of the duty room, turned to see Mike Malloy with something flat in his hands. "No, sorry, I don't do crochet,'' she said politely. "But I do needlepoint, if that's any help.'' Malloy, she knew, wasn't the brightest bulb in the chandelier, but he was her senior in rank, so she tried to treat him with respect.

He, on the other hand, knew she was very bright and suspected she was ambitious. But he couldn't bad-mouth her the way he could male officers with ambitions to his rank and job, not in this era of hair-trigger harassment suits, so he tried to treat her with respect.

With both of them behaving contrary to their beliefs, they tended to talk like actors in a poorly written play.

"Can I show you something?" he asked, approaching with the object held out awkwardly.

"What is it?" asked Jill, not reaching for it.

"A textile expert from the university says it maybe was part of a dress or a handkerchief. It's got homemade lace edging, he says. I want to know what you think. This expert guesses it's crochet."

"Oh. Okay." Jill took the glass sandwich with both hands, careful to hold it at the edges. She lifted it so the ceiling fluorescents could shine through it. "Hard to say," she said after a few moments. "Actually," she added, lowering the glass and handing it back, "I'm not an expert on lace. But I know where to ask for experts. Want me to bring you their names?"

"Are they in town?"

"Probably. All I have to do—or you can do it yourself—is go to Crewel World and ask for Godwin. He knows just about everyone in the area who does things with fibers."

"Yeah, I should have thought of that myself."

Malloy being self-deprecating was unusual, so Jill's stiffness thawed a little. "Say, is this connected to that skeleton we found on the old *Hopkins*?" Jill had just been part of the crowd control aspect of the crime scene, she had no role in the investigation. But she was curious.

"How'd you know?"

Jill smiled. "Well, that thing you showed me is the color of algae."

"As a matter of fact, it's that color because it was under a piece of copper for fifty years—and okay, at the bottom of the lake, on board the *Hopkins*."

Jill bloomed a little bit over being right and Malloy smiled, but not unkindly. She asked, "Was it near the skeleton?"

"Not really. The skeleton was near the stern, the fabric was found more amidships, near where the engine used to be. But with all the tumbling it might've got while those divers were removing rubble, it could've started out anywhere."

"Amidships?"

Malloy's prickliness appeared. "Yes, and deck and gunwale and ladder and so forth. What of it?"

"Oh. Nothing, I guess. I thought you picked up that word talking to the divers, but I guess it's for real with you. What, you were in the navy?"

His small eyes narrowed. "Why do you ask?"

Jill shrugged. "Hey, no reason. It's just that the current owner of Crewel World is also a navy vet."

"That woman who thinks she's a detective?"

Jill wanted to remind him that Betsy had been the one who came up with the solution to Malloy's last case, and so was, in fact, able to detect. But she bit her tongue and then said, "You remember Betsy Devonshire, then. I'm sure she'll help if she can, do whatever you want."

"Yeah, I'd like that, so long as she doesn't get enthusiastic and go charging around looking for clues." Malloy sighed. "Still, thanks again for the suggestion, Jill."

When Jill took her coffee break at Crewel World a few hours later, she found that Malloy hadn't been by yet.

She described what Mike had shown her to Betsy and Godwin.

"I'm surprised he's letting us in, after the last time," said Godwin.

"Hey, slow down, he's not letting you in," said Jill. "He doesn't want you to sleuth, he wants you to answer some questions about something he found on the *Hopkins*."

"What kind of lace do you think it is?" asked Betsy.

"I don't know that it's lace at all. It didn't look like anything but a tangle of threads to me. Mike said the textile expert thinks it might be crochet, though how he figured that, I don't know. But like I told Mike, I bet there are some customers at Crewel World who can look at it and know whether the expert is right or not."

"Are there lace makers around here?" Betsy asked Godwin.

"Heavens yes. Tatting and crocheting and even old-fashioned bobbin lace. Martha Winters used to make beautiful bobbin lace. And Lucy Watkins still does, and tatting besides. Patricia does gorgeous crochet work. There are probably others who do or know someone who does. And most of them are Crewel World customers, because hardly anyone who does one kind of needle-work does only one kind. Even you, Miss Knit, have branched out into needlepoint. After all that complaining, I watched you do a beautiful row of mosaic this morning."

"Oh, all it took for that was learning how to interpret the illustrations in the book," said Betsy. "But I couldn't do it without the open book right there."

"Uh huh," said Godwin, "just like the rest of us. And tell Jill how you've expanded into counted cross-stitch."

"I'm still kind of only thinking about it." Betsy continued to Jill, "Those big patterns Shelly does intimidate me, but The Stitchery catalog had some darling Christmas tree ornaments that looked about my speed, so I ordered a set."

"The little squares of animals wearing Santa Claus hats?" asked Jill.

"Yes, aren't they adorable? The set came over the weekend, but I haven't had a chance yet to take a good look at it."

"You'll like it. I'm working on my second set. I've decided to enclose one or two with some of my Christmas cards. And I'll donate one to the tree."

"What tree?"

Jill looked at Godwin, who shrugged back. Godwin said to Betsy, "Margot used to put up a little artificial tree, and her customers would make ornaments for it, and on Christmas Eve she'd take it to someone who otherwise wouldn't have a tree."

Jill misinterpreted the look on Betsy's face and said, "You don't have to do it, too. I mean, for one thing you're busy, and for another you don't have Margot's connections, so you won't know who needs the tree."

"That's not what's bothering me," said Betsy. "I feel so bad about all the things that won't get done because she's gone."

There was a little silence, then Godwin sighed noisily and asked, "What else did Sergeant Malloy say about the lace?"

"Not much. He said it might be part of a dress or a handkerchief. It's green, but that's because whatever was holding it down was made of copper or bronze, like a section of pipe. It's only about four inches' worth, going around a corner, like maybe the corner of a handkerchief or a collar point. Silk, he says. The expert, not Mike.

But really, it's such a mess I don't know if even someone who makes lace could tell Mike anything useful.''

Malloy hesitated before opening the door. Betsy Devonshire was okay, he was pretty sure. He had a problem
accepting women as equals, and his natural cop attitude
toward civilians overlay that to make him appear a male
chauvinist pig. Which he wasn't, not really. But here,
too, and not all that long ago, Ms. Devonshire had
shown herself willing to interfere in a police investigation. So he'd have to step carefully around her, because
he really wanted to use her as a resource. After all, the
woman had been pretty clever coming up with the murderer of her sister. But he didn't want her poking around
again because that first time was undoubtedly just luck,
and if she tried again, she'd probably only scare off or
corrupt a witness. So he'd have to talk kind of careful
to her.

Malloy steeled himself and opened the door.

Inside the shop, Betsy and Godwin had been staring
at the person standing so dark and still on the other side
of the door. His head was on a level with the Open sign
so they couldn't see his face, but there was a sinister
tension in the stillness of his pose. And one hand was
hidden in the folds of his overcoat.

Then the door went *bing* and it was Sergeant Mike
Malloy. They were both so relieved that their greetings
were especially warm, which made them grin at one another.

Which puzzled Malloy, who started to frown suspi-
ciously.

"We thought you were a robber," explained Betsy,
still smiling. "You were standing there like you were
trying to get up the nerve to come in and demand all
our money."

Mike laughed and gestured dismissively. "Heck, this is too nice a town for something bad to happen to decent people twice in a row."

"Jill was here a little while ago," said Godwin, eager to get down to business, "and she said you might come to ask us to help you with some needlework sample."

Malloy shrugged crookedly. "Well, what it is, I'm hoping you know someone who can tell me if I have an example of handmade lace here, and what kind it is." What Malloy had hidden in the folds of his coat was the glass sandwich. It now had a double seal of tape and a tag with Evidence in big red letters.

Betsy looked at it without touching it and shrugged. But Godwin took it and held it up to the ceiling just as Jill had, then over toward the front window, then close to his right eye. Frustrated, he said, "I'm sorry, it doesn't look like anything to me."

"Perhaps one of your customers could help me. Officer Cross said that everyone in the area who does needlework comes here."

"From your mouth to His ear, amen," said Betsy fervently and Malloy laughed again.

"Still," persisted Malloy, "is there anyone who comes here who is knowledgeable about handmade lace?"

Betsy said, "There are a number of local women who make bobbin lace, do tatting, crochet, and make lace in other forms. The real question is, can they look at what you have there and make sense of it? I'm worried now that Godwin says it doesn't look like anything to him, but he's not a lace maker, so maybe someone else can help. If you like, I can ask customers to take a look at your sample—but wait, I guess you wouldn't want to leave that here."

"I'm not allowed to leave it here." Malloy lifted and dropped the Evidence tag.

"Oh, I see. So how about we arrange a meeting, and you can bring it, and we'll see if someone can help."

"You'll never get everyone to agree on a time," said Godwin.

"Including me," said Malloy. "So how about I get a good picture of it, or maybe just a Xerox for a start. Then if it rings any chimes with someone, I can show the real thing to them."

"Yes, of course. Would it be all right if I taped up the photocopy? Or should I keep it in a drawer and just show it to select customers?"

"I don't see why you can't post it. I'd appreciate hearing right away if someone thinks she can help. I'll drop the copy off later today."

"All right," said Betsy.

After Malloy left, Godwin said, "You know, there are times when he seems almost human."

There's no statute of limitations on murder, and occasionally something will crop up to crack an old case. Even in solved murders, someone convicted many years ago may persuade a judge to order a new trial or a DNA test that proves him innocent, or something will be discovered during another investigation that forces the police to start over. So when it's a homicide case, the records are kept forever.

But nobody can keep records of every crime. So when Malloy wanted reports of a missing woman in the summer of 1949, the missing person reports were long gone. He went first to the public library and searched microfilm copies of old newspaper files. And found nothing, which he thought was a little strange.

Shrugging off his annoyance, he went to his first fallback location, the Excelsior Historical Society, which consisted of three seniors, all women, who met on Tuesday mornings in the vault of City Hall.

City Hall was in the basement of the volunteer fire department, a cramped space with five employees. The mayor was at his regular day job, so the highest executive present was the city comptroller. He smiled and nodded when Malloy stated his business, and Malloy lifted the flap that marked the entrance and made his way to the back of the room, where a large, thick, fireproof door let into a space almost as big as the main room. Three walls were lined with metal shelves stuffed to overflowing with wire baskets, accordion folders, boxes, and files, the official records of the City of Excelsior. The fourth wall was obscured by metal file cabinets and an old wooden map cabinet. Near these stood a scarred wooden table, at which the Excelsior Historical Society sat in session, surrounded by plats, deeds, and old tax records.

"Good morning, ladies," said Malloy. "What's on your schedule for today?"

"Good morning, Michael," said the littlest woman, who was also the oldest. "We're trying to map the location of the fire lanes. The city hasn't kept up its claim to them where they touch the lakeshore, and there's been a lot of encroachment. *Some* of it inadvertent."

This budding problem had made the news recently. When the Excelsior Fire Department was young, its pumper drew water from the lake, and so eight or ten narrow access lanes to the lake were marked off and maintained for its use. The installation of fireplugs in the '50s removed the need for the lanes. Some were turned into public access boat landings. But over the years the others blended into the lawns of the houses on either side of them. A quarrel was developing over what should be done about the lanes. Sold to the homeowner(s) who

had encroached with garden or lawn? Divided equally
between the properties on either side? Reclaimed by the
city? Before anything could be settled, the city had to
first discover just how much land was involved and
where it was located.

"If I might pull you off your work for just a few
minutes," Malloy said, "I'd like to know if you can tell
me if there was a report of a woman gone missing in
1949."

"From just Excelsior?" asked the second oldest
woman, whose name, Malloy suddenly remembered,
was Myrtle Jensen.

"Excelsior and the area close by—unless you can
search other areas easily," said Malloy. "And also, can
you find the month the *Hopkins* was sunk? I assume it
was summer, but it could have been any time there was
no ice."

Myrtle pressed a crooked forefinger to her lips. "I can
tell you that," she said. "It was just before the Fourth
of July. I remember because Jack brought up a bushel
basket of sweet corn from Illinois—ours wasn't ripe yet.
We boiled it up and had a Fourth of July picnic in the
backyard and a neighbor came by for an ear and said
he'd seen the *Hopkins* towed out to be sunk. That was
the best sweet corn I ever ate, and ever after, I associated
corn on the cob with the Fourth of July, even though
it's never ready up here by then. We always have to buy
it from people who bring it from down south. There used
to be a man who would drive to Tennessee—remember
him, Lola?—he'd fill his trunk and the backseat of his
car and drive all day and night and park down by The
Common and sell it. I remember my dad used to put
about half of our garden in sweet corn, each row planted
a week later than the one before, so it didn't all ripen at
once. We used to have a real big backyard garden. I

remember being sent out to work in it when I was a child, weeding and picking caterpillars off the leaves. My brother's son Jimmy worked in that garden, but Jimmy's boy Adam went to college and he uses mulch and organic bug spray.''

Malloy had patiently waited for her to run down, then reaffirmed the pertinent part of her remarks. "So it was July they sank the *Hopkins*."

"Didn't I say that? Yes, early July, before the Fourth, because on the Fourth we heard it had been done, so a day or two before. It was hot that day, just blazing sun. Jack set up a cauldron outside, and was miserable tending the fire. Good corn, though.''

The littlest woman said, "I've got a missing person story. Trudie Koch ran off with Carl Winters, or so everyone said. Maybe he murdered her instead and ran away.'' Her eyes sparkled at the thought.

Malloy looked at her. "Who was Trudie Koch?"

"Waitress down at the Blue Ribbon Café. No better than she ought to be, remember, Myrt? Had a steady boyfriend, what was his name? Vern something. Mean fellow, gave her a black eye once in a while, not that she didn't provoke him something awful. She dated a lot of men, and was very easy, or so everyone said. We were surprised that she ran off with Carl, or rather, that Carl ran off with her. He had a perfectly nice wife and a good job.'' She looked at Myrtle. "Remember?"

Myrtle was looking thoughtful. "But that didn't happen the year they sank the *Hopkins*, did it? Those two ran off in 1948.''

"I thought it happened the same summer. Are you sure they ran off in 1948?"

"Yes, because that was the year Martha had to drop out as organist and they asked me to take her place. With her husband gone, she had to run the dry cleaning store all by herself and she didn't have time for choir. I got in and stayed in. I got my gold pin for twenty years' service in 1968, see?'' She touched one of two tiny round badges pinned to her dress. Malloy took a look and saw the badge said Saint Elwin's Choir and Twenty Years around its edge. A tiny gold chain led from the pin to a tiny rectangle with the year 1948 on it.

The other badge was slightly more elaborate and said Saint Elwin's Choir and Forty Years around its edge. The chained tag also read 1948.

''I stepped down as organist after I got this pin,'' she said, touching the second one. ''My ears weren't what they used to be.''

''Sorry,'' said Malloy, but carelessly. ''Say, maybe the *Hopkins* was sunk in 1948?''

''Oh, no,'' said the youngest woman. She stood and went to a low shelf behind the table. She selected a slim, blue paperbound book and brought it to Malloy. ''It says in here that the boat was sunk in 1949, and this book was written by the man in charge of raising both the *Minnehaha* and the *Hopkins*. He even took a picture of the *Hopkins* at the bottom of the lake.''

Malloy paged through the book, which was locally published and had good black and white photographs in it. Sure enough, there was an old photo of a streetcar steamboat loaded with passengers, and another of an open hatch, this one taken under water. The accompanying paragraph said the *Hopkins* was sunk near her sisters off the Big Island in 1949.

''Anyone know where I can reach the author of this book?'' he asked.

''He's with the Minnesota Transportation Museum's steamboat branch; their office is right down by the lake, in that little row of stores,'' said Myrtle.

"May I keep this?" he asked, displaying the book.

"For $7.95, you may," said Myrtle, producing a cash box, and the best Malloy could do was get a receipt and hope the department would reimburse him.

4

The Minnesota Transportation Museum Ticket Office and Souvenir Store was a little storefront, in a row of them behind Pizza Hut. There was a parking lot in front, and Malloy stood a minute looking at the lake across the street. A gentle slope ran down to the docks—narrow wooden walks into the water, supported on thick wooden piles—now empty in anticipation of winter. Malloy sometimes thought he would like to live in some state where winter didn't take up so much of the year. They had bass lakes as far south as Missouri, didn't they? But in Missouri, they didn't go ice fishing, did they? And Malloy loved ice fishing almost as much as fishing from his bass boat.

He turned, saw the sign, and went up and into the MTM store.

Like most souvenir stores, MTM had lots of T-shirts and sweatshirts. There were also caps, some of them the old-fashioned, high-crowned, mattress-ticking variety that yesteryear's engineers wore. There were bright-colored prints of the lake in its heyday, with streetcar boats taking on passengers in the foreground. Each boat was named after a town on the lake. There were also prints of streetcars, some in small-town settings back when Hopkins and Minnetonka were not merely suburbs of Minneapolis—though even then the main purpose of the streetcars was to take workers to the big city.

A glass case held a big model of the restored *Minnehaha*, showing the peculiar long slope of her stern. Malloy remembered seeing photographs of the Great White Fleet back in Teddy Roosevelt's time, where the ships had that same odd back end. He wondered what its purpose was.

At the far end of the store was a counter behind which a young woman with short dark hair frowned at a computer monitor.

He walked back and she looked up. "May I help you?" she asked. Her features were attractive, but she had made no effort to enhance them with makeup.

"I'm interested in learning about the *Hopkins*," he said. "What can you tell me?"

"It's no longer at the bottom of the lake," she replied with a twinkle.

"Tell me something I don't know."

"Like what?"

"When was it sunk?"

"1949."

"That's what everyone keeps telling me. Who knows that for a fact?"

She smiled. "If everyone's telling you that, then everyone, I guess. What are you looking for, an eye-witness?"

"You got one?"

She looked around. There was no one there but the two of them. "Not here in the office."

He laughed, but then produced identification, which stopped the banter as it widened her light blue eyes. Then she turned abruptly and reached for some books tucked into a shelf under the counter. "These are stories about the lake and the towns on it, and here's one about the streetcar steamboats in particular. They all say the *Hopkins*—well, it was renamed the *Minnetonka* by then—was sunk in 1949. This one even has some pictures of it on the bottom of the lake." This one was *Salvaged Memories*, the blue paperback Malloy already had a copy of.

Still, he took the books and went to a corner of the store that had a chair and looked them over. They all agreed that the *Minnetonka III*, née *Hopkins*, had been sunk on the north side of the Big Island in Lake Minnetonka in 1949.

All right, he'd accept that. He got the phone number for the author of *Salvaged Memories* and left.

Diane Bolles was sorting through a thin stack of cardboard signs when a customer came to the checkout counter. Distracted, she glanced up without at first recognizing the woman, who had a half dozen old books. "May I help you find something else?" she asked—then blinked. "Oh, hello, Shelly!"

"You must have something else on your own mind today, Diane," said Shelly Donohue.

"Well, yes, as a matter of fact, I do. I'm thinking of changing the name of my store."

"What's wrong with D. B. and Company?" Shelly looked around at the store, which looked like an old-fashioned general store in layout. There was even a penny candy counter next to the checkout. But elsewhere were silk flowers, old-fashioned tea sets, doilies, vases, jars, and over by the door a large cement statue of a frog.

"Nothing, actually. Except it doesn't describe the store."

Shelly giggled. "I don't see how you would describe this place in one sentence, much less one word."

"We sell the final touch for your decor, in the house or the garden."

"Oh. Well, yes. In fact, you put that so well, you must already be writing your new radio ad."

"Not until I get the new name." Diane picked up the cardboard squares. "May I try some out on you? I've sorted it down to these, but I don't know which one I like best."

"Sure."

"Belles Choses, which means Beautiful Choice in Italian. Or, there's Nightingale's, after the bird. Or Near Midnight—I like that one because it's romantic. You know, midnight, the bewitching hour. Or Chenille—did you know that's French for caterpillar? And last, My Favorite Year, which was my favorite this morning. This evening I'll like a different one."

Shelly said, "I like Nightingale's. The bird was a symbol of home and hope to the British during World War II, and it has a very beautiful song. I did a counted cross-stitch of a nightingale a couple of years ago for a friend who was born in England, and she just loved it."

"That reminds me. I was thinking of expanding into antique and vintage clothing. And then I found my grandmother's embroidered tablecloths and brought them in to decorate that table with the antique dessert dishes."

Shelly said, "Your grandmother made those? I can't believe you're going to sell those, Diane; they are heirlooms. The embroidery on them is wonderful; those strawberries are almost three-dimensional.''

''Oh, they're not for sale, they're just decoration. But I've gotten so many inquiries from customers that I think I should add stitchery to my line.'' She cocked her head. ''Do you still work part-time in that needlework store down on Lake?''

''Yes, I do.''

''Maybe I should stop in there and ask the new owner if she can put me in touch with people willing to sell their work.''

''Well . . .'' said Shelly. ''Actually, she probably can't help you. She's a terrific person, I really like her, but she's not only new at needlework, she's not from here.'' There was a subtle emphasis on that last part, *not from here.*

''Ah,'' said Diane.

''On the other hand, you could talk to her one full-time employee, Godwin. He knows everyone in the area who has ever done any kind of needlework. But you know something?'' Shelly leaned forward in a mockery of her own posture when imparting a tantalizing tidbit of gossip. *''So do I.''*

Diane's eyebrows raised in surprise, then she laughed. ''Well, of course! So where do I go? Who do I see? I'm looking for vintage, antique, and new items. Not a big selection, just a few things.''

''Tell you what. Let me think about it, maybe ask around. I'll draw up a list. And I think you should come to the shop anyway, meet Betsy—she's really nice. I'll consult with Godwin. He can probably suggest some names I miss. Let's see, today's Tuesday. I'll need about a week, can you wait that long?''

''Yes, of course. I'll come by sometime next week, maybe on my lunch break.''

Diane began to ring up Shelly's selections. "Do you collect old children's books?"

"No, I'm going to encourage my students to read them. I think it's helpful to expose even young children to a variety of reading experiences," said Shelly. She had a variety, all right, from the sweet and innocent *Pokey Little Puppy* to a pre-Disney version of *The Three Little Pigs* that had the wolf eating the first two.

Diane put the purchases into a bag and handed it to Shelly, who wasn't finished talking. "You know about the skeleton on the boat they raised?"

"Yes, I read about it. How dreadful for the divers, finding something like that."

Shelly nodded. "We're involved again."

"Who is?"

"The shop, Crewel World."

"I don't understand."

"You know how we solved the murder of Betsy's sister for the police, of course."

Diane started to object to that but changed her mind and only raised a mildly doubting eyebrow.

"I know the police are acting as if they solved it themselves, but they would still be looking for a burglar if it wasn't for Betsy Devonshire! She has a nose, or is it an eye, for crime solving. And so they're practically begging her to help again. They've left a big clue in our shop, and people are being asked to look at it and see if they can identify it."

"What kind of clue?"

"It's a piece of silk with lace edging, or rather a picture of it. It was found on the boat, which means it went down with it in 1949. No one has come up with anything yet, but you just watch. Of course, Betsy won't suspect you or me, because we weren't around in 1949." Shelly laughed, embraced the paper bag a little tighter, and left, not noticing the way Diane frowned after her.

The Saturday after Thanksgiving is traditionally the best day for American retailers, but for needlework shops, it's the Saturday after Halloween. That's when the procrastinators realize that unless they want to offend their mother-in-law *again* with a store-bought gift, they'd better get down to Crewel World and see if there is something that looks as if it took more than two months to finish, but doesn't.

For the first time, Betsy began to believe she could actually make a go of the little shop. Customers were waiting outside for her to open, and it was nonstop from then till closing. Fortunately, Shelly was able to join Godwin and Betsy.

Shelly was slim, not yet thirty, with long, thick, straight brown hair pulled into an untidy bun at the nape of her neck. She had beautiful eyes, intelligent and compassionate, and was a skilled counted cross-stitcher, a hard worker in the shop—but an incorrigible gossip. "... Linda chose that same cream-colored linen," she was telling a customer, "and frankly, I think iris-blue and purple silk would go even better for your sampler than her shades of pumpkin."

Meanwhile, Godwin was saying, "If the Ott table lamp is too small, you might want to try a light by Chromalux; it's a floor lamp, and comes already on a stand. And if you stitch in the nude—like *I* do—you'll appreciate the heat it puts out." The customer giggled, and Godwin reached for a catalog. "See, here's a picture of it; we can order it for you . . ."

Betsy stopped eavesdropping and looked at the completed piece of counted cross-stitch, Mermaid of the Pearls, lying across her hands. "Wow," she said sin-

cerely, "this is much prettier than the picture of it I saw.
Let's look at the sample mats to pick a color to match,
and then we'll choose a really nice frame. You'll want
to do justice to this, I'm sure."

While Betsy was writing up the order, her customer
noticed the Xerox taped to a corner of the checkout desk.
When Betsy saw her bend over it, she asked, "Recognize it?"

"What's it supposed to be?" asked the customer.

"Lace edging on a collar or handkerchief or sleeve.
It was hauled up from the bottom of the lake, and we're
hoping someone who does lace will be able to tell something about it."

"Looks like a spill of spaghetti to me," remarked the
customer, taking her slip and looking at it. Betsy held
her breath; the finishing, mat, and frame came to over
two hundred dollars. But the customer only said,
"You'll have this back in three weeks? Good, I can get
it in the mail on time, then. Thank you, Betsy."

"You're welcome, Mrs. Liljegren." Betsy had
thought she'd never get used to people calling her by
her first name while she must address them more formally, but at these prices they could call her anything
they liked.

"What's this about some lace you want identified?"
asked a very handsome woman Betsy recognized as one
of the Monday Bunch. She had a fistful of silk floss and
a packet of needles for Betsy to ring up.

"Hello, Patricia. Detective Malloy found something
on the *Hopkins* and hopes someone here can help identify it." Betsy indicated the Xerox copy taped to the
desk. "It's a corner of a handkerchief or maybe a bit of
a silk dress, and that tangle of string may be crochet
lace."

Patricia bent over the paper, frowning. Betsy wrote

the sales slip, then rang up her purchase, but Patricia didn't move. Betsy gave her a minute, then saw Godwin bringing another customer to check out. "Er-hem, excuse me?" Betsy said. "That'll be seventeen dollars and fifty-three cents, including tax. Patricia?"

Patricia said, "Hmm?"

"That'll be seventeen dollars and fifty-three cents."

"Okay."

"Excuse me, Patricia?" said Godwin politely, instead of making a wisecrack. Godwin knew which customers enjoyed him at his outrageous best and which didn't.

Patricia straightened. "I wonder why someone thinks that might be crocheted lace. It doesn't look like crochet to me, the loops are all wrong. It might be tatting, but is more likely bobbin lace."

Betsy looked at the copy. "You mean you can actually make sense of that?" She had thought the original unidentifiable, but the photocopy was even worse.

"Oh, it's definitely lace," said Patricia. "Question is, what kind? There are a number of ways to make lace, but I think I'd want to see the original before I said for sure what kind this is."

Godwin's customer crowded in for a peek but frowned and stepped back again. "I can't see any pattern to that," she said as if in complaint.

"Patricia, Sergeant Malloy is going to be *so pleased* if you can really tell him something helpful," said Godwin.

Betsy added quickly, "That is—would you mind talking to him?"

"No, of course not." She pulled her checkbook from her purse. "I'll pay for my silks and you may copy the phone number on the check to give to him." Her cheeks were pink with pleasure, her brown eyes alight. "This will be a poke in the eye for my husband, who says nothing of real value ever came out of a needleworker's basket.''

Hours later, closing time approached. Betsy, near exhaustion, was trying to rearrange a basket of half-price wool so that it didn't look so picked-over. Her feet were like a pair of toothaches. Shelly and Godwin were in back, quarreling tiredly over whose turn it was to wash out the coffeepot.

The door went *bing* (Betsy gritted her teeth and swore that someday soon she was going to replace that thing), but she forced her features to assume a pleasant look and turned to greet her customer. She was a small, thin woman with dark hair standing up in little curls all over her head. She had shiny dark eyes in a narrow face and a smile as false as the leopard print of her coat.

''Hello, Irene,'' said Betsy neutrally—that being the best she could manage.

''I hear you've had a splendid day, lots of customers,'' said Irene.

''Yes, the Christmas rush has begun, it seems.''

''Won't last till Christmas,'' warned Irene.

Irene Potter was one of the thorns on Betsy's rose. She was an extremely talented needleworker and a steady customer, but she was also opinionated, rude, hyperactive, nosy, and impatient. She thought Betsy incompetent and was watching hopefully, even cheerfully, for any sign the shop might slip into bankruptcy. Because if it did, then she, Irene, could take it over, fire that dreadful Godwin person, and run it as it should be run. Meanwhile, a mass of contradictions, she was also willing to share her considerable business and needlework expertise with Betsy. She was serenely unaware of this and other contradictions in her behavior.

''Why won't the Christmas rush last till Christmas?'' asked Betsy.

"Projects done as gifts or decorations have to be bought well in advance, to be done by Christmas. Once it's too late to get the projects finished on time, they'll stop buying them."

"Oh," said Betsy. "Of course."

"Unless they are given as projects to be done by the recipients," said Godwin. "Hello, Irene."

"Goddy." Irene gave an almost imperceptible nod of her head in Godwin's direction. She was sure of a number of vicious and untrue things about gay people, so vicious she was ashamed she knew about them and so never alluded to them, even obliquely. But the knowledge made her unable to look Godwin in the eye—which was as well, because his reaction to her shame was to grin tantalizingly.

"H'lo, Irene," said Shelly tiredly.

"Why, Shelly, I thought you'd be home grading papers or something."

"Now, Irene, you know that's how I spend my Sunday afternoons, smoking and drinking and grading papers." When she was tired, Shelly could be difficult, too.

"May we help you, Irene?" asked Betsy, anxious to get this over with so she could go upstairs and sit on the edge of her bathtub and do that trick of running cold then hot then cold then hot water over her feet.

"I've come to look at that picture you have of the lace collar."

"What? Oh. It's not a picture, it's a Xerox copy. And we don't know exactly what it was part of. Sergeant Malloy left it in hopes that people can identify it." Betsy led the way to the desk.

Irene studied the copy from different angles, coming beside the desk and even behind it. Betsy, seeking a second to Patricia's opinion, was beginning to feel optimistic when Irene said, "Humph, doesn't look like much of anything to me."

Betsy sighed. "I agree, and I saw the real thing."

Irene straightened so abruptly that Godwin, who had been standing close behind her, was forced to jump backward, which he did adroitly. Irene said, "I thought perhaps I could be of significant help with your second case, as I was with the first one"—she smirked proudly, then her face fell—"but I suppose not."

"This isn't my case, Irene," said Betsy, annoyance lending strength to the assertion, which she had made several times that day. "I am not involved. I am only allowing Sergeant Malloy to leave a request for information here. He probably has also left it at Needle Nest and Stitchville and who knows where else."

"Do you mean to tell me, Irene," purred Godwin, "that there is a needlework style you can't identify? I am *stunned* to hear that, Irene, at a total loss for words."

Irene did look him in the eye then. For about three seconds. Then, silently, she turned and walked out of the shop.

Shelly, giggling, said, "Godwin, you are the limit."

"Thank you, Shelly, I try."

5

Today's Monday Bunch more resembled the usual gathering, with four present. Oddly, one of the most faithful wasn't there: Martha Winters.

Her best friend Jessica explained, "The refrigeration unit in her dry cleaning machine has been acting up for weeks, and Jeff had the repairman over at least once, but now it's broken down completely, and everyone's cleaning is going to be late. So Martha decided to supervise the replacement herself."

"Jeff's her grandson," Alice explained briefly to Betsy.

Jessica nodded. "Her grandson is careless about repairs and replacements, but you can be sure Martha's going to stand right behind that poor repairman to make sure he does it right." Jessica sniffed righteously and then added, "Oh, she said to ask if anyone knows how Emily and her baby are doing, and she'll be here next Monday." The baby blanket Jessica had been working on was nearly finished. It gleamed in soft white folds in her lap, and her crochet hook moved as rapidly as if it were attached to a machine rather than a work-thickened hand.

Alice said, "Emily's named her Morgana Jean. Six pounds, twenty inches, both at home, grandmom's there helping." She sighed and shrugged her big shoulders, fingers working on yet another afghan square.

Jessica said, "Then I'll have that pink wool, Betsy; just one skein, please. I'll embroider little pink daisies around the edge of this."

As Betsy got up to get it, Kate, a trim woman working on a complex counted cross-stitch of a horse-drawn carriage on a rain-wet cobblestone street, asked, "Have they identified that skeleton yet?"

Betsy replied, "I haven't heard anything. But Patricia is going to meet with Sergeant Malloy to take a look at the bit of silk they found on the boat. She seems to think she can tell what that tangle of thread is, or was supposed to be."

The women started talking in low voices as Betsy went for the wool, and as she came back into earshot, a sudden silence fell. Jessica's thin mouth was a mere line, Alice's complexion was a bright pink, and the other two women were trying out poker faces. *Honestly*, thought Betsy, *the way these people gossip! I wonder what they're saying about me*.

She sat down with a sigh and asked a question a customer had brought in, about how to get colors that run out of needlework (soak in frequently renewed ice water or milk, wash in Orvus, rinse copiously, roll in towels, iron dry, don't hang). Then, satisfied they were back on topic, she said she needed their advice getting started on her counted cross-stitch Christmas ornaments. She got out the kit and complained that the cloth was all one big piece, and they wanted her to leave it that way—"Is that right?''—and to baste all around the edge of it, and then across its length every four inches, and then sort the floss, making sure all the colors were there, and on and on. "When do I get to start stitching?"

"But you are stitching," said Kate in some surprise. "I almost like that part best, when you prepare your cloth and sort the colors, and start to see in your head what the project will look like, and even plan little changes you'll make and so on." Her voice had gotten dreamy at the prospect, and the women chuckled.

Betsy said, "Oh, I get it. It's like baking. You find a new recipe or a new version of an old one, and you get out the pans and line up the ingredients. You heat the milk and pour it and the sugar into the bowl, and the smell of the yeast as it starts to work is wonderful."

Jessica said a little dreamily, "Yes, it's a lot like that," and this time there was laughter.

The Monday Bunch began discussing serging around the fabric on a sewing machine or even putting masking tape on it instead of basting, and were just starting on finding the center of a pattern, when the door went *bing* and Patricia entered, Malloy close behind her. She was wearing a green plaid swing coat and her dark hair was pulled back into a ribboned clip, which made her look prosperous and responsible. Malloy was wearing a raincoat that Columbo might have coveted. "Hi, everyone!" said Patricia, looking around. "Where's Martha?"

"Not here today," said Jessica. "Why?"

"Oh, no! I told Sergeant Malloy she was our bobbin lace expert. He wants to talk to her about that little piece of fabric they found, because I told him I think it's part of a handkerchief edged in bobbin lace."

Malloy's face also showed disappointment, but Alice Skoglund said quietly, "I used to do bobbin lace."

All heads came around. Since she had joined the Monday Bunch, no one had seen her do anything but crochet endless afghan squares. She set her heavy jaw and looked back calmly.

"Well, Alice, can you look at this, then?" Patricia gestured at Malloy, who obediently put the square of glass on the table in front of Alice.

She peered at it closely for a few moments, turning it once, then said, "Have we got a magnifying glass anywhere?"

"Yes," said Betsy, and went to the checkout desk. She pawed through two drawers before finding the big rectangular one with its handle on one corner. She brought it to Alice, who bent close and used it to study the glass plates for a longer while.

"Yes," she said finally, leaning back. "This is bobbin lace."

"Are you sure?" asked Malloy.

"Yes."

"How can you tell?"

"If you pick a strand and follow it, you can see how the twists were made. And these are twisted and crossed over like bobbin lace."

Jessica asked, "How sure can you be? Couldn't it be something else? Tatting, maybe? Or crochet?"

Alice looked sharply at Jessica, then said with an air of being patient with her, "No, it's not the loop, loop, loop of crochet." She looked at the blank faces of the other women and continued, "If you found the end of this and pulled, it wouldn't all come undone, would it? So it's not crochet. And it's not tatting, I can't see anything like those circles you get in tatting. But there are twists and weaving in it, and they look like bobbin lace patterns to me." She bent over the fragment under glass again, this time so closely there was barely room for the magnifying glass. "Here, for example, this must have been ground. And here, what do you think, Patricia, the petal of a flower, maybe?''

Patricia looked, the small neatness of her a strong contrast to the large woman bent over the glass. ''I see what you mean, I think.''

Alice said, pointing with a thick forefinger, ''But all along here, the threads have been broken. And here, see how it's pulled; this thread is thinned out to nothing here and here it's thicker and there it's thin again. Same with these. I never saw thread do that before.''

She looked accusingly at Malloy, who shrugged. ''It's silk, if that's any help. A textile expert says if you put animal fibers under pressure under water for a long time, they will stretch. And silk's from worms, which are animals.''

Patricia, still looking at the sample, nodded. ''You know, I think you're right, Alice; it's not just pulled crosswise, the thread itself is stretched, and not evenly.''

Alice said, ''Yes, that alone makes it impossible to see what the pattern was.'' She moved the magnifying glass along the fabric. ''Though here, I think this was a line of picots. I don't think this was torchon. Hmmm, binche?''

''Bench?'' echoed Betsy.

''No, binche, a kind of bobbin lace. Well, maybe not. It's too damaged to tell for sure.'' She put the magnifying glass down and sat back again. ''That's all I can tell you.''

Malloy said, notebook in hand, ''But you're absolutely sure it's bobbin lace?'' Alice nodded, and he wrote that down. ''Is that a common kind of thing? I mean, lots of women knit and crochet. Do lots of women do bobbin lace?''

''No,'' Alice said.

"The question is," said Betsy, "did women make bobbin lace back in 1949?"

"Oh, yes," nodded Alice. "I was making it back then, and I wasn't the only one. I learned it as a child; my Grandma brought it from the old country. My mother wasn't interested, so Grandma taught me. It's very difficult to learn from a book, you just about have to have someone show you, so I doubt there's been a time since it was invented hundreds and hundreds of years ago that someone hasn't been doing it."

"So I guess the patterns have all been passed along, too," said Betsy.

Alice nodded. "Of course, you can make up your own, too. Some people make lace into pictures, like of flowers or animals or trees. You can take a picture with a nice, easy outline, like from a coloring book, and make it into lace. I once saw a Batman, the lace maker handled the cape real nice, all lines and shading. But mostly you do geometrical patterns, repeats of flowers or leaves."

"Were more women or fewer doing it back then?"

Alice considered for a bit. "Fewer, I think. There's a trend back to handmade just now, so more women are learning how to do these things. There's someone teaching it locally. She holds a regular class at Ingebretsen's in Minneapolis."

"Is there something about the way people do this stuff," began Malloy, thinking his way slowly through the question, "so that you can tell who did it? I mean, could you identify a person just by looking at the lace they make?"

Alice nodded. "Sometimes. There are different skill levels, so if someone showed me a sample and said did this person or that person make this, and one was a beginner and the other one was experienced, that would be easy."

Patricia nodded. "Yes, that's true of all needlework."

Malloy said, "What if they were both experienced?"

"Then it would be impossible," said Patricia.

But Alice said, "Maybe not. Some people make up a pattern, or have a signature way of doing it, and if you've seen it, you can recognize it if you see it again. And some people just have a way with lace, so if you see something really well done, you might think she did it."

Malloy said, "Do you think this is a signature pattern?"

Alice frowned massively at him and said, "It was all I could do to say it was bobbin lace. I can't even tell what the pattern is, much less who might have done it."

Patricia added, "And even if she could figure out the pattern, what would that do? This skeleton you're investigating isn't a local person, so what good would it do to identify the pattern?"

Malloy said, "Because there may be a husband or a daughter somewhere who still wonders what happened to their wife or mother. We've already gotten inquiries from other law enforcement agencies about the find. We'll pass along any clues we get to the identity."

There was a little silence as this sank in, that there were people who had wondered sadly for fifty years what had become of their sister or mother.

"Hold on a minute," Alice said in a much kinder voice. "It may be possible to recreate the pattern of this lace. It will take time, but I think I can do it."

Patricia said, "Anything I can do to help, Alice, just ask."

"Thank you," said Alice, and Betsy knew suddenly how rarely Alice had felt important in this group.

Betsy asked, "Are you making any progress in identifying the skeleton?"

"Not much. The problem is, there weren't many clues aboard the boat, no shoes or clothing or a purse with a wallet, any of which would have been helpful. All we have are the bones and that piece of fabric—which might not even belong to the bones."

Betsy said, "There's a police artist in California who can put a face back on a skull. Perhaps you should contact him."

Malloy smiled. "Minnesota has an artist who can do that, too. Kerrie is, in fact, working on that task already."

Alice said, "What do you mean, put a face back on?"

Malloy said, "It's something that's been around for awhile now. She takes measurements and covers the bones with clay according to the numbers, and there's the dead person looking back at you. We've broken more than one case by showing a photograph of Kerrie's work around. It's a science, the way these artists go about this."

Kerrie held a skull between her hands and stared at the face. Although it had been cleaned, it was still faintly green. It had belonged to a woman, one who had been badly used. Pieces of bone had been glued back in place, gaps here and there filled with clay.

Who are you? Kerrie thought, directing it as a gentle question. Sometimes she got a strong feeling about the victim, once even a name, which turned out to be right. But nothing came this time.

She went to a big wooden cabinet against the wall and got a clear plastic box—the one with the red rubber stubs in it. They looked like pencil erasers cut into various small lengths, which is what they were. She also took out a fresh box of Sculpey modeling clay, and a bottle of glue.

As Malloy had said, there was a science to this business. Kerrie had gone through two intense courses in New Mexico to learn it. She would glue the markers on mapped areas of the skull to show the varying thickness of flesh at those points, then lay strips of clay between the markers. She would measure eye and ear and nose openings to determine the shape and length of the nose and ears and placement of the eyes, and as she filled in the spaces, a face would grow on the bone.

But when that was done, there was still the indeterminate to deal with: color of eyes, thickness of eyebrows, hair color and style, whether the face was habitually tense or angry or happy. No science could fill in these variables. Kerrie would keep her work on her desk, waiting to see if she'd get a flash of insight—it amounted sometimes to ESP—before completing the assignment. Sometimes it felt as if her small cubicle were haunted by the spirit of the deceased, so always, always, she handled her charges with respect and humility.

She paused again after gluing the little rubber markers to the skull, holding it cradled in both hands to ask again, "Who are you?"

But again, the answer was silence.

On Tuesday afternoon Betsy had a visitor. Before the electronic *bing* had faded his rough voice shouted, "What's this I hear?"

Betsy was behind a set of shelves that marked off a little area at the back of her shop, rearranging old stitchery magazines in date order—people *would* replace them any old how, if they replaced them at all. She was alone in the shop; Godwin had gone to pick up a shipment of fabric.

She recognized the voice; it belonged to Joe Mickels, her landlord.

"Hey!" he shouted again. "Anyone here?"

"What is it, Mr. Mickels?" she asked, a trifle impatiently, coming out from behind the shelves.

Mickels was a broad man, somewhat below middle height, with a mane of white hair and big, old-fashioned sideburns. He also wore an old-fashioned overcoat, dark gray wool with a fur collar that looked like Persian lamb—the real stuff, doubtless. Mickels would never wear fake fur, especially that of some edible animal. He was old-fashioned even beyond his years, a throwback to the unbridled capitalists of his great-grandfather's day, and as avaricious. And proud of it; that explained the coat, and the sideburns, which for him didn't date to the 1970s but the 1870s. He'd have worn spats if they were still sold, and happily sneered at frostbitten little girls selling matches, if there were any on the streets of Excelsior.

That old-fashioned arrogance showed in his voice.

"You shouldn't leave the front unattended like this; someone could walk in and steal you blind."

"The sort of person who lusts after alpaca yarn and bamboo knitting needles isn't the sort to steal them," she said. "Is that why you came in? To warn me not to leave the front unguarded?"

"It would have been, if I'd known. What I want to know is, what is this I hear about Mrs. Winters?"

"Martha Winters? What about her?" she asked impatiently. More gossip!

"Did she murder her husband?"

Betsy stared at him. "What in the world makes you ask a question like that?"

"That skeleton they found on that boat."

"The skeleton is a female."

He gestured impatiently. "*I* know that! But I heard it might belong to that woman Carl Winters is supposed to have run off with. I suppose it occurred to everyone when they found it that maybe Carl didn't run off with her, he murdered her. But now I hear they're looking for Carl's body, too; they think Mrs. Winters murdered both of them.''

"Where on *earth* did you hear that?''

Mickels looked suddenly less angry, and his voice was less certain when he said, "Irene Potter told me, over at the Waterfront Café, not ten minutes ago.''

"Irene—? And you *believed* her?''

Mickels shrugged even less certainly. "She's not wrong *all* the time. And she was a real help solving your sister's murder.''

What he meant was that it was Irene Potter who supplied Joe Mickels with a badly needed alibi when he was a suspect.

Crewel World's building belonged to Mickels, who had long planned to tear it down and put up something bigger. He had been ruthlessly leaning on Betsy's sister Margot for months, trying to make her give up her lease and move out. His eagerness to dispossess Betsy after Margot's death and his fury on learning that even Margot's death hadn't broken the lease had soured any early chance of rapprochement between him and Betsy.

Now he hoped that when Margot's estate was closed, Betsy would take the money and close the shop. Struggling with the arcana of small business, Betsy often considered doing just that. Among the things stopping her was a disinclination to give Joe Mickels the satisfaction. She was aware that Mickels believed he was being mostly polite and endlessly accommodating. For example, he allowed her to live in Margot's old apartment over the shop and hadn't even raised the rent. Which he could still do, if she aggravated him enough.

So Betsy reined in her impatience and said, "Sit

down, Mr. Mickels. Would you like a cup of coffee?''

Warily, he took a seat. "No, thanks, I just had one."

She sat down across from him. "Why did you think
Irene was right when she told you Martha Winters murdered both her husband and that woman—I can't think
of her name—"

"Trudie Koch. She was a waitress at the Blue Ribbon
Café. Well, when I came into the Waterfront, Irene was
there talking sixteen to the dozen with Myrtle Jensen,
who—I don't know if you know her, she's one of the
Excelsior Historical Society ladies. Myrtle was telling
about how Sergeant Malloy interrogated her over this
skeleton business, wanting to know when the *Hopkins*
was sunk. She—Myrtle—sold him a history book that
said it was 1949, and he wanted to know what month,
and she told him it was the second or third of July.''
Suddenly, deftly, he put on the face of a sweet old lady
and spoke in a soft, old voice. " 'I remember it was July
because a neighbor came over and told me he saw it
being towed out to be sunk the day before, or maybe
the day before that. It was on the Fourth of July he came
over, we were boiling corn in our backyard, it was simply blazing hot, my poor husband was just miserable in
all that heat taking care of the fire, and we gave our
neighbor an ear and he told me he'd seen it being towed
out full of rocks.' ''

Betsy, smiling at his clever impression, asked, "And
what did Irene say?"

And Mickels became Irene Potter of the shiny eyes
and malicious tongue. He said, in a skillful parody of
Irene's rapid speech, " 'I've been talking to people who
remember back then, and what I *conclude* is that Martha
found out her Carl was messing around with Trudie and
she got into a fight with Carl and hit him, and killed
him, and buried him in her backyard, and then she went

down to meet Trudie when Trudie got off work—in
place of Carl, you see—and hit her and hid her body on
the boat, which was tied up right there waiting to be
towed out and sunk.' What was interesting is that Myrtle
said Martha gave up gardening the year her husband
disappeared, her yard went all to weeds, she said. And
then she said everyone always liked Carl Winters, he
didn't have an enemy in the world. He liked to flirt with
the ladies, but it was all in fun, Myrtle said, and he was
a hard worker, always taking on little part-time jobs in
addition to his dry cleaners.'' Again there was a hint of
old lady in Mickels's repetition of Myrtle's report.

Betsy smiled. ''Well, I kind of hate to spoil everyone's fun, but it's impossible that the skeleton is Trudie's. You see, Carl and Trudie disappeared in 1948, and
the *Hopkins* wasn't sunk until 1949. For another thing,
I talked with Sergeant Malloy only yesterday and he
didn't say a word about looking for Carl Winters's body.
And, *one more* thing, if I may be so bold: What's *your*
interest in this?''

''Because I used to own the mortgage on Winters's
dry cleaning store. I bought it after Martha took it over,
and I'm the one who brought the mortgage to her after
the last payment and watched her burn it.''

He seemed to think that was all the explanation necessary and turned away to look around the needlework
shop—though she suspected he was not seeing the shop
but its replacement. Doubtless something in steel and
granite, with THE MICKELS BUILDING engraved in stone
over the entrance.

At last he became aware of something in the silence
and turned back to find Betsy looking at him inquiringly.

His forehead wrinkled while he did a swift dig into
his memory to see where she had stopped following his
chain of reason, and said, ''Mrs. Winters took over the

dry cleaners and ran it by herself after Carl disappeared.''

But Betsy still looked at him inquiringly.

He said impatiently, ''Don't you see? If she killed him, she couldn't inherit that place, not legally! I don't know who should have inherited it, but she couldn't, because you can't profit from a crime! I may have to run this through a court, and going to law always costs a fortune!''

Betsy sighed. Of course, if it was important to Mr. Mickels, it involved money.

He continued, ''How sure are you about the discrepancy in the year?''

''Mrs. Winters sat in that very chair a week ago yesterday and told me and three other women that Carl disappeared in 1948. So if the history books say the *Hopkins* was sunk in 1949, then the skeleton can't be Trudie Koch's, unless the murderer saved her up for a year in his basement.''

Mickels's enormous sandy eyebrows lifted, then something almost like a smile pulled his wide, thin mouth. He smacked his hand gently on the table and got to his feet. ''I guess I should have known better than to believe Irene Potter. Thank you, Ms. Devonshire.''

After he left, Betsy sat for awhile, thinking. Why had Mickels come to her about this? Did he think she was investigating again? Well, why wouldn't he? Everyone else did! She grimaced and went back to sorting out magazines. This one looked tattered. Look, someone had torn four pages out of it, stealing a pattern. What nerve!

But as she continued, she had trouble concentrating. Something was waving its hand from the back of her mind. What? Something about fishing from a boat.

She tried to dismiss it, but again the thought waved for her attention, and she sat back on her heels. She could picture the *Hopkins*, stripped of its superstructure, waiting to be towed out—no, pulled up onto the shore and abandoned. Ah, that was it! Martha Winters had said something about the boat sitting on the lakeshore, being used by boys as a fishing pier. How long had it sat there before being towed out and sunk? Two years or more, according to Martha. Betsy considered that. Perhaps it was something she should mention to Malloy. A murderer certainly wouldn't keep a body in his basement, but he might stuff it into the bottom of an old wreck. And if he had, it might remove that discrepancy of a year between Carl and Trudie disappearing and the boat being sunk behind the Big Island. Malloy should be told so he could look into it.

She went to the library table and phoned the police department. Sergeant Malloy was out, so she left word for him to call. But, haunted by doubt, she dialed another number.

This time, she called Mayor Jamison at his day job. "Excuse me for bothering you with a stupid question, but do you remember back when you were a kid and you used to fish off the *Hopkins*—well, I guess it was the *Minnetonka*, then—over by the dredging company?"

Jamison laughed and replied in his flat midwestern twang, "You bet! Why, has someone been telling you about the time I played hookey?"

"No—"

"Good, because I didn't start playing hookey until the third grade, and the boat was gone by then." Jamison laughed again.

Betsy, smiling now, said, "No, I wanted to ask you if you remember a terrible smell coming from that boat one summer."

"A terrible smell?"

"You know, like something died on board her."

"No, it never smelled like anything but water weed and fuel oil. We used to crawl all over the inside of that thing and come out looking like we was part mermaids and part oil riggers. Well, we did find a drowned rat in there once. And I guess it did stink. What's this all about, anyhow?"

"Nothing much, especially since you tell me you climbed all over the inside of the boat. That's right, isn't it? There wasn't a room or something below decks you couldn't get at, was there?"

"No. Anyway, there wasn't a room under the main deck to start with. Why, is it important?"

"No, no. Not from what you tell me."

"Say, listen here, are you—What?" This last query was asked away from the receiver. "Gosh, I forgot, thanks for reminding me. Betsy, I've got a meeting to get to. Talk to you later. Good-bye."

Betsy hung up, and this time when she went back to work, her mind was clear and at ease. If someone had stuffed a body into that boat while it was pulled up on shore, Jamison and his childhood buddies would have found it. She smiled to think of the sensation that would have caused in this town; no one would ever have forgotten that! She pictured the slightly shy mayor as a boy crawling around on a big old boat, tearing his clothes on rusty nails, coming home smeared with algae and traces of antique fuel oil. Perhaps he'd caught a nice bass to mollify his mother; Lake Minnetonka has long been famous for its bass.

But she was positive now; the skeleton couldn't be Trudie Koch.

The front door sounded, and Godwin came in, a bulky package in his arms, all amused about something. "Guess what I heard?" he asked. "The police are going to arrest Martha Winters for the murder of Trudie Koch and dig up her yard to see if her husband is buried there."

"How dare you go carrying outrageous tales like that?" she demanded. "Poor Martha, she's a very nice woman who probably never killed anything bigger than a fly in her whole life."

Godwin, taken aback, said, "Well, she does seem an unlikely candidate for that sort of thing, since I've never seen her lose her temper. But I heard from two different people that Malloy is going to arrest her." His eyes narrowed. "Of course, maybe she's been afraid to show her real self in case people suspected."

"Godwin, listen to me, this vicious rumor-mongering has got to stop! I don't want to hear one more word from you or anyone else about Martha Winters murdering people. It isn't true. It can't possibly be true. That skeleton can't be Trudie's." She explained the discrepancy in years, concluding, "Now you see why it can't be true, and why I want you to stop spreading that terrible story."

Godwin said with admiration, "I might have *known* you would investigate and come up with the truth. You are *so* clever! I can't wait to lay this on Irene next time I see her. I hope she comes in this afternoon."

But Irene didn't, and Godwin had to be satisfied with sharing Betsy's cleverness with other customers, though only when Betsy wasn't close enough to overhear.

Godwin had gone home, and Betsy actually had the two-sided needlepoint sign in her hand, ready to turn Closed to face the street, when Jessica Turnquist appeared outside the door, one gloved hand upraised and a pleading look on her face.

Betsy opened the door.

"Thank you, Betsy. May I come in? I really have something very important to ask you."

Betsy stepped back, but she dropped the Closed sign in place as she closed the door. "What is it?"

"You've probably heard the rumors about them arresting Martha."

"Yes, I've heard. It's ridiculous, of course."

"I'm glad you agree! Martha wouldn't murder anyone! That's why I'm here. I want you to prove it."

Betsy nearly laughed out loud. "I don't know how many times I'm going to have to repeat this. I am not a detective, I am not a police officer, I am not a private investigator. It's not my job, and I don't want the job of proving anything about anybody."

"But everyone says—"

"Everyone is wrong. Just because Sergeant Malloy asked me to ask my customers if they could recognize a bit of fabric edged with lace doesn't mean I have become a peace officer sworn to uphold the law. He put that photocopy in Needle Nest, too; why don't you go ask Pat Ingle if she'll investigate for you?"

Jessica, her eyes worried and sad, put a hand on Betsy's arm. "Because Pat Ingle wasn't the one who realized how a missing piece of needlepoint pointed to a murderer. I'm not sure why you don't want to help Martha. Perhaps it's because you're working so hard in the shop. And of course Martha isn't a relative, so you don't have the same motive you had when Margot was murdered. But please, think about it. Please. She's my very best friend and I can't bear the way the town is talking about her."

Later, pouring Sophie's little scoop of Iams Less Active cat food into her bowl, Betsy had one of those flashes of too-late insight. She *had* helped Martha! She'd proved the skeleton wasn't Trudy at all, right? Godwin doubtless had told some customers, who went eagerly to share the news with friends. For once, Betsy blessed the grapevine. By tomorrow afternoon, it would be all over town, and people would stop talking about Martha. Betsy smiled. She really had done a little deducing, and even some investigating, hadn't she? After supper she'd call Jessica and put her mind at ease.

6

On Wednesday, Diane Bolles used her lunch hour to visit Crewel World. The temperature was above freezing and the sky was sunny, so it was a pleasant walk from the Old Mill shops.

Diane was a tall, slim woman with dark hair and eyes. She wore a navy blue coat with a bright yellow scarf, a pleasant complement to the day. It was only three blocks to the bottom of Water Street, to the lake, then right on Lake for another two blocks, and she was in front of the old, dark-brick building. There were three stores on the ground floor: a sandwich shop, a used-book store, and Crewel World.

An irritating electronic *bing* sounded when she opened the door, but then she stopped short, because the shop itself was very attractive.

The first thing she noticed was how pleasantly quiet it was. Fibers are sound absorbing, and here were not only a carpeted floor, but heaps of fibers everywhere. Hanks and skeins of wool in autumn colors filled baskets of all sizes, thin wool skeins in every possible color hung from spindles on one long wall, and circular spinner racks carried floss in clusters of·greens, purples, golds, reds, and other shimmering colors. Here and there were sweaters knit in complex patterns; the booklet containing the pattern was next to each, along with a selection of knitting yarns.

The shop was fairly narrow but deep. Halfway back was the checkout counter in the form of a big old wooden desk, and temptingly near the cash register were last-minute items such as packets of needles, a pretty display of little scissors, and a shallow basket of small kits marked Sale.

A hidden sound system played classical music.

Track lighting picked out items: here a sweater, there a basket of wool, over there a spinner rack of silky floss. Though Diane was not a needleworker, the colors and displays attracted her eyes ever deeper into the place. Beyond the desk were boxy shelves laden with more wool, magazines, books, and needlework accessories Diane could not imagine the use of. But she nodded in appreciation; as a fellow shop owner, she knew a good layout when she saw it.

There was a library table in the middle of the room, at which sat a slim, fair-haired man in an expensive-looking sweater, and a plump, attractive woman in a peacock-blue dress that, while a little light for the season, suited her. The woman was putting down a mitten she'd been working on; the man was looking up at her while continuing the motions of knitting a white sock.

"May I help you find something?" the woman asked.

"No, but if you are Betsy Devonshire, I'd like to talk to you."

"Yes, I am."

The woman had a pleasant smile and a look that invited questions. Diane smiled back, and said, "My husband and I own The Old Mill on Water Street."

"Ooooh," said the slim man, and to Betsy, "It's that sweet collection of gift shops halfway down Water Street."

"Yes," Diane nodded. "I also run the gift shop at the front of The Mill."

"I've looked in your window," said Betsy. "I really like that big vase, the one filled with silk roses."

"Thank you. My place is the reason I'm here. I want to add something to my line: needlework. I spoke to an employee of yours, Shelly Donohue, who said she would make a list of prospective needleworkers for me, but I see she's not here."

The slender young man said, "Oh, *you're* the one she talked to! I can tell you she's been having trouble with that list. I'm so sorry."

Betsy was looking confused, so Diane said to her, "I brought in some antique embroidery just for display, but it seems to have created a demand, so now I'm looking for needlework to sell." Diane looked around the shop. There were four or five completed pieces framed and hung on the wall, and some pillows on display in a rocking chair, but none of them impressed her as the kind of collectibles her customers might be interested in. Beyond the checkout desk hung a collection of thin doors, each slightly more ajar than the next, and attached to them were canvases painted with Santa Clauses, angels, puppies, kittens, and mottoes. Again not what she wanted—except one. "Like that garden with the gazebo, for example," she said, pointing. "That's quite nice." She walked over for a look. "I suppose the idea is to cover the picture with embroidery?"

"Needlepoint," said the young man.

"What would it cost, if I bought this stamped cloth and the yarn or floss, to have someone else do the work? I'm sure I could sell several of these a month."

The young man frowned and shook his head. "Those aren't stamped. Each one is hand-painted, and that brings us to the problem of Shelly's list. I'm sorry, but I don't think you could afford to carry a piece like that in a finished state."

Diane felt her cheeks flame. "What do you mean? I don't sell cheap things in my shop!"

"Of *course* you don't!" said the young man. "But—"

"What Godwin is trying to say," interrupted Betsy, "is that these canvases are not inexpensive to start with. Each is not only hand-painted but done in a special way to make it possible to needlepoint over it. Even so, it takes skill to do the needlepoint properly, and a fair amount of time. I believe the going rate for needlepoint is three dollars per square inch, and that's just to cover the painting in a basic stitch like basketweave." Betsy went to the swinging door set and looked at the painting Diane had liked. "That picture is twelve by sixteen, so that would be—" Betsy rolled her eyes, trying to multiply in her head.

"Five hundred and seventy-six dollars." Diane had a gift for numbers.

"All right. Fancy stitches and beadwork would cost more, and to make a really beautiful project, you'd probably want both. Add that to the cost of that particular canvas, which is two hundred and twenty-five dollars, plus wool or silk and beads, plus two hundred dollars to be finished and framed, and you're getting pretty high in cost for a piece of needlework."

"A thousand and one dollars," said Diane. "Plus materials. Yes, you're right, that is a lot of money." She bit a thumbnail and thought. "But what about something that doesn't involve hand-painted canvases? An embroidered apron, for example? Or a tea cozy?"

Betsy said, "A favorite topic among my customers is what they might charge for what they do, if they were to do it commercially. And what it comes down to is, very few people would pay that much for an apron or a tea cozy. The work my customers do is often very beautiful, as you have realized, and takes considerable time and talent. They don't do it for money, but out of love. They most usually use finished pieces as gifts for friends and family or to ornament their own homes."

The slim young man—Godwin—said, "And on a *commercial level,* people who do needlework wouldn't be excited at the prospect of doing *twenty copies* of the same project."

"Oh, but I wouldn't want twenty copies!" said Diane. "In fact, if there's just one of something, that makes it more likely to sell! Especially since, from the way you describe it, these are original works of art. And I assure you, I have customers who might be willing to pay a good price."

Godwin said, "But wait. If you're talking embroidered aprons, you're talking iron-on patterns that are *virtually identical.* If you're talking about *original designs,* then you're back up into the four-figure price. More, *lots more,* if you want an original design that is to be worked only once." He gestured airily. "And even if your customer *had* the money, it's still not something you'll be able to *provide* them, not reliably. As Betsy said, these things are made for the pleasure of working them. Putting a price on them takes away the whole *cachet.* I mean—" He dived under the table to unzip and reach into a sports bag. He came up with a large, magnificent, nearly completed stocking with a Christmas scene on it.

Diane came closer, the pangs of covetousness curling her fingers. This was more like it! The scene was cleverly adapted to the shape of the stocking, crowded with a Christmas tree and part of a stair railing. Santa Claus's head was peeping out from behind the tree at the upper halves of two children coming down the stairs. The boy's Dr. Dentons were done in something that looked like brushed flannel; Santa's beard was a collection of tight curls; some of the ornaments on the tree were tiny glass or metal objects, and the garland was made of microscopic glass beads. Santa's sack and wrapped presents filled the toe of the stocking; like the little girl, they weren't done yet.

Diane reached a very gentle forefinger to touch the subtly rough surface of Santa's mitten. "Yes, something like this wouldn't last a day in my shop. Would you think of parting with it?"

"Not even *Bill Gates* could buy this from me," said Godwin. "It has taken me over *two hundred hours* to get this far. I did Santa's beard *three different ways* before deciding on French knots—there are ninety-two of them, you may count them if you like, and I can't tell you how grateful I am that only a third of his beard is showing, because I may not *ever* want to do another French knot. I haven't decided how to do the little girl's hair yet, but it will probably be something difficult and tedious and wonderful to look at. I'm sorry"—Godwin did not sound the least sorry—"but it's not for sale. It's a gift for someone I love, that's the *only thing* that makes it all worth while."

Diane turned and saw the helpless, commiserating look in Betsy's eyes. "I see," she said.

"That's not to say you couldn't have someone do a really fine embroidered or counted cross-stitch apron for you," said Betsy. "It's just that the price would make it the kind of apron you drape over a chair or hang on the wall as an ornament, not the sort you tie on to protect your clothing while you decorate cookies.''

Diane smiled. ''Some of my customers have kitchens with a full set of copper-bottomed pots no one is allowed to use. An apron also there strictly for show is a definite possibility.'' She opened her purse. ''How about I leave you my card? Perhaps you can ask some of your customers if they would be interested. They can call me or just drop by.''

''Certainly,'' said Betsy, taking the card. It had the crisp clean look of a new coin. NIGHTINGALE'S Enchanted Vintage for Home and Garden, it read. *Diane Bolles, Proprietor*. She smiled suddenly. ''Maybe there will be some people interested in selling some of their projects. I have customers who complain that they just can't stop doing needlework, even though they have a closet full of things and no room left to display any more of it.''

''They should rotate their work,'' said Diane. ''That way, their eyes are always refreshed by the display, instead of getting bored and not even seeing it anymore.'' She had used that reasoning to increase her own sales of prints and silk bouquets.

''What a good idea!'' said Betsy. ''I'll suggest it; it makes my heart sink when a good customer starts in about having no more space.''

''Good idea, certainly,'' drawled Godwin, ''but *I* think Diane just shot herself in the foot by sharing it.''

Diane laughed. ''I've done that before.'' She looked around again. ''You have really done some thinking in your layout.''

Betsy shrugged, her eyes suddenly sad. ''No, it was my sister who did this. I only inherited it.''

Diane said, ''I was very shocked when your sister

died in that awful way. But I've heard nothing but good things about you. I'm certainly glad you were here to assist the police in solving your sister's murder. Have you always done that kind of thing?"

Betsy smiled. "Never before in my life. It was beginner's luck, I assure you. And not likely to happen again."

"Really? But I understand you are involved in that skeleton business, helping the police with a major clue."

"Not really. The police brought me a photocopy of some fabric they found on the boat, and I've been asking my customers if they can identify it. And, as it happens, just yesterday someone did. It appears to be a sample of bobbin lace."

"Oh, I saw some bobbin lace once! It was *so* gorgeous. May I see the photocopy?"

Betsy indicated the Xerox copy still taped to the desk, and Diane looked only a moment before saying, puzzled, *"This* is bobbin lace?"

"I know, it doesn't look like anything to me, either. But a customer assures me it is water-soaked bobbin lace."

"It must have been soaking for a very long time."

"Ever since that hot, dry Fourth of July in 1949," drawled Godwin, making a sort of rhyme of it.

Diane turned to face him, her eyes blank.

"Don't look at *me,* my *mother* was a toddler in 1949!"

"Hmm?" said Diane. As part of her gift for numbers, when someone said a year that came within her lifespan she automatically subtracted to see how old she was. In 1949, she had been six years old.

"I said—" began Godwin.

"You said it was a hot, dry Fourth of July," interrupted Diane brusquely. "It wasn't. In 1949, the Fourth of July was cold and wet. I remember because my Aunt Faye and Uncle James were in town and they were going to take me to the amusement park and then out on a boat to watch the fireworks, and we couldn't go because it rained all day.''

Betsy said sharply, ''Are you *sure?*''

''Yes, why?''

''Because our police investigator is using an eyewitness to close in on the exact day the *Hopkins* was sunk. The eyewitness says someone came to her on the Fourth of July in 1949 to say he'd seen it towed out to be sunk a day or two before—and she described the day as blazing hot.''

''Then she's wrong,'' said Diane. ''I cried all afternoon because we couldn't go, and Aunt Faye said I mustn't make it rain indoors as hard as it was raining outdoors. It rained all that day, and all evening, too, so we couldn't go see the fireworks, either. I was *so* disappointed.''

Godwin said, ''You were just a little kid; I bet you don't remember the year exactly. It could have been 1948, or maybe 1950.''

''No, in 1948 my Aunt Faye wasn't married yet, and in 1950 my parents took me to Yellowstone. So I am absolutely sure the Fourth of July of 1949 was cold and rainy.''

''Oh, my,'' said Betsy. ''We'd better call Sergeant Malloy right away.''

Malloy and his investigative partner stood in the doorway of the motel room, just looking. A uniformed officer was standing at parade rest just outside the door, the perfection of his stance slightly spoiled by the clipboard he was holding in one hand poking out from behind his back. Malloy's partner would sign in on the clipboard—

Malloy had handled the skeleton, so it was his partner's turn to handle the physical inspection of this body—but neither went in just yet.

A thin, elderly man lay on his back across the bed, whose white chenille bedspread was slightly rumpled. He was wearing an old brown suit, more than slightly rumpled. His legs were off the end of the bed from about mid-calf, and his right hand hung off the bed on the near side. A semiautomatic handgun was on the floor under the hand.

A small table had a lamp on it, the lamp turned on, though it was broad daylight outside. Of course, the heavily lined curtains were pulled shut, so when the door was shut, perhaps the light was necessary.

The state crime bureau had sent a crew—"Getting to be a habit, isn't it, Malloy?" one had wisecracked—and had photographed and videotaped everything. The medical examiner was on the scene.

Malloy held out his hand for the clipboard and asked the cop, "Were you the first responder?"

"Yessir."

Everyone seemed to have signed in and out properly; Malloy gave the clipboard to his partner to sign. "Have you checked the other rooms?" he asked the cop.

"Yessir. There were only two other customers checked in last night; one up next to the office and the other down at the corner. Both checked out before nine this morning, and the room down at the end's been cleaned up already. The other one doesn't seem out of the ordinary, and none of the rest of the rooms looked disturbed."

"Did you turn any lights on when you went in here?"

"Nossir."

"Is the condition of the room now just as you found it?"

The cop came to attention before stepping around to peek in. You could always tell the ones who came to the police from the military. "Yessir."

"Who found the body?"

"Cleaning ladies. Two of them."

"Where are they?"

"In the office."

"Your witness," said Malloy to his partner and went to talk to the cleaning ladies. He detoured on his way to the unit at the end, the one also guarded by a uniformed officer. He didn't go in, just opened the door and looked. Bed mussed, one pillow used, no luggage left, towels on the bathroom floor, smell of aftershave, empty pizza box standing slantwise in the wastebasket. Nothing odd or out of place. His partner would do a more thorough search, of course.

The cleaning ladies turned out to be a pair of middle-aged women. Sitting with them on a couch, equally scared and distressed, was the owner of the motel. Her husband, she said, was at his part-time job in Excelsior.

The Hillcrest Motel, which was not located atop a hill but at the foot of one just outside Excelsior, was owned and run by an older couple. It had twelve rooms and an office along two sides of a blacktop parking lot. A small, shabby laundromat, also owned by the couple, occupied the third side. All the buildings were coated with faded pink stucco crumbling around the edges.

The cleaning partners were locals who lived just up the road. They'd worked here two years, but only while school was in. They were dressed in those aprons that cover all your clothing, even in back. These were a matching set in mint green. Patterned scarves were tied around their heads, à la Lucy Ricardo and Ethel Mertz. They had their heavy rubber gloves in their laps and they were smoking up a storm, their way of handling the fright, sickness, and excitement of this event.

They said they had knocked on the door of room seven about two, checkout time—it was now quarter after three—and when there was no reply, Lise had unlocked the door and they had seen the body and run pell-mell for the office to tell Mary to dial 911. No, they hadn't gone in, no they hadn't turned on any lights or checked to see if the man was really dead—of course he was dead, it only took one look to tell he was dead. Their little wheeled cart was still right outside the door— it wasn't? Well, they hadn't moved it, they had come right here as fast as they could and had been here ever since and did Malloy know when they might be able to finish their work and go home?

Malloy questioned them closely, but their answers were decidedly innocent. He asked if they could stay here for awhile, until the room on the end had been searched. Then they could clean it.

He turned to the owner, Mary Olsen. She said the man had checked in alone late yesterday afternoon and seemed all right, except all tired out from driving. She produced the sign-in card the man had filled out.

Malloy took it, a little five-by-six piece of thin white cardboard, and sat a few moments staring at it, because the name on it had a certain familiarity: Carl Winters. And from what Malloy remembered of the death scene, this Carl was about the right age to be the other Carl, the Carl that was Martha Winters's husband. The address on the card was Omaha, Nebraska. Hadn't run far, then. Hadn't done well, either, by the shabby suit and the tired old Chevy with Nebraska plates that was parked outside his unit. Trudie, it seemed, wasn't as valuable a partner as Martha had been.

"He check in alone?"

"Yes, and I watched his car pull up to his unit and he was the only one who got out."

"Did he make any phone calls?" asked Malloy.

She checked. "Just one, a local call."

Since he hadn't gone through a switchboard, she had no record of the number the victim had called. Malloy noted the time of the call in his notebook.

He got the names and addresses of the other two guests, then went back and stood again in the doorway and watched his partner. The medical examiner was with the body, taking measurements.

"Whaddaya think," said Malloy, "he comes home to commit suicide?"

"So you know who he is?"

"Unless he signed in under a false name, our victim was one Carl Winters, who was alleged to have run off with a waitress back in 1948, leaving his wife Martha to run the dry cleaning store and raise their son all by herself. So now he's old and sick and sorry, so he comes home, calls his wife, who tells him to get stuffed, so he suicides."

"One problem with that theory," said Malloy's partner.

"What's that?"

"This wasn't a suicide."

On his way back to the station, Malloy put in a call for Jill Cross to meet him there. She was standing beside her squad car when he pulled into the parking lot and approached at his gesture, breath gently steaming, to bend with the awkwardness imposed by a Kevlar vest and heavy winter police jacket to look in his window.

"You heard about the gunshot victim at Hillcrest?" he asked.

"Yes, I did."

"Identification on the body and the registration card both say it's Carl Winters."

"Oh, lord," said Jill.

"He made one local call after he arrived yesterday. The motel can't say to who, but it isn't hard to guess."

"So you want me to come along when you tell her?"

Malloy nodded. "It may be an arrest situation. It's not a suicide we're dealing with here, unless he had the rare gift of being able to shoot himself from across the room."

Jill stared at Malloy, who stared calmly back. She said after a bit, "We're going to arrest Martha Winters?"

"No, we're going to go talk to her. Carl Winters isn't exactly the rarest name in the world, so we're not even positive it's her husband. I'm going to go talk to her about what happened, see which way she jumps. She's not a professional criminal; if she did it, she may be waiting to tell us all about how she murdered Trudie Koch all those years ago and hid her body in that boat, and now has rounded things off by shooting her husband."

Jill was even more surprised. "I thought the skeleton couldn't be Trudie."

"Here, get in, I'm letting all the heat out through this window."

Jill came around and got in the car which, though without markings, proclaimed itself a public safety vehicle on the inside with a two-way radio and a red light with a magnet that could be stuck on the roof or dash.

Jill by now had another question. "If it is Martha Winters's husband, what brought him back to town?"

"The story of the skeleton they found on the *Hopkins*. It's been turning up in papers all across the country; I've got inquiries from as far away as Fort Meyers, Florida."

"But I thought there wasn't a connection between the

body hidden on the *Hopkins* and the disappearance of Carl and Trudie Koch. I thought they happened a year apart.''

"Everyone thought so—except Irene Potter, whose lunatic speculations to a local columnist inspired a story about small-town gossip that apparently got picked up and reprinted. Our victim had a clipping in his wallet from the Omaha *World-Herald*. Irene would blow a gasket if she could see how she's described in that story—though the columnist was careful not to give her name. But you know how it is, even a stopped clock is right twice a day. Here, buckle up; I'll tell you the rest on our way to Winters Dry Cleaning.''

They pulled out of the parking lot, and Malloy began to unwind his theory. "Around twelve thirty today I got a call from Diane Bolles, who owns Nightingales, over in the Old Mill. She says she was talking to Betsy Devonshire and somehow the subject of the Fourth of July 1949 came up—and Ms. Bolles is as sure as she can be that it rained all day the Fourth of July 1949. I have a witness who told me that the day she heard about them sinking the *Hopkins* was the Fourth of July, and it was a blazing hot day. I called the Minneapolis public library, which keeps weather records, and guess what?''

"What?'' said Jill.

"The Fourth of July 1949 *was* rainy. *But* the Fourth of July in 1948, the year Carl Winters and Trudie Koch went missing, was stinking hot. Every book about the streetcar steamboats and the raising of the *Minnehaha* I've looked at says 1949. But I wonder if maybe they're wrong, every damn one of them.''

Jill said, "How did that happen, that they're all wrong?''

Malloy gestured sharply. "I wondered the same thing, but the chief says he read just the other day about that

sort of thing, which happens all the time, he says. Someone researching the history of a town asks a local what
year something happened, and the local says, '1949, I
think,' and the author writes that down as fact, and for
years after that, other history writers use his book as the
source instead of asking around. The chief was about to
send me out to find more people who were here in 1948
when the call came in about the body at the motel. But
the upshot is, where before it wasn't possible, now it is
entirely possible that the skeleton on the *Hopkins* is Trudie Koch.''

Jill sat back in silence. She thought about Martha
Winters, who seemed to be such a nice, quiet, competent
lady. Her grandson was nice too, a good-looking young
man who seemed content to take over the dry cleaning
business his grandfather had founded. Jeff's father was
an executive with 3M, and reportedly disappointed in
the boy's lack of ambition.

Jeff had been only a year behind Jill in high school;
she'd actually danced with him once or twice. And she'd
sat on more than one occasion at the table in Crewel
World with Martha and the rest of the Monday Bunch.
It gave her an odd feeling to think she might be about
to help arrest a Monday Bunch member for murder.
She'd ask Malloy to get someone else, except she was
the only female cop on the little force, and they needed
a female cop to do this because Martha was a female.

Jill had never arrested anyone for murder. The worst
arrest she'd ever made was the time she'd brought in a
teen high on drugs who had thrown a plastic garbage
can full of trash at her. And that had been hard because
she knew the kid's parents really well.

Of course, in a small town, any arrests you made were
likely to be of people you knew or at least knew about.
But Martha Winters? A murderer? That seemed im-

possible. Surely there was some other explanation.

"Do we have to go talk to her right now? Maybe there's some other explanation."

"Maybe there is," agreed Malloy, "but we have to talk to Mrs. Winters anyway. Tell her that her husband is a murder victim. But I kind of think she might be able to help us figure out why."

7

It wasn't far to the dry cleaners, a small, flat-roofed building whose entire customer area was plate glass. They walked into a reek of cleaning fluid and Malloy said to the young man behind the counter, "Hi, Jeff. Is your grandmother here?"

"She's home this afternoon," the young man replied. There was no hint of reserve or nervousness in his voice. He seemed only as surprised and curious as anyone would be when the police come asking for a grandparent.

So they went without undue haste to the modest house, a two-story brick with a small front yard shaded by a towering blue spruce.

Jill saw Malloy heave a deep breath and felt for him. And herself. Martha Winters had never earned so much as a parking ticket and was a good, churchgoing Lutheran. If they made a slip here, the town would have their badges. Yet the questions had to be asked.

They went up the brick steps to the front door, and

Malloy rang the bell. It was opened by Martha in a gray housedress and slippers. With her round, pleasant face and white hair, she looked like Norman Rockwell's model of a grandmother. But when she saw Jill's uniform her hand went to her mouth. "What's happened?" she asked. "Is it Jeff?"

"No, ma'am," said Malloy. "We just left him at the store; he's fine. May we come in?"

"All right." Martha stepped back.

The tiny area immediately inside the door was tiled, and there was a coat closet on the left. The immaculate living room was to their right, carpeted in a powder blue plush that was pleasant to the feet. Most of the wall facing the street was a box-pleated drape in a matching color, open in the center to show a big square window. The couch was ribbon-striped, green, beige, and blue. The recliner was vinyl in a green that didn't quite match—that's Jeff's, I bet, thought Jill—and there was a velvet easy chair in beige. Martha sat in the easy chair and motioned them to the couch. On the wall over the couch, pressed behind glass frames, were three ecru handkerchiefs with elaborate lace edging.

"Thanks, I'll stand," said Malloy, and Jill braked and turned to stand to the left and a little behind him. But her eye wandered again to the handkerchiefs; were those edgings bobbin lace?

"Mrs. Winters, do you know where your husband is?" asked Malloy.

Martha started to pretend to be surprised at the question, but discarded the attempt immediately. "He's at the Hillcrest Motel out on Seven," she said in a low voice.

"Did he call you from there yesterday?"

She nodded. "But I don't want to see him. I told him that and told him not to call me again." Her lip trembled. "Is that why you're here? To talk to me about him? I don't want to, you know. Except to ask if I'll have to divorce him, now I know he's alive. Or will I?" Her faded blue eyes moved from Malloy to Jill and back again. "I mean, he's legally dead, isn't he?"

"Ma'am, I'm sorry to be the one to tell you this, but we think he's really dead. A body was found in his room this afternoon, and the driver's license we found on the body has his name on it."

Martha sat back, and her lips began to move in a very odd way. A smile came and went, came and broadened, and suddenly she began to laugh. Jill and Malloy looked at one another in wonder.

The laughter quickly became hysterical, and Jill went in search of a bathroom. She found one and wet a washcloth in cold water, which she brought back along with a small glass of water. She applied the cloth to Martha's face, speaking soothingly to her.

"Here now, here now, it's all right, it's all right. You're going to be fine. I want you to drink this."

The laughter caught on a sob and stumbled to a halt. Martha took the glass from Jill and took a sip, then another. "Thank you, Jill," she said at last. "I'm all right now." But her hand trembled, and her face was white.

"You sure?"

Martha nodded. She took the washcloth and wiped her eyes and mouth, then folded it carefully into her hand.

Malloy said, "What can you tell us about your husband's return?"

Martha closed her eyes. "Nothing. I was surprised, of course. I really thought he was dead." Her eyes opened. "I don't know why he came back or what he wanted. He's an old man, let's see, he must be seventy-seven—no, seventy-eight. I don't know what he thought I would say, calling me like that right out of the blue, saying he

wanted to see me, would I come over. To a motel? I ask
you! And I told him not to come here, either. The idea!
He tried to coax me, argue with me, and I said, 'I don't
want to talk to you, now or ever!' and I hung up on
him.'' Her face changed from an echo of the indignation
she must have felt to concern. "What, was he sick? I
thought about it after I went to bed last night, maybe I
should have listened to him, maybe he's sick and *she*
left him and he's all alone . . .''

"Who left him?" asked Malloy.

"Why that waitress, what was her name, Gertrude
something. Trudie, she was called. The young woman
he went off with—I suppose that's true, now, isn't it?
She probably left him a month after they ran off together. So what was it he died of? Heart? Cancer?''

"No, ma'am, he was shot.''

Her eyes and mouth became three round *O*s. "Shot?
I don't understand. You said he was dead."

"He is," said Malloy patiently. "He was shot to death
in his room and someone tried to make it look like suicide.''

"Oh. Oh! Yes, I should have thought of suicide—but
you say it wasn't suicide.''

"No, ma'am.''

"But then, who shot him? Was it her—Trudie? Surely
he wouldn't have brought her along and then called
me." Her expression was verging on the indignant
again.

"We don't know who shot him. That's what we're
trying to determine. But before we go any further, I think
we have to be sure the deceased was Carl Winters. How
sure are you that the man you talked to on the phone
was your husband?''

"Oh, it was Carl, all right. His voice was pretty much
the same, and he talked like he always talked, kind of

bossy and sure of himself. He said he had something important to tell me, he wouldn't say what it was, except it was something I needed to know. He talked just like he used to, telling me to just hush and listen to him. As if what he did to me didn't matter, as if after all these years I hadn't gotten over letting him talk to me like that!''

''Yes, ma'am,'' said Malloy. He reached into his coat pocket and pulled out an old wallet. ''Do you recognize this?''

''No.''

He opened it, found the section that holds photographs or credit cards, turned it around and held it out. ''Do you recognize this?''

Jill leaned forward just a bit and saw it was an old photograph of a woman in a ruffled apron standing in front of a freshly planted evergreen tree.

Martha turned her face away. ''That's me,'' she said. ''He used to carry that photograph. He took it the day after I told him I was pregnant. He bought that tree, it's the one out in the front yard. He said he wanted it to remind him of the days before I lost my figure.'' Her mouth quivered. ''I didn't lose my figure until Carl ran out on me.'' She looked toward the wallet. ''Funny he kept it, isn't it?'' Her eyes were hurt and puzzled.

''Do you know if Carl called anyone else but you?''

''I have no idea. I shouldn't think so, but Carl did have the capacity to surprise me.'' She blinked twice then said, ''What are you going to do with him—his body?''

''There will be an autopsy, and then the medical examiner will give you a call and you can tell him what you want done with the body.''

A very odd expression crossed Martha's face, but all she said was, ''Very well.''

"Have you any idea who would want him dead after all these years?"

She thought briefly. "No. Not even me."

"Well," said Malloy, "thank you very much for your cooperation. I'm going to leave you one of my cards," he added, handing it to her. "If you think of anything, please contact me. And if I have any more questions, may I talk to you again?"

"Yes, of course. I'll be at the store tomorrow morning."

Malloy was obviously finished, so Jill asked, "Martha, those handkerchiefs over the sofa. Did you do the lace on them?"

Martha nodded. "I won a blue ribbon at the State Fair with the one in the middle. I gave it up after Carl left. I was too busy with the store and raising Henry. Probably my eyes are too bad now to take it up again."

Jill went to the couch and leaned toward the middle one. "I can't imagine eyes good enough for this kind of thing to start with. I mean, look at the thread—such delicate work—oh, and look, the corner has a butterfly."

"I always put that butterfly in the lace I was keeping for my own use. It was kind of a signature."

"This is bobbin lace, isn't it?"

"Yes, why?"

"The subject came up at the last Monday Bunch meeting. Did you know Alice does bobbin lace?"

"She does? Why of course, I remember she used to. I didn't know she still did. How interesting." Martha did not sound very interested, and appeared suddenly to realize that. She stirred on the chair and said more positively, "I'll have to talk to her some time."

They did leave then. Outside, Malloy said, "Slick, Cross. I was wondering how to ask without getting her all suspicious."

"Thank you," said Jill, gratified. Compliments from Malloy were rare. She wondered if she'd get mentioned in his report. Probably not. And after all, the way Martha reacted to Malloy's questioning, it was obvious she was innocent.

For all the skull's lack of cooperation, Kerric finished it rapidly. She got out her box of glass eyes and looked at them, and the half-formed face, for several minutes. White folks' eyes were so variable! She finally picked out a blue pair and fitted them into place, then worked the eyelids over them. She wasn't satisfied with the result and tried lowering the lids a bit, which was better but still didn't quite do it. She took the glass eyes out and put brown ones in, which was another improvement, but still not right. She couldn't think what else she could do, and sat staring at it, baffled.

She had given the lips a hint of a smile, and had found evidence of an old break in the nose and so had made it a trifle crooked, with a bump. There was a rakish air of reality in these details somehow not reflected in the eyes. She wished she were a better artist, able to capture such subtleties. She sketched eyebrows onto the forehead, hoping that would help, but it didn't, much. She colored the lips deep red—lipstick in the forties was red, red, red—and got out a selection of wigs.

Eyes were merely variable; hair was infinite in its variety. Blond, she decided, though she'd given the face dark eyebrows. What were the hairstyles of fifty years ago? Not that it mattered, all she had were modern wigs. She picked a medium-length one and tried tying it up in various ways, then finally left it loose.

She put the completed head on a shelf over her desk, sat down in her chair, and looked up at it. There was a face looking back, all right.

Who are you? she asked one more time.

And still the answer was silence. But now it was a sullen silence. The eyes said she really hated the hair.

Malloy got a fax of an eight-by-ten photograph of the face on Monday morning. It had the almost-real look of such re-creations, with a pleasant expression that didn't reach the eyes, which had a sullen glare.

Still, it was a whole lot better than the fractured skull he'd started with.

He took the picture along on another visit to the strong room in City Hall. The Historical Society women weren't in session today, but he would catch them later. Right now—Yes, he was right; among the books on the shelves were high school yearbooks, from back when Excelsior had its own high school.

It took some searching. He didn't know when Trudie graduated from high school or even if she had. As it turned out, she hadn't, but she'd been a cheerleader as a sophomore.

Trudie as a sophomore had been a brown-eyed bru-nette, her face a little plumper than the re-created face. But there were undoubted similarities; the general shape of the face, the line of jaw, and the slightly crooked nose with a bump. Both faces had a hint of the sensual, with full lips and slightly heavy eyelids. To Malloy's think-ing, there were far more similarities than differences, enough to call it a match.

Identification of a skeleton from a recreated face wasn't admissible in court, but Malloy was now sure that it was Trudie Koch who had died violently fifty-one years ago, and her body hidden on the steamboat *Hopkins*, just before it was taken out and sunk. In 1948.

Malloy had thought it possible that Carl Winters mur-dered Trudie and fled. In fact, it was still possible. But it was also possible that someone else had murdered Trudie, someone with a hatred so deep and bitter that it reached out again to take Carl's life. And there was only one person Malloy knew about who might reserve her hatred and bitterness over that many years. He'd check further, of course, because if he was right in his surmise, it was also clear that Martha Winters was one hell of a dissembler.

The Monday Bunch meeting was in order, the chair was serving hot cocoa in honor of the first snowstorm of the season. It was very bad out, because yesterday had been very cold, so what had begun as a thin rain today froze the instant it landed on street and sidewalk. The official weather reports had predicted rain turning to snow by evening, but this hadn't waited until evening. The rain had quickly become sleet, and now was snow, the gorgeous, feathery stuff every white-Christmas-lover dreams about.

But snow over ice can be a lethal combination. The schools realized what they were faced with, and students were sent home at noon. So Shelly was present, and very pleased about it. "Two inches, they said this morning, but it turned to snow before they thought it would, and the storm system isn't moving through like they said it would, either, so now they're saying more like six, maybe seven. Late start tomorrow, I bet."

"Late start?" said Betsy.

"Schools will start late if kids have to bus from a distance. It will take awhile to clear the roads."

"If it snows six or seven inches by tonight, I bet school won't start at all tomorrow," said Betsy.

"She's not from Minnesota," explained Godwin, showing compassion for her ignorance, and there were friendly chuckles.

"I don't understand," said Betsy.

"That means," said Shelly, "that it takes a blizzard to close a school in Minnesota, and six inches isn't quite a blizzard."

"Too bad," said Betsy, having fond memories of school closings.

"Lots of accidents, however," said Jill, thinking ahead to her night on patrol. "Always are with the first storm, until people remember how to drive in this stuff."

This set off a round of complaints about Minnesota winters, with an undertone Betsy had come to recognize as boasting. "We can take it, bring on your worst," they seemed to be saying.

Betsy, who had only to walk up a flight of stairs to be home, and who had not seen snow like this for many years, ignored all that. She was filled with warm pleasure every time she looked out her window. It was so incredibly beautiful. How could these people not appreciate how magical it was to see snow falling?

A huge dump truck with a gigantic plow on its front pushed down the street. As it went by, Betsy could see little whirly motors spinning sand out from the bin in back. It spoiled the opaque whiteness of the street, but of course it had to be done.

She looked around the table. There were more than the usual four or five present—seven, in fact. The carpet under the table was crowded with discarded boots and blue plastic Crewel World bags. There was a pleasant air of anticipation among the women, which seemed focused on Betsy. Since there had never been any presiding done at these meetings, she was at a loss to know what they were waiting for.

She said, "I got in a shipment of embroidery hoops and some iron-on patterns, and it inspired me to try out some old skills." She reached into her work basket and

pulled out a white apron with a fifties pattern of vegetables with smiling faces half embroidered on it. "Diane
Bolles is looking for work like this to sell in her shop.
Actually, she's looking for much better work than this;
I won't pass this around because I know how you all
are about the back." That got an agreeable laugh; the
Monday Bunch thought the back of needlework should
be as presentable as the front, and Betsy had never been
that fussy.

"I think my mother had an apron like that," said
Kate.

Jessica, who was sitting in the first chair at Betsy's
right, said, "You do beautiful French knots. And you
have a good eye for centering and layout of the pattern."

"Thank you," said Betsy, pleased.

Then silence fell again, and again they all seemed to
be waiting for Betsy to do something, but just as she
was about to cry, "What? What do you want of me?"
Martha stood and lifted a big paper bag onto the table.

"We have something for you," she said. "We want
you to know how much we appreciate your keeping
Crewel World open. And we want to show how much
we loved your sister, all of us." They all nodded sol-
emnly. "And we came up with this way of telling you."

She opened the bag and brought out a box about
twenty-four inches square and about three inches deep.
It was wrapped in red foil paper and tied with golden
ribbon and matching bow. She handed the box to Betsy,
who stood to receive it. It was so heavy she nearly
dropped it—and that gave a hint to its contents.

Her comprehension showed on her face and the
women laughed softly. Shelly said, "The hardest part
was finding a finisher who wouldn't automatically send
it back here to you."

Betsy sat down and admired the wrapping awhile.

"It's very pretty," she said. Someone handed her a pair of scissors from the basket of needleworking tools in the middle of the table, and she obediently cut the ribbon and used a blade of the scissors to open one end of the paper. The box inside was heavy cardboard, and again the scissors were needed to cut the tape.

Betsy lifted the box lid. Inside, double matted with cutouts and in a black oak frame, was a motto done in needlepoint, a fragment from the last chapter of Proverbs, which had been read to enormous effect at Margot's funeral. "Her light does not go out," it read in gold lettering on a deep blue background. Betsy did not recognize the quote at first, but then she looked at the symbols surrounding the motto and began to smile. There was a ring with a real red-glass stone ("She is worth far more than rubies"), a sheep standing in tall grass ("She selects wool and flax"), a hand grasping a kind of stick wrapped in thoroughly brushed satin stitching ("In her hand she holds the distaff"), a tiny decorated Christmas tree ("She . . . extends her hands to the needy"). There was a bright red ribbon surrounding and connecting the symbols, its meaning probably both the sashes Margot supplied to merchants and the scarlet clothing supplied her servants so they were not afraid of the cold.

"We did it as a round robin," said Martha. "Everyone in the Bunch had a hand in it."

Betsy wanted to thank them but found, to her dismay, that she was crying. The women gathered around to pat her on the back and shoulders and speak comforting words, and after awhile she realized her weeping was a more effective thank-you than anything she could have said.

When at last everyone was settled down again, and

projects were brought out to be worked on, Betsy asked, "Whose idea was this, anyway?"

Martha said quietly, "Mine. But actually it was inspired by something Jessica gave me when Carl disappeared. Remember?" she asked Jessica.

Jessica bowed her head as if embarrassed and murmured, "Yes."

"When she gave that to me, it was the beginning of our friendship. She's been such a comfort to me over the years."

Jessica blushed and said nothing.

"What was it?" asked Shelly.

"It was cross-stitch, a heart with Carl's and my initials in it, and the word *Forever* underneath. All those years ago." She sighed. "I still have it."

Jessica looked up, surprised. "You do?"

"Of course. It's in my bedroom where I see it every morning first thing when I wake up. You know, though, I think sometimes I see your initials instead of Carl's. Yours is the love that proved to be the forever one."

"Awwww," everyone sighed, even Godwin.

Such a surge of emotions overwhelmed the Scandinavian breeding of the Monday Bunch, and soon after, the group decided they'd had enough and would go home.

Jessica said to Martha, "That was one of my earlier efforts at cross-stitch. What people would think if you showed it to anyone! I wish you'd let me redo it properly."

Betsy smiled. She'd heard of people going back to undo and redo work they weren't satisfied with, but not at this remove of years.

Martha said, "Oh, when I first saw it, I thought it was the most beautiful thing I'd ever seen! And it's the sentiment that still counts. And don't worry about it being seen, I'm not going to enter it in a competition." Laughing, the two friends went out together.

"We didn't get much work done, did we?" Shelly remarked.

"We'll do better next time," said Kate.

But Alice Skoglund had leaned to murmur in Jill's ear, and the two stayed behind. When everyone had left, Alice said, "Betsy, maybe you should see this, too."

"What is it?" asked Jill.

Alice, her chin even more prominent and her glasses winking with importance, brought a sheet of graph paper out of her purse and unfolded it. "I've been working on that bobbin lace pattern, and I've got a big part of it figured out." She put the sheet on the desk and said, "Here is the ground, mostly spiders." There was a pattern of solid blocks, each with thin "legs" growing out from it—twelve legs, Betsy noticed, not eight.

"And here, this was very difficult, because it's weaving and open spaces, and the outline was broken and it's not complete, the bottom portion is mostly gone. But see? A butterfly."

Jill asked sharply, "How much of this was guesswork?"

Alice replied in kind, "None of it! I just took what was there and figured it out. I didn't add anything. That's why it's not complete. Where the threads were pulled thin, I tried to think what it would look like shorter, closed up, and I only connected the broken threads in a way they most likely joined. I didn't guess, I restored." She looked defiantly at Jill.

Jill said scornfully, "And you've never seen Martha Winters's work!"

"Of course I have! Why?"

"Because she always put a butterfly into her lace."

"Are you sure? *I* never saw one."

"She has three samples hanging in her living room, and all three have butterflies, and they look a lot like this one you've drawn."

"I've never been in her living room. I saw some gorgeous stuff she made for Mrs. Allen's baby's christening cap twenty years ago, and there's no butterfly on that. And I saw the pieces she made as shelf fronts for the Sutter House restoration, and there's no butterfly on them, either."

Jill frowned, then nodded. "Okay, okay, that's right, she said she put the butterfly only in pieces she meant to keep for herself."

Alice sniffed righteously, but Jill didn't apologize.

Betsy stared at the pattern on the graph paper. Jill had told her about the butterflies in the bobbin lace that edged Martha's handkerchiefs on her wall. This was bad, this was very bad.

8

It was a teachers' conference day, schoolchildren had the day off. But the portion for elementary school teachers ended at noon, and Shelly came to Crewel World after a hasty sandwich in the Waterfront Café.

"I, uh, wanted to see if you had any work for me," she said. She was looking very earnest—Betsy might have described her as desperate.

Betsy looked around doubtfully. The shop wasn't very busy; Godwin was seeing the first customer in an hour to the door.

"You see, there's that Carol Emmer counted cross-stitch pattern, and with the hours I put in last Saturday and my employee discount, I could buy it and the floss with just a few more hours' worth of work." Shelly glanced toward the front of the shop. "And, that front window isn't as good as it could be. I could redo that."

Betsy frowned at it. "I think it looks very nice."

"Well, then, how about I get out the Christmas decorations and put them up? There's lights for the window and some fat candles with needlepoint and cross-stitch decorations, and some artificial holly garland.''

"I can't afford to buy—" began Betsy.

"No, they're in the storeroom, in a big cardboard box.''

Betsy looked at Godwin, who nodded. "Well, all right," she said, wondering if perhaps Shelly needed the money for something more necessary, like groceries or car repairs. Though Shelly *was* a very avid counted cross-stitcher.

Godwin came to help her get out the box of decorations. They had been at it only a few minutes when the real reason Shelly had come to Crewel World was revealed. She asked, cautiously because of Betsy's aversion to gossip, "Did you hear about Martha Winters?''

"Hear what?" asked Godwin immediately, but then he also glanced at Betsy.

But Betsy looked inquiring as well, so Shelly burst out, "Martha is under arrest for murdering Trudie Koch!''

"Nooo!" wailed Godwin.

Betsy also made a mourning sound but said, "I guess I've been expecting that.''

Godwin said, "You have? Honestly, Betsy, I don't know how you managed not to become a private eye years and years ago! You know everything before it happens.''

Before Betsy could object to this, the door went *bing* and Jill, in uniform, entered. "Have you heard?" she asked.

"Shelly just told me. Was it the lace?''

Jill nodded.

"What lace?" Shelly asked.

"Were you there?" asked Betsy.

Again Jill nodded

"How did she take it?"

"Utterly surprised. She didn't do it, Betsy, she couldn't have, or she would have been more careful what she said when Mike interviewed her the second time. He walked all around that handkerchief, and she just kept on talking, innocent as a baby chick. I had to go stand behind her, or my face would have warned her. I couldn't believe she couldn't see what he was doing."

"What was he doing?" asked Shelly.

"She said she never rode the *Hopkins*, she didn't visit it while it was aground or while it was tied up waiting to be towed out and sunk. She said she never gave away any of her personal handkerchiefs, and that she never put butterflies in any of the lace she gave away. She said that when a handkerchief would get worn out, she'd take the lace off and put it on another handkerchief. Bobbin lace lasts forever, did you know that? Mike asked if she ever missed any handkerchiefs, and she said of course she'd lost some, but mostly got them back because people knew about the butterflies. Only two she never got back. One she lost at the State Fair in 1944, and another at the Guthrie Theatre ten or twelve years ago. She was laughing about them; she was pretty sure she dropped the one in the biggest-pig display in the pig barn and was glad no one tried to bring it back to her, because you never get the smell of pig out; and the other she thinks she saw the next season, onstage, in a production of *Othello*."

Betsy smiled, then sobered. "So she didn't understand what Mike was getting at?"

"What was he getting at?" asked Shelly.

"Yeah," seconded Godwin, "what?"

Betsy said, "Alice Skoglund worked out the pattern of the lace edging on that piece of silk and showed it to me and Jill. There was a butterfly in the pattern. Martha used to do bobbin lace, and she always put her own design of a butterfly in the lace she meant to keep for herself. And the pattern Alice figured out looks an awful lot like Martha's butterfly.''

"Oh, no," groaned Godwin.

Betsy continued, "And so Mike gave her every opportunity to explain how a handkerchief with a lace butterfly on it came to be on the *Hopkins*—other than that she left it there after hiding Trudie Koch's body on it.''

Jill said, "And Martha said she'd never taken a ride on the *Hopkins*, or gave a handkerchief to someone who later complained of losing it on the *Hopkins*.''

Shelly said, "Poor lady—but I see what you mean. If she had lost a handkerchief while hiding the body, she would have realized what Sergeant Malloy was doing, and at least tried to make up a story.''

Jill said, "Of course, he didn't ask her directly, because that would have alerted her, and she might have lied. But you're right, Shelly, if she *did* lose a handkerchief about then, even more especially while moving Trudie's body, Mike's questions would have put her on her guard. But they didn't. So he thanked her and let her get back to her baking while he went and got a warrant. They're booking her now. I think she still hasn't got a clue why.''

Godwin said, "Gosh, *Martha Winters* in *jail!*'' He turned to Betsy. "So, what do we do first?''

Betsy frowned at Godwin and said, "What do you mean?''

"*Martha,* of course. What are we going to do about her?''

"What could *we* possibly do?''

"We can *investigate*, of course! Where do we start? Who do you want to talk to?''

Betsy said, "Are you serious?"

Shelly said, "If he isn't, he should be. The nerve of Sergeant Malloy, arresting Martha! Why, nobody with a functioning brain cell could believe she's a murderer!"

Betsy said, "He's an investigator. He'll investigate, find out she's innocent, and let her go. Meanwhile, it's awful for Martha, and I'm very sad and sorry for her, but I don't think there's anything *we* can do."

"You can help me find out about the lace," Jill said, to Betsy's surprise. "Seriously, Betsy, I'd like you to talk to some people. You would be giving me a hand here. No, no, I'm not an investigator, but Mike considers me his expert on lace, and God knows I'm nothing of the sort. I'm going to ask around, but I'd like you to ask, too; help me find out about who was making lace in 1948. And while you're about it, maybe you can find out if her pattern was hard or easy to copy."

"Oh, my!" said Godwin. "I didn't think of that!"

Shelly said, "And so long as you're asking those questions, you might as well find out who else had a reason to want Trudie Koch dead." Seeing objection in Betsy's face, she hastened on, "Since it's all tied together, isn't it? If Martha didn't murder Trudie, and of course she didn't, how *did* that handkerchief get on the *Hopkins*? Someone stole one of hers, right? Or made one just like it. Why? To frame Martha. Why frame Martha? Because if poor, dumb Malloy weren't looking so hard at Martha, even he could see who really did it."

Betsy said, "That handkerchief was left on the *Hopkins* before Mike Malloy was born."

Shelly gestured. "You know what I mean, it was so the police would think Martha did it. A frame."

"And who do you think was the author of the frame?" asked Godwin.

Shelly said, "*I* don't know. That's why Betsy has to

try to find out, isn't it? But Carl Winters knew. That's why he came back, right? He learned about the skeleton on the *Hopkins*, and he knew right away who did it. He came back to tell what he knew, and that same person who killed Trudie killed him.''

Godwin said, ''Then I think we should start with Carl's murder; it's newer, so everyone's memory is fresher, there's more to find out, and more people to talk to.''

Jill said, ''There's nothing to find. The only person he called when he got back was Martha. Nobody else knew he was in town.''

Betsy said, ''Has she been charged with Carl's murder?''

Jill shrugged. ''Not yet, though the fact that only she knew he was back in town may be damning enough. I think Malloy is going to try to tie the gun to her.''

''But we *know* she didn't do it!'' said Shelly. ''So there must be some explanation. Betsy?''

Betsy thought while the others watched. ''He phoned her from the motel, right?''

Jill nodded.

''Well, he could have phoned or written or E-mailed someone else from Omaha before he left, couldn't he? Or, he could have stopped on the road and called, or he could have gone out to supper and called from the restaurant.''

''See?'' said Godwin, pleased. ''See? She's *so* clever! That's probably what happened. So how do we find out? What do we do first?''

Betsy said in an annoyed voice, ''*We* are not going to do anything! Because *you* are going to help Shelly finish with those lights and the other decorations, which had better look as if the two of you worked hard on them. And if there is any time left after that, you are going to change the yarn in the baskets to winter colors.''

"Yes, ma'am," said Shelly and she took Godwin by the elbow and led him off to the front window. But she was smiling.

Betsy said to Jill, "How about if I go talk to Alice Skoglund? She's the one who figured out that pattern from that little piece Malloy found. She couldn't be a suspect, could she? Because I don't know from lace, either, and she could tell me just about anything and I'd believe it.''

"Alice, a suspect?" murmured Jill, her pale eyebrows raised. *"Alice?"*

"Yeah, yeah, okay. But I imagine she could tell me the name of at least some of the people who were lace makers back in 1948, and who of them were familiar with Martha's work.'' She raised her voice for the benefit of the pair up front. "But I hope I've made it clear that I am *not* out to prove Martha isn't a murderer. I'm just giving you a hand with some research, so you can pass it along to Mike Malloy.'' She dropped her voice again. "Because at least one other person who poked his nose into this affair got himself *shot.''*

The day was overcast, the temperature in the low thirties. There was still some snow on the ground, and more was forecast for tonight. Betsy rummaged through her memory and came up with memories of early-winter snow in Milwaukee melting before more fell. But this was Minnesota, where the snow piled up to the eaves of houses. Apparently that didn't happen in one spectacular blizzard, it was cumulative.

She pulled the bright red muffler tighter around her neck, snuggled deeper into the navy blue wool coat she'd finally bought at the Mall of America, and crunched across the frozen parking lot to where her car waited, doubtless bewildered by the new viscosity of its oil.

But it started bravely, and Betsy drove off to Alice Skoglund's house, a charming but very small white house on Bell Street, four blocks from the lake. It had a picket fence that needed painting. Stiff, dead tops of flowers poked up through the crusty snow to trace the curve of sidewalk to the tiny front porch. Frowzy juniper bushes crowded the space under the front windows, whose green trim needed paint.

Betsy rang the doorbell. There was no answer. She rang again. When there was still no answer, she came off the porch and would have gone away but heard an unmusical clank from around back. She followed the narrower cement walk, stepping over patches of ice, around the side of the house. She stopped when she saw a man in a heavy overcoat shoving something into an old-fashioned metal garbage can, one of two. As she watched, he bent and picked up the lid, which he replaced with a loud clank. Then he turned toward the house—and it was Alice Skoglund.

"Hi," said Betsy, both startled and shy.

"Hello, Betsy," called Alice. "What can I do for you?"

"I—I need to talk to you," said Betsy, approaching. When close enough to speak without raising her voice she continued, "Do you have a few minutes?" Close up, she felt even more awkward. The coat Alice wore was a man's overcoat, her boots had low, square heels.

"I wondered when you'd come to ask me questions," said Alice. "Well, come on in, there's coffee on the stove."

Betsy followed her in the back door, which let into a little stairwell leading to the basement, so they had to go up a step to get into the kitchen. The linoleum on the

floor had been scrubbed so often for so long that the
pattern was nearly worn off, and the markers for the
stove burners were partly gray and partly gone. Even
the walls were a very pale yellow—though that might
have been the original color. White curtains with yellow
stitching and a pattern of square holes near the hems
covered the only window, which was over the tiny
kitchen table.

"Have a seat," said Alice. "How do you take your
coffee?"

"With everything, I'm afraid."

"You say that like you're ashamed of it. Why, don't
you like coffee?"

"Not much, actually. I like fruit and vegetable juices,
herbal teas, and cocoa, and when I have a cold, I like
hot lemonade, but I'm not that fond of coffee. But everyone around here sure drinks a lot of it."

"It's a Scandinavian thing," nodded Alice. "I'm
British myself, half English and half Scot. But after all
those years married to a Norwegian, I got converted. I
have some herbal teas around here somewhere, I can
heat a mug of water in the microwave for you."

"No, don't bother. I'm fine, really. But you have your
coffee." Betsy glanced over her shoulder at the hook by
the back door with the man's overcoat on it. "Was that
coat your husband's?" she asked.

Alice stopped in the progress of the step and a half
from the stove to the table and looked at the coat as if
seeing it for the first time. "No, it's mine. Bought it at
a rummage sale." She sat down. "A big woman like
me, with shoulders like I got, regular women's coats
don't fit me. They bind under the arms and at the elbows
something painful, and my wrists stick out and get
chapped. I've been wearing men's coats almost all my
life. Oh, once in awhile I'll find something, usually in a

real ugly color or priced so it takes me all winter to pay it off. And when I do buy one, do you know I have the worst time buttoning it? It buttons the wrong way—or at least what's become the wrong way for me, for coats. Everything else I wear that buttons, I can button right the first time. But I always go to buttoning my coats from the men's side.'' She chuckled at herself, then took a drink of her coffee. "But you didn't come here to ask about why I wear men's coats.''

"I keep hearing about bobbin lace, but I wouldn't know it if it came up and bit me on the knee," said Betsy. "Do you have any you can show me?''

Alice smiled. "Yes, I have some. You just wait, I'll go get some samples of my work. I'd invite you into the living room, but the light's better here.''

Alice was gone several minutes. Betsy took advantage of her absence to look into the living room. It was nearly as small as the kitchen, and as worn, and as clean. Faded chintz curtains hung at the two windows, and a big rag rug made a shades-of-green circle on the hardwood floor. An old television set stood on a metal frame in one corner, with an upholstered chair close to it. No cable box in sight. The chair and a loveseat were both covered with afghans, doubtless made by Alice, in shades of green. On the wall were framed photographs, of Alice with a strong-looking man in a clerical collar, the man alone in front of a stone church, Alice very young in a wedding dress, and a single, sad photo of a very frail looking little girl.

Betsy saw another door off the living room start to open and scooted back to the kitchen table.

Alice came into the kitchen with a big round cushion supporting a little stack of magazines and a loose-leaf binder.

When she put the cushion on the table, the magazines

and binder slid off, revealing that it wasn't quite a cushion after all, more like a flat-bottomed doughnut. It was covered in a tan fabric that looked like twill. The opening in the center held a cylinder covered with the same tightly woven fabric, and around the cylinder was a strip of paper with a pattern of dots and squares drawn in ink. The uppermost part of the pattern was clogged with dozens of straight pins, and woven through the pins was thread, dozens of threads, each stretching from the pins to three-inch wooden pegs shaped something like the bishop in unelaborate chess sets.

"Bobbins!" said Betsy. "That's why it's called bobbin lace!"

"Yes," said Alice.

"How many bobbins are there in bobbin lace?"

"It varies. This lace pattern calls for sixty-two. I've worked as many as a hundred and forty."

"Wow. I had no idea."

Coming out the other side of the cylinder and draped across the cushion was a strip of scalloped lace about an inch and a half wide, perhaps seven inches long.

"How does it work?" asked Betsy.

Alice said, "The idea is to move among the pins according to the pattern. You're only working with a few bobbins at a time." She picked up four that had been lying side by side. "You would move this one over this, then these two like this—" She moved the bobbins deftly, like a three-card monte dealer, then scooped them up and pulled the threads attached to them to the left. She reached to the back of the pattern covered with pins, plucking one and putting it at the front, pushing the newest twist of threads into position behind it.

"Then you do this—" She stopped and bent forward, peering at the pins. "No, that's wrong, I think. In fact, I think I did the last two—No, that one is— Ach, never mind!'' She dropped the bobbins and pushed the cushion aside with an angry gesture, and a little wooden clatter. That immediately calmed her, and she ran her fingers across the bobbins again. ''I miss that sound. When a lace maker is going fast, the bobbins chatter to her in a kind of rhythm. I used to recite nursery rhymes to the rhythm when my little Fifi was restless.'' She sat down heavily.

''Who was Fifi?''

Alice put a big hand in front of her mouth, as if afraid to let the words out. ''Our little girl,'' she murmured through her fingers. ''Phyllis Marie was her name, but I called her Fifi. She was born with a hole inside her heart. They called them blue babies back then, before they invented the surgery that could fix the hole. Because their little fingers and toes and lips were blue from lack of oxygen. She was a fighter, our Fifi. They said she wouldn't live past her first birthday, but she was four years, three months, and sixty-one days old when she died. She was our only child. I remember when they invented that surgery, it was just amazing. They had it on the *Today Show*, an actual operation. They showed the open chest, and how the doctor stopped the heart, cut it open, did a few quick stitches, then sewed the heart back up. It was fascinating, he held the stopped heart in his hand, and when he was done operating, he squeezed ever so gently, and it started beating again. That baby, they said, had been dead for the time it took them to operate, but now she was alive again, and would grow up like a normal child. It was like a miracle, that surgery—and I was *so angry!* Because they didn't dare to do that back when my Fifi was still alive, and she died. No one knew then you could stop a living heart and then start it again. It was a sin how angry I got, I think I actually hated those mothers who got their babies back healthy, and all I got was a little tombstone with a lamb on it.''

Betsy could not think what to say. She was embarrassed at the naked emotions on display, and ashamed that she thought Fifi a silly name. She wanted to be big herself, and emotionally kinder, so she could gather the woman into strong arms and let her weep on a capacious bosom. She reached out and put a hand on Alice's shoulder. "I am so very sorry," she said.

"Thank you," said Alice, sniffing hard. "And I'm sorry, too, for letting go like that. I think this mess we're in is bringing up all kinds of old emotions. How about another cup of—oh, that's right, you don't drink coffee.''

"Well, I do, once in a great while, but not after noon, because it keeps me up all night."

Alice smiled as one who often sits up at night and said, "Now, what else did you want to ask?"

"You said you'd show me some examples of your work.''

"Oh, yes, of course." Alice opened the loose-leaf binder, which was about a third full of blank paper. "Mine isn't as fine as some." Between the leaves were samples of lace. The first piece was as delicate as a daisy chain of snowflakes. It lay almost weightless across Betsy's fingers, about seven inches of lace perhaps half an inch wide, the pattern an abstract suggestion of a blossom, repeated over and over.

Betsy smiled at it; that mere human fingers could create something so delicate and perfect was amazing.

Before she could say anything, another piece was added to the first. This one was shorter and narrower, with a curve. It was also stiffer, the pattern more dense without being less delicate, done in ecru threads, with just a few threads of palest pink and a single thread of pure green.

"How can you say your work is not fine? This is lovely." Betsy wished she could put it more strongly; the work was exquisite, delicate, like photographs of snowflakes.

Another piece was offered, this one much broader. It had lots of open spaces connected with braids or twists of thread. "This is what I think of when I think of lace," said Betsy. She experimentally crunched it up a little, seeing it gathered along the edge of a collar or running as a frill down the front of a dress. A shame such things were not fashionable anymore.

"I suppose there are all kinds of lace and ways to tell one kind from another," said Betsy.

Alice began to speak of binche and torchon, of picots and ground. Betsy nodded gamely, but without real comprehension.

When Alice ran down, Betsy handed the lace back, saying, "Why don't you make this anymore? How can you just give it up?"

"I can't see as well as I used to," said Alice. "It was hard, stopping. But I can't do the pricking of the patterns like I used to, and so I keep making mistakes. Even making lace from old patterns already pricked, I have to do it very slowly and carefully, and pretty soon I have a headache. When there's only pain and no joy in making lace, it's time to quit. So I do afghans. One day there won't be anyone without an afghan or a pair of mittens in the whole county, and I'll stop making them, too."

"So long as people keep having children, you'll never run out of little hands needing mittens. And, of course, there are adults like me, who move to the frozen north and can't learn how to knit mittens."

Alice, who had been putting the lace samples back

into the binder, glanced over at Betsy. "Are you hinting for a pair?"

Betsy laughed. "Actually, I bought a pair at the Mall of America, went out to my car and started driving out of the ramp—and went right back and bought a pair of leather gloves for driving—mittens are so slippery on the steering wheel! But perhaps at the next Monday Bunch meeting you could show me what I'm doing wrong trying to knit my own. I just can't get that thumb to work."

"I don't think I'll be coming to any more meetings."

"Why not? Martha will be there—" Actually Betsy had no idea if Martha would be there; she had some kind of notion that people arrested for murder didn't get out on bail. "At least, I think she will. I don't understand why you think you shouldn't come."

"I can't face those people anymore. When they hear that Martha has been arrested because of something I did, figuring out that lace pattern, they will likely think badly about me. This is a *filthy* thing that's happened to us! I wish those people had never taken it into their heads to raise that boat!"

"No, no," said Betsy. "You can't wish a murderer to get away with his crime."

"Hmph," snorted Alice. "I imagine wherever he is, Carl Winters has more serious trouble than mere human justice."

"You are one of those who thinks Carl did it?"

"We all thought he eloped with Trudie, which almost stretched my imagination to the breaking point when I heard about it. So it's not any harder to think he murdered the creature. He was a man like most men, with his off-color jokes and flirting." She pulled herself up short, closed her eyes as if in prayer, and said, "I'm sorry. I shouldn't have said that. I'm so upset." She took a deep breath and a drink of coffee, and said, "You know, I'd have bet the church he was true to his wife, because under it all he really seemed to love her. She nearly died having their boy, got an infection that took away her ability to have any more children, and Carl was there for her the whole time she was sick, practically slept at the hospital for weeks. So when he disappeared and Trudie Koch did, too, I thought maybe it was a coincidence. Gossip had it they'd been seen together, laughing and flirting, but gossip is wrong at least as often as it's right. Besides, Carl was like that—and Trudie was notorious. No reputation at all."

"But now you think he murdered her?"

"What other explanation is there for his running away? And, I think the police are wrong, I think he came back and committed suicide."

"What else can you tell me about Carl? As a person, I mean."

Alice frowned. "Well, he was a member of our church, but one of those who mainly occupies a pew on Sundays—refused to serve as usher or on the board of trustees or sing in the choir, even though his wife played the organ. A hard worker at his store, very friendly with everyone who came in, good at remembering names. Took his boy to ball games and fishing, taught him to swim and shoot skeet. But some men didn't like the way he talked to their wives, and neither did some of the wives." Alice frowned some more, but that was all she had to say.

"What can you tell me about Trudie?" asked Betsy. "Did you go to school with her?"

There was a moment of silence, then Alice said, "All the talk going on right now about those old times, someone is bound to say something and stir this old mess up, sure as I'm sitting here. Maybe no one knows, but in a small town, people pay more attention than they ought to their neighbors, and I don't want you to hear it from someone else. I think it's time to set the record right, so I'll tell you something I haven't told a mortal soul before. I used to cry myself to sleep for shame about it.''

Betsy tried to keep her face muscles in neutral while wondering wildly if she was the right person to be hearing a confession. And what she ought to do if she was sitting in a murderer's kitchen.

Alice took a big breath and began, speaking slowly. "I was always the biggest child in any of my school classes. Even when I got into high school, I was taller than most of the boys. And clumsy and goofy looking. And I wasn't very good in my studies, either, so I didn't have that to comfort me. I'd see the posters go up advertising a dance and yearn and yearn to go, but no boy would ask me, and I was just miserable.

"Then, in my junior year, Trudie Koch said something halfway sympathetic to me, and I just poured out my grief to her. She said she was going to a party where you didn't need an invitation, and there would be plenty of boys to choose among, all of them glad to see me. She said I wasn't really ugly, I just didn't know how to use what I had to best advantage. She said she'd come over and help me dress pretty for it, show me about makeup.

"I knew it was wrong right from the start, but I wasn't making any progress at all with nice boys or with being nice myself and it seemed kind of exciting, to be naughty and flagrant and welcome at a party. I followed her instructions and bought a pair of high heels and some silk stockings. I talked my parents into going out to a movie, so we had the house to ourselves when Trudie came over. She put all sorts of rouge and powder on my face, piled black mascara on my eyelashes until it was hard to keep my eyes open. She put my hair up and she pinned my good dress in a way that showed I did have a figure after all. I didn't even recognize myself in the mirror.

"We went to a house in Shorewood that was kind of isolated, and I had the first beer of my entire life five minutes after I got there. I had another to keep it company, and pretty soon I was dancing with some boy I'd never seen before in my life. He took me out on the porch and I learned a great deal about—"

Alice stopped. Her face was a red so deep Betsy was alarmed for her blood pressure, and her hands were clasped very tightly on top of the loose-leaf binder. "About life, I guess," concluded Alice lamely. "It seemed like great fun, and I became very popular for several hours. But it got later and later, and at last I began to be afraid that my parents would be waiting on the porch for me to get home. I finally persuaded one of the more sober young men to drive me back to town. I gave him an address a couple blocks from the real one, and I sneaked into our backyard and through my bed-room window. As it turned out, my parents were in bed. They had come home to a silent house and thought I'd turned in early. I was particularly attentive in church the next several Sundays, which drew the attention of a young man who was about to graduate from Luther Seminary."

Alice looked into Betsy's eyes. "We had a very happy marriage. He never knew I was only technically a virgin. I recognized two of the young men at school later, but they didn't seem to have any idea that had been me; at least neither of them ever said anything to me about it. Trudie dropped out of school a month later, and I didn't see her for awhile. I married Martin a week after I graduated, and a week after that Trudie came calling. She'd lost her waitress job and was about to be evicted and could I help her? It was just five dollars. Just this once.'' Alice grimaced. ''It's never just once with something like that, of course. But she was careful not to drain my budget to the point where I had to tell Martin. And when she had a boyfriend with money, she'd leave me alone for months. But she'd always come back. Always. Until she disappeared. I used to pray for God to strike her dead, to open the earth so it could swallow her up, and when she vanished, I was happy for the first time in a long while. She was gone a year before I finally believed she would never come back.''

She reached out and took Betsy by the wrist. ''But I didn't kill her. I prayed to God to take her out of my life, but I wouldn't dare do anything myself to get rid of her; it never occurred to me to pray for the strength to kill her.''

9

Betsy went back to the shop. She thought she was maintaining a poker face over Alice's startling confession, but Godwin read something and asked, "What did you learn?"

"I can't say, for sure," she replied.

"Why?" asked Shelly.

"Because I want to talk it over with Jill first."

"Hey, I'm your friend, too, aren't I?" demanded Godwin. "You can tell me anything."

"It's not because she's a friend, it's because she's law enforcement," said Betsy, and retreated from their suddenly serious expressions. She was worried, too.

She went into the shop's little back room, where a bathroom took up half the space and the other half was crammed with a coffee machine and boxes of stock and folding chairs. She hung up her coat and put her purse in a locked cabinet. She came out, but still wasn't ready to face her employees or a chance customer. She looked

around for something to do in the back of the shop. It
was nearly three o'clock.

From the front she could hear Godwin and Shelly
talking, their voices swift and urgent, but not loud.

Speculating, thought Betsy, *about what I learned from
Alice. Thank God they don't have a clue. Poor Alice!*

Back here was a little area set apart from the front by
two sets of box shelves, double sided, filled with fabric,
yarns, books, and magazines. There was a small round
table and two comfortable chairs on the left, where customer and employee or salesman and owner could sit
and plan really big projects or a substantial increase in
the credit limit.

There was a cordless phone on the table; Betsy picked
it up and dialed Jill's home phone number. She got a
recording, and left a message: "Jill, can you call or
come over as soon as possible? I have something to tell
you. It's kind of urgent." She hung up and thought
about calling Malloy, but what could she tell him? She
was not going to reveal Alice's secret, and it would be
useless to just tell him that Alice had once hated Trudie
without telling him why. No, the person she needed to
talk to was Jill.

She straightened the chairs and moved some catalogs
back to where they belonged. Then she decided to tackle
a spinner rack near the box shelves that held counted
cross-stitch patterns and supplies. The items on the rack
weren't moving well—perhaps because the rack looked
so disorganized, like a collection of remnants. She took
the items off the rack and laid them out in various ways
on the table. Scissors all together? No. Arranged in sets
of scissors, needles, thimbles, patterns? No. She finally
decided to treat the rack like a Christmas tree, which
meant the bigger the item, the nearer the bottom it
should go. She swiftly put things back on the spinner,
big scissors and floss organizers on the bottom, chate-

laines and smaller scissors in the middle, and thimbles and scabbard needle holders on the top row of black metal arms. That at least looked better than the original arrangement.

She was near the end of her task when she heard the sound of the front door opening, and Godwin calling gaily, "Hiya, Myrt! How's ever' little thing?"

A woman's voice giggled and said, "Now who would have thought anyone would still remember that?"

"Remember what?" asked Shelly.

But Betsy remembered, too, and, smiling, came into the front part of her shop. "It's from *Fibber McGee and Molly*," she said.

"Who are Fibber McGee and Molly?" asked Shelly.

"It was a radio show way back when," said Godwin. "Betsy, this is Myrtle Jensen. She's president of the Excelsior Historical Society."

"Hello, Mrs. Jensen," said Betsy, coming forward. "How may I help you?"

The woman, short and very thin, wore a long wool skirt, low-heeled boots, and a plaid wool jacket. She moved briskly, but her face and hands were those of an elderly woman. She met Betsy halfway, hand extended. Betsy, leery of arthritic fingers, took it gently.

Myrtle had a small head, clear brown eyes, a tiny nose, and a wide, thin mouth. She made Betsy think of a chimpanzee. "What a pleasant store you have," she said, looking around.

"Thank you."

"I've come to talk to you about Alice Skoglund."

Betsy felt her smile vanish, and suppressed a sigh. "What about her?"

"The police are sure the skeleton they found on that boat is Trudie Koch, and I'm sure they're right. She and Carl Winters disappeared the night before it was taken out behind the Big Island and sunk. It's embarrassing how that error about the year got into all the accounts of its sinking, and we're going to prepare an errata slip to go in the books. Thank God for photocopy machines. I'm old enough to remember the days of mimeographs and ditto—that smell would give me the biggest headache! Now you just put the original facedown on the glass and punch buttons.

"But that's not the subject here. I understand the police have decided Martha murdered poor Trudie, and while it's true Martha had what some might think a good reason to do that, I don't believe for one minute that she did. She was a respectable Christian wife and mother in 1948, and it would never have occurred to her to murder some silly young woman just because her husband was canoodling with her."

"Canoodling?" echoed Betsy, amused at the term and Myrtle's lengthy way of coming to the point.

"You know. Canoodling." Myrtle rolled her brown eyes and tossed her head. Betsy nodded, and Myrtle continued, "When people hear some story from history, they tend to see just the people named in the story. They don't see all the other people who were around them, whispering in their ears, carrying tales, applying pressure, working on their own reasons for doing things. In this case, people are talking about Martha and Carl and Trudie as if they were the only people in town in 1948. And they don't pay attention to context, or make connections between stories. Like people don't realize the connection between Henry VIII and Christopher Columbus."

"What was the connection?" asked Betsy.

"Henry's first wife was Katherine of Aragon, who was the daughter of Ferdinand and Isabella of Spain, who financed Columbus's first voyage. It's also like peo-

ple calling that boat the *Hopkins*. For twenty-two years,
from 1926 until 1948, it was the *Minnetonka III*, owned
by the Blue Line Café, the same restaurant where Trudie
worked. She was a waitress there, and a very immoral
person. Of course, she was popular among a certain set
of people, not nice people but drinkers and philanderers.
She came by her lifestyle honestly. Her mother was a
tramp and her father ran off before she was born. She'd
been an impulsive sort of person since before she got
into high school. She had a boyfriend, a bad-tempered,
jealous young man named Vern Miller, who went away
to the army and came back years later married to a sweet
little Japanese woman who turned out as American as
any of us.''

She leaned forward and said, ''I understand you went
and talked to Alice. Instead of just listening to what she
has to say, you should have asked her some hard questions.''

''Such as what?''

''Well, for example, why did she purely hate Trudie
Koch?''

Myrtle nodded several times, wriggling her eyebrows,
until Betsy said, ''Hate is a strong word, Mrs. Jensen.''

''I'm saying what I mean. I remember while it was
still during the war, I saw Alice on two separate occa-
sions looking at Trudie, and if looks could kill, Trudie
would have fallen down on the spot and never moved
again.''

Betsy hoped her poker face worked better this time.
''Have you any idea why?''

''Not one. They were in high school together, but I
don't think they ever did anything together. They
weren't friends, of course; Alice would never be friends
with someone like Trudie. Trudie had a reputation that
made all the nice girls steer clear of her. As my mother

put it, Trudie was no better than she ought to be and a sight worse at times. I heard Trudie called on Alice several years later, but that may not be true because this was while Martin was being considered for pastor, so she had to be careful of her behavior.''

"Martin?''

"Her husband, the Reverend Martin Skoglund. He was hired as pastor of Saint Elwin's soon after, so like I say, it may not be true that Trudie visited Alice.''

"What do you know about Reverend Skoglund?''

"He was a wonderful pastor, quite wise, a good preacher. He had some old-fashioned ideas about morality, but that was expected of a pastor back then. He retired in 1987 and died five years ago, still very respected. And it was as if Alice had died, too; in a month she was forgotten by the people who'd acted like her friends and depended on her all those years. After all she and Pastor Martin had done for Saint Elwin's, it was a real shame. I always thought Alice should have gone to nursing school or become a teacher, but she set her cap at Martin, and he married her when she was barely nineteen. She was a big girl, and homely as a mud fence, but a good, good person, and they seemed very happy together, even though she was rather shy to be a pastor's wife. She never got proud, and she was a good cook, and a terrific housekeeper. It was so sad their one child died, she was a little bit of a thing, very frail, something wrong with her heart.''

"Yes, Alice told me she was a blue baby.''

"Yes, that's the term. I'd forgotten it. Alice turned out yards of embroidery and knit scarves and made beautiful lace. She gave most of it away or put it in the rummage sale. Half the Lutheran women in town wore her aprons or dried their dishes with her towels, the other half trimmed their dresses with her lace. And there was

never a Saint Elwin's child going without mittens, not
if Alice knew about it. So it doesn't seem fair, does it,
that she should get cataracts and have to give up her
needlework.''

"Alice had cataracts?"

"Years ago, had surgery and all for it.''

"She hasn't given up needlework. She comes to our
Monday needlework gatherings, and she crochets afghan
squares.''

"I don't do needlework, and even I can crochet an
afghan square. Those big hooks and the yarn in all those
colors, it's not hard.''

"You make it sound as if she's blind.''

"No, not blind. But she can't do fine work—''

"You're wrong!'' The speaker was Godwin, who had
appeared as if by magic behind Myrtle's shoulder.

The old woman jumped, then gave Godwin a stern
look. "It isn't polite to eavesdrop!''

"Who's eavesdropping? I'm at work right over there,
and you're not exactly whispering. I couldn't help hearing what you were saying. And I say you're wrong about
Alice. She identified the threads on that piece of silk as
bobbin lace right in front of us, and she figured out the
pattern, down to a little butterfly in it.''

"Well, I heard about that, and I'm here to tell you
she had to give up making lace twenty-five years ago
because her eyes went bad on her. She had surgery, and
wore thick glasses for years. Then she got lenses put
right into her eyes, I don't know how they do that, and
after that she got regular glasses. But I've known other
women with cataracts, and no matter what the doctors
do, you never get the good vision back. But on top of
that, she hated Trudie Koch. I think you should wonder
if she has a good reason for trying to make the police
suspicious of someone else over this skeleton business.''

"Have you talked to the police about this?" asked Betsy.

Myrtle nodded. "And Mike Malloy listened to me, just like he always listens to people. Then he goes and does what he likes. He's already made up his mind about this, just you watch him."

After Myrtle left, Betsy called Shelly over to join Godwin.

"All right, what do you think?" she asked.

"What do I think about what?" asked Shelly, not willing to be the one to start another round of gossip.

"What Myrtle said, about Alice Skoglund having good reason to want the police to look anywhere but at her."

Shelly hesitated. "I don't know. The things she's talking about happened before my time."

"Is Myrtle inclined to stretch the truth?"

Shelly considered this. "No. In fact, one reason she's so involved with the historical society is because she wants the facts known and kept straight. She's just curling up inside over that 1948–49 business. Irene Potter told me it's given her a whole new bee in her bonnet, about taking different collections of stories and cross-referencing them."

Betsy said, "I think she made one important point. We've been looking at Carl and Martha and poor Trudie as if they were the stars in a movie, as if everyone else were extras, there to make the place look inhabited."

Godwin said, "And as if it's history, like Columbus discovering America—not that he did, really—but as if it happened so long ago that everyone is dead. If Myrtle and Martha are still around, and Alice, who else is still here who remembers what was going on at that time?"

"Vern's still here," said Shelly. "You know, the man Myrtle said was Trudie's boyfriend. They trained him to fix jeeps in the army. He did that for them for thirty years, and then they gave him a pension and sent him home, where he opened his garage. It's Miller Motors, over on Third, near Morse. It says right on his sign, 'Since 1978'. It used to be a livery stable, his building.'' Shelly lifted her head a little, having made a historical connection of her own.

Betsy said, ''He was in the army for thirty years, you say?''

''That's what he tells people,'' said Shelly. ''I take my car to him to be serviced.''

Betsy said, ''Subtract thirty years from 1978 and you get him joining the army in 1948, the same year Trudie disappeared. And Myrtle says he was a mean and jealous boyfriend.''

Godwin murmured, ''I wonder if he joined up in July. *Early* July.''

The three looked at one another, but before they could say anything more, the door alarm went *bing*, and Jessica Turnquist came in. She saw the trio staring at her and looked down to see if she'd come out with some private parts showing.

''Hello, Jessica,'' said Betsy. ''I'm afraid I've caught the Excelsior Virus, which turns people into gossips.''

Jessica smiled her thin smile and said, ''And I'm afraid there's no cure, either. Betsy, I'd like four hanks of that hand-spun yarn I was looking at last week.''

Betsy went to one of the yarn bins in the box shelves. ''What color?''

''That pale yellow.'' Betsy got down the yarn, which was full of blibs. The yellow was an uneven and dispirited shade, a sorry imitation of the soft color onion skins produce.

Jessica shook her head over it. ''I don't much like this myself, but I have a good friend who just loves sweaters made of it. It's to be her Christmas present.''

"You know," said Betsy, ringing up the sale, "it's interesting how handmade has gone from meaning especially well done to meaning full of obvious mistakes, even if you have to make them deliberately. Listen, do you have to go right away? I have some questions for you.''

Jessica hesitated, obviously wanting to say no, but compassion—or curiosity—won out. "If it won't take too long. I've got to go grocery shopping today. What do you want to know?''

Betsy leaned forward and asked quietly, "You knew Carl Winters, didn't you? What was he like?''

"Well, I didn't know him really well. I saw him around town, and I took my dry cleaning to him, of course. And he worked for me every August during State Fair. I used to have a food concession, and he would sell while I would cook.''

"Did you really? How interesting! What kind of food did you sell?''

Jessica smiled. "Corn dogs on a stick. One of the things our State Fair is famous for is food on a stick. Steak on a stick, fish on a stick, pork chop on a stick, fried cheese on a stick, shish kabob on a stick.''

Betsy laughed. "I think I've heard of that last one.''

Jessica's smile had some life in it this time, and Betsy suddenly realized that she'd once been really beautiful. "You'd be surprised how much money you save not having to supply paper plates. I sold corn dogs, French fries wrapped in newspaper, and three kinds of pop in a deposit bottle. You wouldn't believe the grease inside that stand; the floor would get so slippery we had to mop it a dozen times a day.''

"What was your husband's role in all this?''

"He bought the stand for me as a kind of wedding

present in 1941, but we only ran it together that first year. He joined the Army Air Corps right after Pearl Harbor, and they made him a navigator in the flying fortresses. He was killed in a mission over Germany.''

''I didn't realize that's how you became a widow. I'm sorry.''

''I'm more sorry we decided not to have children in case he didn't come back. We were very young but trying hard to be grown-up about things. I was so sure he would come back that I didn't mind putting off having a child.''

''You know, this may seem like an impertinent question, but I wonder why it was you didn't marry again. You must have had lots of suitors.''

Jessica's eyelids dropped as she simpered just a little. ''Well, I did,'' she said. ''I thought about it, but I just didn't . . . connect with anyone. And then one morning it was too late. I've had a good life anyway, good friends, a nice town to live in, my own home, my church, my needlework. It's enough.''

''Did Carl Winters flirt with you?''

For just an instant those prominent eyes flashed. ''I should say he did! He was notorious! 'Hiya, sweetheart, you're looking mighty fresh and tasty this morning,' he'd say. And until you put a stop to it, he'd get worse and worse. But it was never more than talk, really; he didn't mean anything by it. He loved his wife, I know that now. But at the time I felt sorry for her, even though I didn't really know her. It wasn't until Carl disappeared that we became close. She was kind of standoffish, I thought, but now I know it was because of Carl; compensating, I'd guess you'd say, for his being over-friendly.''

''Would she get mad at him for acting like that?''

''She never said a word to him, not where anyone

else could hear—though of course he wouldn't behave like that in front of her, that would have been going way too far. He did call her 'the ball and chain' and 'my *first* wife' and things like that when she wasn't around.''

"God, I'd've murdered him," muttered Betsy.

"Yes, well . . ." said Jessica, and looked away.

Betsy said, "Now wait! You came to me and begged me to prove she *didn't* murder him!"

"No, I came to you and begged you to prove she didn't murder Trudie Koch," said Jessica. "It broke my heart to hear the talk going on around town about that. But now Carl comes back and right away he's shot dead, and it isn't suicide, the police say. So now I'm not sure what to think."

"Could it have been someone else?"

"Who?"

"I don't know. Anyone. Alice Skoglund, for example?"

Jessica's well-shaped eyebrows lifted. "I think Alice might have been the one person in town Carl didn't flirt with."

"Because she was the minister's wife?"

"No." Jessica let that stand by itself while she gathered up the bag with the her wool in it. Then she added a rather peremptory "Good-bye," and left.

"Well!" said Godwin. "Talk about *rude!* Why didn't she just come out and *say* she thought Alice was too ugly for even Carl to flirt with? Humph! I bet she was never as pretty as she thinks, not with that attitude."

Betsy thought to scold him for sneaking up, and for poking his oar in, then decided it didn't matter. Besides, she was inclined to agree with him.

A half hour later, Betsy pulled into the parking lot beside Miller Motors. The old wooden building did look like something out of a western movie, with its false front and general air of impermanence. The back of the shop was right on the edge of a gully. Betsy pulled her car up to the edge and looked over, expecting to see mechanical debris—it was, after all, so handy; just open the back door and toss. And just what one might expect of a place like this.

But the gully was clean. Down its center ran some new-looking railroad tracks. Just as she became aware of footsteps crunching on the frozen gravel of the parking lot, a low, gruff voice said behind her, "Them damned volunteers are gonna run a trolley car down there."

"What volunteers?" she asked.

"Same ones that run the trolley steamboat." The speaker was a man built approximately like a shell a battleship might fire. He was about five feet eight inches tall, with a domed head shaved bald and no hat to protect it from the chill air. His powerful, sloping shoulders and thick neck added to the gunshell effect. He was not a young man: his face was deeply seamed, and as he turned to gesture at the gully, she could see the start of a stoop as well as a thinness to his legs inside the filthy denim trousers. He wore a heavily lined denim jacket and in one large, dirty, chapped hand carried a plastic bucket full of old oil cans.

"The same ones who raised the *Hopkins*?" she asked.

"That's them." He spat, more in opinion than from need.

"Where did they put the boat after they took it out of the water?" she asked.

"Big ugly barn over on George Street. You gonna be one of them volunteers?"

She smiled. "No. Are you Vernon Miller?"

"That's right." He spat again, less definitively. "Who are you, then?"

"My name's Betsy Devonshire. I inherited Excelsior's needlework shop, Crewel World. I was wondering if I could talk to you."

"I don't know from needlework. I do car repairs. That your car?" he nodded toward the elderly white hatchback.

"Yes, that's mine." Betsy had an inspiration. "And it needs an oil change and whatever kind of tune-up you give a car that's not used to the winter."

"Bring 'er up to the door." He nodded toward the set of double doors on the side of his building. "We'll have a look." He walked off with his burden to the row of wheeled gray garbage cans lining the other side of the parking lot.

Betsy obeyed and soon was admitted to the interior of the shop. If the floor was not dirt, it had become so thickly layered with oily dirt that it made no difference. A young man in need of serious dental work came over and listened to her story of a car bought used in San Diego and only recently driven to Minnesota.

"But I need to talk to Mr. Miller first," she said, not wanting to tell him just yet that there was no way on earth she would trust her car to this place, these people.

Miller shrugged and let her go first into his office, a room formed out of a corner of the work area with plywood and used boards. Much of its interior was taken up by a desk buried in paper, both marred by black fingerprints. There was an office chair, dirty and so broken into the shape of Miller's lower extremities she would no more sit in it than his lap, and a metal stool with a composition seat she took instead. The office was perhaps twenty degrees warmer than the shop area, so both of them unbuttoned their coats.

"What can I do for ya?" asked Miller, sitting in the

chair. His eyes were small and watchful under the heavy brow.

"I'm curious about that skeleton they found on the *Hopkins*," began Betsy. "Apparently, the police are sure it's Trudie Koch."

"What's that got to do with changing the oil in your car?"

"Nothing. But I'm hoping you'll talk to me about her."

Miller shrugged his heavy shoulders and turned the chair away from her. "I suppose someone told you I was her boyfriend way back then."

"Yes."

He heaved an insincere sigh and turned the chair half-way back, glancing at her as he did so. "That was a long time ago."

"What can you tell me about her?"

"What do you want to know?"

"What was she like? Who were her friends? Who . . . who were her enemies?" She saw him start to get up and said hastily, "Please, you loved her, didn't you? You were probably the one person who really understood her. If Martha Winters didn't murder her, and I don't think she did, then who else might have done it?" He looked up at her from under that massive, frowning brow, and she tried a winsome smile along with a look of friendly, sincere inquiry.

A little to her surprise, the frown faded and he sat back in his chair. "I did love her," he said after a bit. "People didn't understand how much, because we had a lot of fights. Worst of all, I don't think Trudie understood."

"Wasn't she the understanding sort?"

"She was the kind of girl who always asked, 'What's in it for me?' She could be sweet and charming when she wanted something, and she could turn cold as—well, as January in International Falls when she didn't get it. She liked having a good time, she liked men to bring her presents, and she could be real grateful when the present was something special.''

''Like money?'' asked Betsy.

''No, she wouldn't take money, that was going too far. But something she could return for money was okay.''

''Was this before you became her boyfriend?''

He nodded. ''And when we'd have a fight, she'd go take up with someone she knew would give her things. And she made sure I knew about it.''

''And I suppose that would set off another fight.''

He nodded. ''It sure would. Sometimes she'd pick a fight with me because she got to wanting a jacket or a hat or a piece of jewelry and I couldn't afford to give it to her. I'd blow up and say we are through, I never want to see you again; and she'd take up with a fellow who would buy it for her, but in a day or a week, I'd hear the new fellow was out on his ear. And there'd I'd be with a bouquet of flowers or some candy, saying I was sorry and would you take me back.''

''And she did?''

''Every damn time. Neither of us any smarter for it.''

''Why did you love her?''

He shrugged, then said, ''She was smart and sassy, and real pretty. I thought she was beautiful. She had that sexy shape, like a woman oughta be shaped. And always laughing, teasing—'' The frown returned, but not directed at Betsy this time. ''Her last job was waitressin' at the Blue Ribbon Café. She was a waitress most of the time, once she got off the farm. Complained her mother worked her to death, but on her own she worked about as hard. Course, the money she earned on her own *was* her own. She was a hard worker. On her feet all day, but she could still dance half the night. She was a good dancer, liked to dance.'' He glanced up at her and something almost like a smile lightened his features. ''Boogie-woogie. You ever hear of it?''

''Of course. There was swing, then boogie-woogie, then rock and roll. Where would you go dancing?''

''Different places, sometimes to a ballroom that was part of the amusement park. Huge dance floor, biggest I ever seen, it was the biggest in the midwest at one time. Lawrence Welk came there once, during the war. I went and I danced with Trudie. She was just a kid then, her ma had to bring her, but she already was giving her fits. She was a wild 'un.'' Smiling, he shook his head.

''Was she popular in high school?''

He nodded proudly. ''Had the boys standing in line.''

''I bet the other girls were green with envy.''

He nodded. ''Some of 'em. Some of 'em was downright mean to her about it. But it didn't bother Trude. She'd sass 'em back, and walk off laughing. She didn't care. She just didn't care.''

''Did you care?''

He looked at her, seeking suspicion, but Betsy's look only begged for a good answer. ''Yeah, I cared. She was wild from the start, and I knew it, but I kept on coming. She dropped out of high school the end of her junior year, got a job, a good job in a factory, moved into a rooming house. But she flirted with the line supervisor and his wife found out, and she got fired. She said she didn't like that job anyway, and got another as a waitress, and she was always a waitress after that. She'd work six months, a year, then she'd move on. Sometimes it was the boss, sometimes it was the customers, it was never her fault. I think she'd just get bored. She knew it didn't matter; she could lose her job and turn right around and get another.''

''Did she make enemies over losing her jobs?''

''I don't think so. She wasn't one to carry a grudge, and I don't think her bosses cared that much.''

''But someone finally got angry enough to kill her.''

''Yes, you're right. Y'know, all these years I thought she just up and left town, and that's how I thought about her, living in some other town, still waitressing, flirting with the customers. Or maybe she roped some jerk into marrying her, maybe she even settled down, had five or six kids. I used to think about her a lot for a long time. And I never quit thinking about her altogether. And all this while she was in that damn boat, a skeleton. It's like my mind got into a rut, thinking about her in some big city, sassing the customers in a café, so it's hard to change that into knowing she's been dead for fifty years, that she's forever twenty-two.''

''Is that why you joined the army? Because you thought of her in some other town, flirting with someone else?''

He said, surprised, ''Hell, no! I left before she went missing. We'd had another fight and I decided I wasn't gonna go crawling back this time. Besides, I wasn't gettin' anywhere in this one-horse town. So I decided to give the army a chance. I'd like to tell you we made up, that she came down to see me off and begged my forgiveness and promised to write, but she didn't. She had her pride, too, I guess. I know I did, once I made up my mind.''

''So how long were you gone before she disappeared?''

He thought a long while, scratching his chin, then said reluctantly, ''I guess I was still in boot camp when someone wrote and said she'd run off with Carl Winters.

She'd been gone a couple of weeks by then."

"But you're sure you were in army basic training when Trudie disappeared."

"Hell, I could dig out my old service record and show it to you. My dates of service are July 3, 1948, to July 3, 1978. I got that letter, and I couldn't believe it, flat couldn't believe it. Mr. Winters was a married man, with a business and a kid and a house. I thought it was a crock, I thought she'd gone off on her own, at the most let him give her a ride to somewhere. I just couldn't believe those two had a serious love affair—and I guess I was right."

"What do you think really happened?"

"I think Trudie was flirting with him at the Blue Ribbon, just like she flirted with every man, and he took it serious. I think he waited till she got off work and tried something with her, and she slugged him, and he killed her." Miller shrugged, holding his heavy shoulders up for a bit before dropping them. "I never knew Winters, so I don't know how much that sounds like him, but it sounds a whole lot like Trudie."

"Did you come home on leave from boot camp?"

"Naw, they sent me to San Francisco, so I went right there from Kansas and had so much fun in Chinatown all my pay was gone before I reported to Presidio. The army took me in and cleaned me up, sent me to school and taught me how to repair every kind of motor there is, from motorsickle to tank. After a few wild years I started saving my pay, and a few years after that I married Miyoshi, who finished my drinking for good. Then I retired, came home, and started this business, built it from the ground up, with Japanese savvy, army money, and my own muscle. The army taught me all I know, God bless the U.S. Army."

Betsy went out to find the gawky young man leaning

deep into the interior of her car. He straightened when she cleared her throat behind him. "Engine's in good shape for the mileage you've got on her," he said. "But your brakes are leaking. Better let me fix that."

"Not today," said Betsy, who was sure her brakes were not leaking; they worked fine.

"I bet you have to press kind of hard to get yourself stopped, don't you?" he asked.

"Not at all," she said firmly, going around and getting in.

He closed the hood and went to open the doors of the old garage. She noticed as she backed out that he was looking at the car and shaking his head.

That won't work either, she thought, and pulled out onto Third Avenue.

10

It was after five when Betsy drove past her shop—
darkened and, she hoped, properly locked up for the
night—and went on down to Excelsior Boulevard (a pre-
possessing name for a narrow, unprepossessing street) to
the McDonald's, where she bought a regular hamburger,
a small fries, and a Sprite. She found a much-fingered
copy of the Minneapolis *Star Tribune* and perused it, so
by the time she left the restaurant, it was fully dark. An
icy little breeze that smelled of snow flirted with the
curls on her forehead. Her feet crunched on the parking
lot, gritty with sand. She thought of her cozy apartment.

Oh, Lord, she remembered that Sophie was waiting at
the door!

Godwin said he would push Sophie out into the hall
when he closed up. Margot, he explained, did this, too,
when she left before closing time. Sophie knew to go
upstairs and wait outside the apartment door for her mistress to come home.

Feeling guilty for loitering over her burger, Betsy

drove quickly up Lake Street to the narrow entrance to the parking lot behind her building. She let herself in the back door with her key, hustled down the back hall and up the stairs to arrive breathless in front of her door. A muzzy whiteness opened its pink mouth in complaint and greeting, a long, drawn-out cry.

"Yes, yes, Sophie, I see you, it's all right, here I am," she gasped, stooping to stroke the thick fur.

"Rewwwwwwwwwwwwwwww," complained Sophie. She had a high-pitched voice for an animal that weighed twenty-three pounds, not including the cast on one hind leg.

Betsy unlocked the door, Sophie shot through and ducked into the kitchen to stand beside her bowl, gleaming empty on the floor. "I'm sorry," Betsy apologized, reaching into the cabinet under the sink for the metal can that held the Iams Less Active dry cat food. She filled the little scoop and poured it into the bowl. Sophie fell to crunching her way to the bottom of the bowl with swift efficiency. One would think she hadn't eaten in a week; but Betsy had seen Godwin and two customers slip the animal tidbits.

Jill had not come to the shop nor had she called. So now Betsy checked her own machine and found a message from Jill that she would come over, but not until around nine: "Lars is taking me out to dinner."

Betsy went into her bedroom and changed from her good work clothes to jeans and a faded-pink sweatshirt with cut-off sleeves. She'd had her supper, so she filled half an hour with some housecleaning, then remembered that in the rush to get home to Sophie, she hadn't checked her mail.

She went back down the stairs to the front entrance and unlocked her mailbox with a little brass key. There were six or eight first-class envelopes—mostly the depressing kind with windows—some magazines, catalogs, and a fistful of advertising.

Back in her apartment, she began sorting. Margot was still getting mail, of course. Betsy put those aside. She would return the personal ones unopened with a brief letter explaining that Margot had died in unexpected and tragic circumstances and that she, her sister Betsy, would be at this address for at least the next six months. Doing this invariably triggered sympathy cards and even the occasional written letter of condolence, the latter requiring a thank you note. Betsy was getting used to crying over some parts of her mail.

All the catalogs were of items related to needlework. Betsy kept these in the shop for her customers to peruse. She was beginning to realize how useful they were to her in finding out what was big or popular or new—and make sure Crewel World carried it.

As she was sorting through them, a picture postcard fell to the floor. She picked it up. The picture was of the huge and ugly fruit bats in the San Diego zoo. Turning it over, she saw the message: "Going bats in Minnesota yet? I hear you have snow. Brrrrr!" It was signed *Abbey*.

Betsy sat down at the little round table in the dining nook, the mail scattered before her. Light from the kitchen shone through the window beyond the table, catching little dancing movements. It was snowing, the flakes dancing in a light wind. It was very dark out, very quiet in the apartment. If she was in San Diego, she could call Abbey and they'd go down and walk on the beach, or drive out into the desert and look up at an immensity of sky and stars. They'd talk about life after divorce, hair dyes, and estradiol versus Premarin. And the perils of dieting. Betsy felt suddenly quite alone.

Almost automatically, she looked toward the kitchen.

There was leftover chicken salad in there, her favorite kind of chicken salad, with cashews and red grapes. And some of Excelo Bakery's wonderful herb bread. Betsy had a tendency to eat when she was troubled or lonely. And right now she felt both.

But just a few days ago she had gotten a glimpse of her naked self in a mirror and been appalled. Everything seemed to be puffy or sagging. Really sagging. How on earth had she let herself get like this?

So no more Quarter Pounders, no more desserts, and one day soon look into joining a health club, or do some mall walking. There was a fortune of several million dollars coming her way some time next year, and when Betsy invested in a new wardrobe, she didn't want to buy it from some mail order catalog sent to women ashamed to be seen going into the Women at Large shop at the mall.

So instead of eating a second supper, she got out the fabric, floss, and pattern for the little Christmas tree ornaments, then went to put the kettle on. Tea had no calories, she could have tea. She went into the living room and turned on the Bose, tuned to KSJN, the local public radio station. Fortunately, they weren't being experimental or operatic this evening. She listened only long enough to determine it was probably Brahms, sat back, and looked around.

The living room in the apartment was rectangular and low-ceilinged, its triple window heavily draped. The rug was a deep red on a pale hardwood floor, the walls a light cream with black baseboards. The room was furnished sparingly with a loveseat, upholstered chair with matching footstool, and some standard lamps. The low ceiling, the shaded light of the standard lamps, and the covered window made a cozy haven. Betsy had felt comfortable here from the first moment she'd entered.

But looking around reminded Betsy that while Margot had been a fine decorator and a terrific housekeeper, Betsy wasn't. She stood and debated getting out the vacuum cleaner, but decided against it. Instead, she went to the dining nook, sat down at the table, and tried again to work on the counted cross-stitch pattern. She counted very carefully with her threaded needle, both pattern and fabric, but after ten minutes a line of stitches that was supposed to join an earlier line didn't. She groaned. This was always happening! She consulted the pattern and her stitching and found the error was a dozen stitches back. She stuck the needle into the fabric and shoved it aside. Why did women insist that doing counted cross-stitch was relaxing? It was a lot of things: frustrating, aggravating, stupid, and impossible. But not relaxing.

She glanced into the kitchen but resolutely turned and went to the hall closet and got out the vacuum cleaner. She was about halfway around the living room when Sophie came out of the bedroom. Unlike many cats, Sophie had no fear of the vacuum cleaner. She got in front of it, looked up at Betsy, and opened her mouth. Betsy shut off the vacuum cleaner.

". . . ewwwwwwwwww!" Sophie was saying.

"What do you want?"

Sophie started for the kitchen, the too-long cast, designed to keep her from running or jumping, lifting her left back end up a little higher. The vet tech at the clinic described it as having "square wheel syndrome." She stopped and looked back hopefully at Betsy, then at the kitchen, but Betsy said firmly, "No."

If Betsy was giving up snacks, Sophie was, too.

Sophie limped to her cushioned basket under the window draperies. She gave Betsy a hurt look, then climbed into her basket, lying down with her injured leg pointedly on display.

Betsy felt for the animal but didn't yield. She flipped the switch on the vacuum cleaner and went back to work. It was bad enough that her employees and customers vied to see who could bring the tastiest tidbit to the cat. Betsy wasn't going to. At twenty-three pounds, Sophie was proportionately far more overweight than Betsy.

The vacuuming finished, Betsy considered dusting, but instead went to the comfortable chair with the cross-legged canvas needlework bag beside it and got out her knitting. Not the mittens, she needed something soothing. The red hat was at a section that was just knit, knit, knit—no purl to complicate the action, no increase or decrease. As she had noticed before, there was something calming about knitting. One sat down to it with a jumbled, disordered mind, started in, and after a few minutes, the pulse slowed, the fingers relaxed, the mind, like a troubled pool, settled and cleared.

She wondered if Jill would just take her word for it that Alice hated Trudie without Betsy having to say why. Betsy remembered something her mother had frequently said: "Three may keep a secret if two of them are dead." Alice had kept her secret for fifty years; it seemed a shame it couldn't be kept just a little longer, until Alice was safely dead, beyond hearing the wagging tongues of Excelsior.

And what about Vern Miller? His date of entry into the army was July 3. The *Hopkins* had been towed out and sunk with its grisly cargo on July first or second—and Trudie had been murdered the night before that. Was it what he said, an attempt to get away from a town that didn't appreciate his talents?

Or from an arrest for murder?

11

The kettle had been refilled, heated to boiling, and turned down to simmer long before Jill arrived a little after nine. "Sorry I couldn't get here earlier," she said as she peeled off her uniform coat, dappled with melting snow. "But I figured I might as well change into uniform, in case this runs long. I'm still on the graveyard shift, so we have till eleven-thirty."

"How was your dinner with Lars?" asked Betsy.

"Okay. He asked me to marry him tonight."

This was said so casually, Betsy nearly missed it. "He did? What did you say?"

"I said what I always say when he asks me: No."

"Aren't you in love with him?"

"Oh, I'm mad about the boy," she said, still casually. "But he wants kids right away, and I'm not ready for that yet. Have you got English tea?"

"Yes. And the water's hot." Betsy went into the kitchen, Jill following.

Betsy used a Twinings tea bag, but heated the heavy

mug with a splash of boiling water which she dumped out before putting the bag into it and pouring more water over it. Jill added sugar—two spoonfuls—and a dollop of milk.

"Bad out?" asked Betsy.

"Not yet," said Jill. She leaned against the refrigerator while Betsy made a cup of raspberry-flavored tea for herself. Jill's Gibson Girl face and her invisibly pale eyebrows made her, as usual, hard to read. And that cryptic way of talking about Lars—what was that about?

Did she want Betsy to ask questions? Or was she being cryptic because she didn't want to talk about it? Or did she think Betsy already knew enough about the two of them to understand what Jill meant?

Betsy wondered if Jill often had trouble with that enigmatic face, with people reading into it whatever they were most—or least—comfortable with. Perhaps Jill wasn't cold or unemotional at all, just reluctant or even unable to share her feelings with the world. There had been times when she'd seemed very friendly, such as that other morning on her boyfriend's boat. *Perhaps,* thought Betsy, *if I reached out a little, I'd find her easier to understand. So try to think that there is a friendly interest.*

And, actually, there must be, or why else was she here?

"Tea all right?" asked Betsy.

"Yes, thanks. You make it just like Margot."

Betsy smiled. "We both learned how from our father; he loved tea."

"With a name like Devonshire, that's not surprising."

"Yes, I suppose so. Jill, why don't you want children?"

"I *do* want children. But I want to continue in law enforcement, and when I have a child, I'll want a year or two off, and that would put my career in jeopardy. Also, I can't drive a squad while I'm pregnant, but I could manage a desk. When I make sergeant, then I'll marry Lars.''

"Does he know that?''

"I've told him that, which is not the same thing.''

Betsy smiled. "I see.'' She sipped her tea. "Is Malloy making any progress?''

"Only against Martha,'' sighed Jill. "How about you?''

Betsy said, "Yes, that's why I called you. I've found out something that may be important. Alice Skoglund told me that in 1948 she wished with all her heart that Trudie were dead. She told me why. She also said she didn't kill her, but she did have a good reason to. And after I called you, I discovered Vern Miller, who had been Trudie's jealous boyfriend, joined the army approximately one day after Trudie disappeared.''

Jill said, "I ask you to find lace makers, and you find suspects.''

"I didn't mean to, honest. Well, maybe I did go looking at Vern Miller. But all I did with Alice was ask her about her lace. She made an assumption that I was sleuthing and confessed about Trudie.''

"Why would Alice Skoglund hate Trudie Koch enough to wish her dead?''

Betsy hesitated, then said, "What she told me would be nearly nothing by today's standards. But by her own, it was shocking and shameful. And Trudie was blackmailing her over it. She said she hadn't told anyone until today, when she told me. I felt so awful, listening to her pour her heart out. All that wretchedness—I had no idea. And all I wanted was for her to tell me who was making lace in 1948—oh!''

"What?''

"I forgot to ask her that." Betsy glanced at Jill and noticed a slight quiver of the shapely mouth. She smiled herself, and Jill's quiver became a genuine grin.

Jill asked, "And did Vern Miller just pour his heart out to you, too?"

"No. What happened was, Shelly said he retired from the army after thirty years, came home and opened Miller Motors. His sign says, 'Since 1978.' If you subtract thirty years from that, you get 1948. So I went to talk to him. He said he was halfway through boot camp when he got a letter about Carl and Trudie running off together. He says he didn't believe it, because Carl was a respectable businessman with a family and not likely to fall for someone like Trudie. Vern thought she might have accepted a ride from Carl to somewhere, but that's all. He said he used to think about her waitressing in some other town, sassing the customers and going home to her six kids."

"What do you think?"

"I don't know what to think. He said she used to pick fights with him whenever he couldn't buy her something she wanted, and then she'd temporarily take up with someone who would, then she'd let Vern back into her life. It sounds like it was a volatile relationship, and that can end in murder. And he did leave town at a very significant moment."

"Hmmmm," mused Jill. "You know, you have come up with two very solid alternatives to Martha. I wonder if there's a way to get Mike to look them over."

"You think I should go talk to him?"

"No, let me have a go, first. He didn't like you poking around that first time, remember? And he wouldn't listen to you until you had proof. Which you don't have, right now. He's pretty sold on Martha being the killer, you know."

"I can't believe he really thinks she did this."

"Well, look at it his way," said Jill. "Trudie works at the Blue Line Café, just yards from the dock where the *Hopkins* is tied up, waiting to be towed out and sunk. Carl is having an affair with her, he meets her after work that night in The Common, which is right there next to the docks.

"It's all over town that Carl is messing with Trudie. Think how embarrassing that must have been for Martha! It's not hard to see the obvious, that Martha comes roaring out of the darkness to smite Trudie on the head with a tire iron or a hammer—at least that's the ME's opinion.

"Now, rather than trying to stop her, Carl runs off- "

"The coward," said Betsy.

"Well, if my spouse and my lover got into a fight, I might not care to interfere. Both of them might remember who they really should be mad at."

"Oops," said Betsy.

"Right. So Carl's gone and Trudie is dead. Martha drags or carries Trudie's body onto the boat, the effort shifting her dress around so a pocket opens, or a sleeve unrolls, and her handkerchief falls out. It's dark, she's busy, she doesn't notice. And either when she's moving rubble it gets covered up, or she steps wrong in the dark, and a piece of pipe rolls under her foot, covering the handkerchief."

"But think of that big boat filled with rubble," said Betsy. "It would have been an enormous effort for a woman to move enough of it away to uncover the deck and then move it back again in order to hide the body."

"Malloy has found someone who remembers that they didn't fill the boat at the dock, but hauled maybe half of it out on a barge, since they didn't want the boat to tip over or sink before they got it out behind the Big Island.''

"Oh," said Betsy, deflated.

"But there was enough that she had to clear a space, and enough that when she put it over the body, no one noticed when they tossed the rest in. It was hard work, but not an impossible task. Remember, she's scared. I'm sure you've read the stories about women who have lifted whole automobiles off their husbands or sons after the cars fell off jacks onto them. Malloy has.

"Meanwhile Carl gets into his car, drives off—"

"The *car!*" exclaimed Betsy.

"What about it?"

"All these years Martha says she thought Carl had been mugged and his body thrown into a boxcar or into the lake. How did she reconcile that notion with the fact that his car was missing?"

"His car wasn't missing," said Jill. "It was found behind the dry cleaners. I'm assuming he drove down to the lake, and then drove back again. There was a pretty fine train and streetcar service out here in those days. He left his car behind the cleaners, then caught a street-car or a train into Minneapolis, and caught a train out of town."

"Oh," said Betsy.

"He arrives in Omaha and decides to stay awhile," continued Jill, picking up Malloy's scenario. "He finds work, tries to forget. But fifty years later, the boat is raised, the skeleton found, and a story about it gets picked up by the wire services. The story says Martha is suspected. Carl is overjoyed. At last, he can come home and tell what really happened, see to it his wife is at last punished for her deed.

"But coming back opens old memories. Maybe, he thinks to himself, he'll give his wife the same chance he took, to run off. He phones her from a nearby motel, telling her he's back and she'd better get out of town. But Martha plays it cool, asks to come and talk to him. And she's not leaving town. She goes out there with a gun and shoots him. She leaves the gun beside the body, thinking the cops will conclude it was an accident or suicide. But she's no forensic expert; she doesn't know from powder burns and angle of entry and all that sort of thing. Her hasty little plot doesn't work. She's found out; she's going to prison."

Betsy put down her cup of tea. That was very plausible. So plausible, in fact, that it might be true. Was it true? Was she on a fool's errand thinking it was otherwise?

Jill went to the pig-shaped cookie jar and lifted the lid, then turned with it in one hand. "Do you mind?" she asked.

"No, of course not. I'd love to get rid of them; I'm trying to cut back."

Jill put down the lid, selected a raisin oatmeal cookie, put it down, put the lid back on. As she did, she looked toward the dining nook and said, "That your counted cross-stitch project?"

"Yes, and I'm giving up on it. You want it?"

"What's wrong with it?"

Betsy took her to the table. "I did what everyone said I should do, I basted the edges of the evenweave, and I marked off the divisions with more basting and I folded it per instructions so now it's marked into the squares each ornament will fill. And I found the middle of the first square, and started stitching. After about ten stitches, I realized I'd counted wrong and had to frog—"

" 'Frog'?" interrupted Jill.

"Isn't that a term? I see it on RCTN all the time."

"RCTN?"

"An Internet news group for needleworkers. When they have to pull out stitches, they call it frogging. As in 'rip it, rip it.' "

Jill actually chuckled. "That's cute," she said. "I'll remember that. I've done some frogging myself." She took a big bite of her cookie and drank some tea. "You're lucky you're not working with metallics. You can pick out the little raggedy ends floss leaves on your fabric, but metallics leave a mark you can't see."

"A mark you can't see?" said Betsy, expecting a joke.

"It develops over time." Jill saw the incipient laughter on Betsy's face and said, "I'm serious. The metallic floss comes out clean and you think it's gone, but in a few days or a few weeks or even sometimes in a few months, there are these dark marks, like dirt. And on that piece you're doing, you leave some areas blank. So if you frog an area you should have left blank, pretty soon it will look like you were handling it with dirty fingers."

"Oh. All right, I guess I should be grateful that these patterns don't call for metallic. I've done this one part about four times, and there are two areas I crossed into territory I think should be blank. I'm about out of one color, and there's not a stitch of it left on the ornament."

"You'll have to buy some more."

"No, I won't. You see, *you* eventually get it right, but *I* don't; I just keep getting lost in one direction, then another. I count and count and check and double-check and still I make mistakes. And these are supposed to be *easy*. I'm giving up."

Jill picked up the patterns, which were printed all on one big sheet. "You shouldn't be having all this trouble. I've done one set of these, and they aren't all that difficult.'' She looked at Betsy's cloth. ''Where's your gridding?''

''Gridding?''

''Yes. I hate to have you do yet more setup, but if you mark off every ten squares on your cloth and every ten squares on the pattern, it's a whole lot easier to keep count.''

Betsy looked at the cloth, then at Jill. ''Well, dammit, why didn't they suggest that in the instructions?''

''Because not everyone needs to grid. Especially on something as easy as these patterns.''

''Sit down, why don't you? I've got a marking pen somewhere, I'm going to go get it.'' She walked away, muttering, ''Of all the damn, dumb, stupid things. Why didn't I think of doing that myself? I'm never going to get counted cross-stitch. I don't know why I keep trying.''

When she got back, Jill was looking at the color pictures of finished patterns. ''I did the duck first. The one I like best is the polar bear with the Saint Lucy wreath on its head. There's a town in Ramsey County—that's where Saint Paul is—called White Bear Lake. Very nice place to live. I'll give the white bear to the tree.''

''Thanks,'' said Betsy. She sat down with the marker and a ruler and began counting the paper pattern.

''What's this?'' asked Jill after a minute, picking up the postcard. ''Someone you know likes bats?''

''It's a joke. When I told my friend Abbey back in San Diego that I was moving to Minnesota, she said, 'Are you bats?' ''

Jill turned the postcard over and read the message. She asked, ''So, are we driving you bats?''

Betsy laughed. ''Too early to tell. It sure is different here.''

The wind outdoors threw a handful of sleet against

the window, and Jill said, "Tell me about it."

Betsy laughed but thought she heard an invitation as well as a comment in that, so she put down her marker pen and said, "San Diego has the perfect climate, it really does. Warm all year round, but not hot in the summer. There's only about ten degrees' difference between winter and summer, so there's not a big change in the seasons like here. Even in dry season, with that wonderful ocean breeze the air is always fresh and clean, the sky an incredible blue. And then when it rains, everything flowers. It's rainy season now, so every leaf, every flower is pouring out a scent, the air is like perfume."

"Mmmmm," said Jill covetously, and Betsy wondered why she had thought Jill unemotional.

"It's a military town, a lot of sailors and marines, so by California standards, it's conservative politically. But not by, say, Montana standards. On the other hand, it's not L.A., which is dirty, crazy, only ninety miles away, and approaching fast."

"Is the ocean nice? I've always wanted to swim in the ocean."

"The water's too cold to swim in, at least for me. Even surfers wear wet suits. But I miss the beaches, especially Coronado Beach, and I miss the sun, and the fruits and vegetables being so cheap and having more varieties. I mean, I went to this great big grocery store up the road. Big as a warehouse."

Jill nodded.

"And when I looked over the fresh vegetable section, I just about cried. Apples, potatoes and onions, unripe peaches, sweet bell peppers, and four kinds of lettuce if you count iceberg. Oh, and, carrots. Pitiful!"

"Pitiful," echoed Jill, but this time her voice was dry.

"I know, I know, I can almost kind of remember my

childhood, when fresh fruit all but disappeared during the winter. Still, I looked and looked and couldn't find a mango or a cactus pear . . ." Betsy sighed. "And I miss Balboa Park. There's this big tree, I love to go visit it, it's like a friend, all spreading branches like it's holding out its arms. An army could camp under it—" Betsy stopped, dismayed to find her eyes filling with tears.

Jill said, "When the money comes, are you going to move back?"

"I don't know. Yes, I do. I can't go back. It was my life for fifteen years, but my ex-husband poisoned the well for me. We did so many things together, and his college world became my world, and it's all still there. Everything I'd see or do would remind me of the pig, and he was *such* a pig. The pig." Betsy sobbed once, and took a gulp of her tea to forestall another.

"A real pig, huh?" Betsy looked up and saw Jill looking back so gravely that she had to giggle. Jill's mouth quivered, and suddenly the two of them were laughing.

When the laughter slowed enough to talk again, Jill said, "I'll take you cross-country skiing in a few weeks. I know a place so quiet and so beautiful, the air smelling of pine, you will actually start to fall in love with Minnesota."

"Yeah, I think we missed our chance to ride herd this year."

"Oh, I have a friend who has horses, so we can still ride, if you like. But I think you'd better get hardened up to the cold first. Downhill skiing, or cross-country skiing, will do it. I love both."

"How about a snowmobile ride?" asked Betsy, who wasn't big on exercise.

"I don't like snowmobiles," said Jill. "Too noisy and smelly. And some snowmobilers get drunk and try to cross the road ahead of cars and trucks. Talk about poisoning the well; those crazy snowmobilers totally put me off the sport. Especially when it got to be my turn to tell the next of kin.''

"You've done that?''

"Twice. Once the jerk survived, but with about half the brains he had that morning. And that wasn't a whole lot to start with.''

"Jill, why do you do this job?''

"Because it makes a big difference. It's important—no, it's essential. I always was a take-care, take-charge kind of person, and this way I can put that trait to good use.''

"But sometimes it must break your heart.''

"Sometimes it does,'' nodded Jill. She finished her tea and said, "Would there be any way to prove what day Vern Miller joined the army?''

"He says he can produce his service papers.''

"Why would he still have his service papers?'' asked Jill.

"Because he stayed until he could retire, and he gets all kinds of benefits, but he has to be able to produce his service record on demand. I still have mine, because if I get sick I can go to the Veterans Hospital, even though I was only in four and a half years.''

"Four and a half—?''

"President Johnson extended every service person's enlistment six months during the Vietnam War.''

"So I guess that makes you a veteran,'' said Jill with a note of admiration in her voice.

"Ha! I never got any closer to Vietnam than San Francisco, and I personally don't think of myself as a veteran. But that's not the point. Vern Miller may be the real point of this discussion. I wonder if he has a gun. I didn't think to ask. I keep focusing on Trudie Koch's murder, but maybe I should look at what happened to Carl Winters.''

"I think it's likely they were killed by the same person," said Jill. "And Carl was probably killed because he knew something about who killed Trudie, or why she was killed, and came home to tell what he knew. So you're not mistaken to focus on Trudie.''

"Oh, something else. Myrtle Jensen told me Alice had cataracts removed some years back, and she can't see very well. Alice said her eyes had gone bad and that's why she quit making lace—not that she couldn't, but that it was painful. That makes me wonder if she might not have fudged a little bit about figuring out that lace pattern for Sergeant Malloy. She showed me some samples of the lace she used to make. It's really beautiful, so she does know what she's talking about. Are you sure she didn't know about the butterflies in Martha's lace?''

"If she was a lace maker, I should think she knew. Martha didn't keep it a secret, and as a fellow lace maker, it seems to me Alice would pay attention to things like that. I wonder if her husband knew Trudie was blackmailing her.''

"Oh, I don't think she told him. Think of the climate back then, prefifties. I bet Martin Skoglund, seminary graduate, wouldn't have married her if he knew what she'd done, so I don't think she could have told him about Trudie.''

"What did she—?" Jill raised both hands. "Sorry, sorry, I didn't mean to ask. But I *am* curious.''

"I know. And I'm sorry I can't tell you. Did you know Pastor Skoglund? What was he like?''

"He was my pastor while I was growing up, and as a kid, I liked him. He seemed like one of the good grown-ups, big and strong, but kind and friendly. A little bit distant, too important to be teased or to tell a joke to. Like what I imagined God to be. My mother loved his sermons, but if he was coming for a visit, she cleaned for two days and treated him like royalty.''

"Yes, I see. Poor Alice; he might have been giving off unconscious messages like, 'Don't get messy,' or even 'I don't want to know.' ''

"Pastors get messy stuff all the time. Other peoples' troubles are his work. Like cops. Which reminds me—'' She looked at her watch and stood.

"Jill, thanks for coming over. Just talking to you helped a lot.''

"I'm glad you asked me over. Do it again, any time you need to talk.''

"Do *you* ever need a shoulder?''

Jill hesitated. "Once in awhile.''

"Then call on me. I'm glad you're my friend, and I'd like to be one to you.''

"Thanks,'' said Jill, and she left.

Betsy sat down with the counted cross-stitch pattern and the evenweave cloth. She finished gridding her fabric and then the pattern—a cat—then picked up her needle and threaded it with pink for the nose. It was much easier now to find the center of the fabric. She made a stitch, and another, and crossed them. She counted and stitched, and after awhile, she sat back to double-check her work. Definitely a cat's face looking back, and from under a Santa Claus hat, and exactly like the pattern. This was more like it!

But it was still a tension-making exercise, and she needed to relax her mind or she'd never get to sleep. She put the cross-stitch aside and went to the living room's comfortable chair and got out her knitting. Let's see, where was she? Here, with still two inches of knit and knit to go. That should just about do it.

But in another minute, she began thinking again about

the mystery. Jill was very sure Carl's and Trudie's murders were related. And indeed, if they weren't, there were a lot of coincidences connecting them. They were both locals, they were in the midst of some kind of relationship, they had disappeared on the same day fifty years ago. Trudie had been murdered, and when Carl came back to the scene after fifty years, he was promptly murdered, too. Did they have something else in common besides that relationship? Had they been "canoodling" (to use Myrtle the historian's term) in The Common and seen someone doing something illegal? And had that someone seen them? What could someone be doing that kept alive the murderous determination to prevent its telling fifty years later? Smuggling? Hardly. Murder? No one else was murdered that night in Excelsior. Or mysteriously disappeared. Rape? Hmmm . . .

But then Carl was not murdered the same way Trudie had been. Trudie had been bludgeoned, Carl had been shot. Was that significant? Maybe there were two different murderers. No, more likely, after fifty years, Trudie's murderer was so old he simply didn't have the strength to batter Carl's head in.

Vern Miller had been surprised to hear that Carl had run off with Trudie because of the difference in their social status. Which brought up the question, what *was* Carl doing flirting with her? Not just everyday flirting, he was known for that. Everyday flirting with Trudie wouldn't have the gossips' tongues wagging so vigorously as to anger his wife.

Betsy's needles slowed. That was interesting. Was Carl genuinely taken with Trudie? Enough to risk his marriage? His business? Having lived in the small-town world of college life, she knew how important a reputation could be, and how devastating it could be to have friends and colleagues turn on you. As they had done on Hal the Pig—and, less directly, on Betsy.

No, she could never go back there.

She looked at her watch. Holy smokes, it was way past eleven! *Hey,* she thought, as she packed up her work, *this may be the answer.* Fabrics showed everything, so no snacks around the needlework. But when she got really absorbed, she didn't miss the snacks. Remembering Margot's trim figure, Betsy wondered if she hadn't stumbled onto her sister's secret to a trim waistline.

Feeling heartened, Betsy went to bed.

12

B etsy had a night full of odd dreams. When the
radio alarm went off, instead of the strange and
eclectic selections of KSJN's *Morning Show,* she got
Antonín Dvořák's Symphony number eight. Occasionally the *Morning Show* remembered it was public radio
and played something classical, but usually just a move-
ment. This went on and on, the entire symphony. After
awhile, she realized it wasn't the *Morning Show,* so this
must be Saturday.

But Saturday is a workday for shop owners. She did
not turn off the radio.

There was a heavy thump and a continued wobble of
the mattress as Sophie came for her morning cuddle. She
rubbed her face all over Betsy's hand until Betsy began
rubbing back. The two lay in comfort for a few minutes,
then Betsy got up to start the day.

By 9:30 they were through the back door into the
shop. Betsy turned on lights, started the coffeepot going
and the plug-in teakettle for tea or cocoa, put the start-

up money in the cash register. The Christmas decorations looked nice, she noticed.

She checked the desk for notes and found she would have to order more alpaca wool, bamboo knitting needles, and little stork scissors. Godwin noted that he had sold *two* needlepoint Christmas stockings, the two underlined three times. Shelly noted that there had been inquiries about spring knitting lessons. "I think we should ask Martha," she wrote. "Show our confidence."

Betsy put the note aside.

Godwin came in just before ten looking at peace with the world. "Don't you look nice!" he said.

Betsy had worn a new wool dress she'd found on sale. It had a simple A-line skirt and was a deep cranberry color. "You like it?"

"Are you losing weight?" he asked, narrowing his eyes.

"Not yet," said Betsy.

"You should get a gold scarf to go with that dress," he said. "With a gold scarf you could take that dress anywhere." He looked around as if for eavesdroppers—though how, without the door alarm's *bing,* he could think someone might have come in—and leaned toward Betsy. "What did Vern Miller tell you?"

"He joined the army in early July, the third, to be exact."

Godwin looked genuinely surprised. "You mean, I was *right? He's* the murderer?"

"I don't know. I told Jill, and she's going to tell Malloy, if she hasn't already."

Godwin's smile lit up his entire body. "We did it again!"

"Did what?"

"We solved a murder!"

"We haven't solved it!" Betsy said sharply. "All we've done is supply Sergeant Malloy with another suspect to look at. We don't know that Vern Miller did it."

"Are you going to look for proof that he did?"

"I think I'm going to wait to see what Sergeant Malloy does. If Vern Miller is a murderer, I don't want to be the one to confront him about it."

Half an hour later, Shelly came in to work. Betsy told her the decorations were excellent and reminded her to mark her hours on her time card, as she was doing payroll tomorrow.

Then Betsy went into the back room to poke into cardboard boxes to see if what was written on their outsides coincided with their contents. She was standing on a chair to reach a box stacked near the ceiling when she heard a man's inquiring voice and Godwin's brief reply, then silence. She got off the chair and backed up a step to look through the open door. A slim young man was standing awkwardly in the opening between the box shelves.

"Hi, Ms. Devonshire?" he said shyly. "I'm Jeff Winters." He had light brown hair and his grandmother's faded blue eyes.

"Ah . . . hello," said Betsy. "I'm very sorry about Martha. We all are."

"I know," he said. "That's why I've got the nerve to come and ask you for an important favor."

"Of course," she said, coming out of the back room. "Anything we can do. Would you like to sit down?" His face showed signs of the strain he must be under.

"Thanks."

She sat him in one of the comfortable chairs at the little round table. "How is your mother holding up?"

"She'll be home tonight. A judge allowed bail, and I

got one of those quick mortgages on the dry cleaning business for that and a good lawyer.''

"Getting her home is something at least. Would you like some coffee?"

"Please. Thanks. Black." He ran thin fingers through his already mussed hair.

She went to fill two pretty porcelain cups, his with coffee, hers with a lemon-flavored herbal tea.

He took only a token sip, then put his cup down and sighed. "I know you've told people that you aren't investigating anymore because you aren't a real private eye, but—" he began.

"It's not that I don't want to help your grandmother," said Betsy quickly. "Because I do. I'm sure Martha is frightened half out of her mind, and your whole family must be suffering terribly over this."

"Yes, we're all wishing we could be braver. Except Grandmother; she's amazing."

Betsy continued, "It's funny how people seem to think I enjoy playing amateur sleuth. I don't, because I don't know how. I got involved with my sister's case because I was very angry and sad and it was my own strange way of coping with my grief. I couldn't believe she was murdered by some kid who needed a desk calculator, so I started asking questions and just got lucky."

"Yes, I understand that."

"So I hope the favor you want to ask for isn't for me to go looking for clues."

He looked at her, his face at once determined and wretched. "The problem is, the lawyer we hired says we need a private investigator to look into the case. And between posting bail and hiring that lawyer, I can't afford a private detective. I went to my dad, but he's working out some stuff of his own. You see, he was thinking his father was dead all these years, and then he heard,

'He wasn't dead after all, but now he's murdered, and the police think your mother did it' all in one sentence. It really messed him up. He isn't talking to me or Grandmother right now.''

''That's very sad.''

''Oh, he'll come around, but maybe not very soon, and we need to do something right away. I understand how you think you can't do anything, but you did so splendidly for your sister, I want you to try again for Grandmother. Just ask some questions, like you did the first time, and maybe it will happen again, you'll understand from the answers what really happened to my grandfather and to that other woman all those years ago.''

Betsy picked up her cup of tea and took several sips while she thought what to say. She'd been lucky again already, finding out about Alice and then Vern. But that might be the end of her luck. Anyway, finding another suspect wasn't the same as proving Martha innocent. And there was another bad thing about all this.

''Suppose I do go sleuthing, and I find out things—bad things—about people? Rooting around in other people's lives can really hurt them. And if they're innocent, too . . .''

''Ignore the stuff that doesn't matter, can't you? There has to be something to find that will help, because Grandmother didn't do this. I know it. And I know you'll find it. You should start with the Monday Bunch. Those women know everyone in town, and everything that's going on, and everything that's happened, too. They've been around for years and years, most of them. And they know Grandmother better than anyone. They can tell you she didn't murder that Trudie person, or Grandfather.''

''I don't know if they'll want to—''

"Are you kidding? Of course they'll want to help! Grandmother is practically the oldest member of the Bunch. The first Monday Bunch meetings were held in your sister's home, before she started Crewel World, did you know that? And Grandmother was one of the first members."

"No, I didn't know that."

"Margot used to organize trips to other towns—other states, sometimes—to buy yarn or patterns or go to conventions, and Grandmother went every time she could get away. She was devoted to your sister and just devastated by her death. She was also very proud of you for solving her murder. Please, won't you help her now?"

Again Betsy lifted the cup of tea to her lips as an excuse not to answer immediately. She didn't want an official involvement with this case. If Alice's role had to be revealed—Betsy foresaw trying to explain herself in a court of law.

But then a memory swam up, of that first Monday after her sister's funeral, when four members of the Bunch came and worked for hours to help clean up the mess in the shop left by the murderer. Martha had been the one sorting out yarn. Yes, and she had been the one who called the Humane Society and the one who designed and printed the posters asking for information about Sophie, who had gone missing. Betsy remembered what a wretched mess she herself had been, and how patient they had been with her, Jill and those four members of the Monday Bunch. They hadn't been afraid to just pitch in.

"Yes," said Betsy. "All right. I'll do what I can. But remember, I really am an amateur. You mustn't get your hopes up."

But Jeff was on his feet, extending a long-fingered

hand. "Thanks! Thank you so much! I'll tell Grandmother, and she'll be so grateful and comforted."

After he left, Betsy sat back down on the chair and
sighed.

"Well?!?" said a voice and she jumped.

It was Godwin, appearing as if conjured, agog with
curiosity. "I just can't stand it anymore!" he said.
"What's going on?"

"Jeff Winters wants me to ask some questions, see if
I can find out anything that will help his grandmother's
case. I said I would. Now, go away, get back to work.
And please stop sneaking up on people!" she added
crossly, but an indulgent smile teased her lips.

Betsy worked through the lunch hour so her employees
could go out, but as soon as they came back, she left.
She was hungry but had an idea she wanted to try out
before she bought some lunch. She got her car out and
drove up Water Street to Oak and followed it north to
where George angled into it. As she made the steep angled turn back, she could see the barn belonging to the
Minnesota Transportation Museum. It was more like a
big, windowless shed, two stories high, made of corru-
gated fiberglass in an ugly beige color. Several cars had
forced their way up a narrow, unplowed lane to park in
front of it.

As Betsy followed suit, she went past an enormous,
ancient, military-style tow truck. That must be how they
got the boat over here, thought Betsy.

She got out and found a small door on the back side
of the barn. It wasn't locked. She opened it, went inside,
and found the entire interior was taken up by a boat. Its
mustard-colored bottom rested on a big cradle built onto
a trailer. She looked up and saw that the upper structure
was surrounded by a kind of mezzanine built out from

the walls of the shed. A set of wooden stairs led up to it.

The air was warm and smelled of freshly cut wood and varnish. Men's voices indicated there were people on the upper level working on the boat.

The boat, of course, wasn't the *Hopkins*; this was the *Minnehaha*. She knew it was pulled out of the water for the winter, but it hadn't occurred to her to wonder where it was kept.

She went up the stairs. A half dozen men in coveralls or jeans were measuring or painting or consulting a very large hardcover catalog of pipe fittings. One looked around at her. "You the new volunteer?" he asked.

"No," she said. "I'm looking for the *Hopkins*."

He laughed. "Not here, obviously. Not only because there's no room, they told us it's the scene of a crime. The police hauled it up onto the Big Island until they finish with it."

"Oh," she said, disappointed.

"You sure you aren't a volunteer? We sure can use someone to varnish the slats of the upper deck seats," he said, and stuck out a hand. "I'm John Titterington. This is Pete Weir, and that fellow in love with the catalog is Virgil Behounek, and over on the deck are Jim Hewett and Leo Eiden."

Betsy waved vaguely at the men, who nodded vaguely back and continued their labors. "Some other time," she said to Mr. Titterington and retreated back down the stairs.

I should have known, she told herself as she got back into her car and wallowed back up the lane. They wouldn't allow the public to go crawling over the boat.

And what did you think you'd find on the Hopkins, *anyhow? You're just trying to act like a real private eye,*

*which you're not. Go do what you can, which is ask
nosy questions.*

She drove back to the shop in a grump and picked up
a salad with double croutons in the sandwich shop next
door. The dressing she selected wasn't diet, either.

But a big special order came in that afternoon, and
going through it with the customer and finding it all
there, as ordered, brightened Betsy's spirits—and the big
check the customer wrote helped, too.

Just before closing, the phone rang. It was Jeff Winters. "Grandmother's at home," he said, "if you want
to talk to her."

So Betsy ate a hasty supper, called Jill (who wasn't
home) to leave a message saying she'd be home by
eight, then got back in her car and drove down Lake
Street to what she called "the *other* Lake Street." At its
north end, Lake Street went around a corner and became
West Lake Street.

The west end of West Lake Street made another sharp
turn that led it down to the lakeshore. Betsy negotiated
the curve carefully, wary of ice. She'd once been a good
winter driver, but that was many years ago.

Martha Winters's attractive brick house was the second from the end on this segment. A streetlight gleamed
on the snow clinging to an enormous blue spruce in the
front yard. Martha's driveway was gritty with sand.

Bushes beside the little porch had been covered with
cloth tied close with twine. Betsy, no gardner, wondered
if they were roses. She went up the brick steps to the
front door and rang the bell, feeling uncertain about the
conversation she was about to have.

The door opened, and there was Martha, her face pale,
its folds and wrinkles looking freshly carved. "Jeff said
he'd asked you to come over and talk to me," she said.

"Oh, Betsy, I'm so worried! I do hope you can help me. Please, come in."

Betsy stopped on the little tiled area just inside the door and took off her coat. She glanced past Martha at the virginal blue carpet and said, "Shall I take off my boots?"

"Yes, if you don't mind," said Martha, and she hung Betsy's coat and scarf up in the little closet, then led the way into the living room. "Would you like some coffee? It'd just take a minute to make a pot."

"No, thanks. But you have some, if you like."

"No, I had three cups with my supper, which I ate in my own kitchen, *thank God,* and that's two more than I usually have in the evening. I won't sleep a wink to-night."

Martha sat down on the very front edge of a pale, upholstered chair, so Betsy started for the couch. But her eye was caught by the framed handkerchiefs, and instead, she leaned forward for a look. Sure enough, there was a butterfly, plain in the design of each corner. The lace itself was two inches wide around the center handkerchief, very elegant and rich-looking. "These are amazing," said Betsy. "Jill told me about them, but they are even more luscious than I thought. I pictured the butterflies as a subtle pattern, but they're as clear as drawings. How old is this work?"

"Years and years. I stopped making lace a long time ago—soon after Carl ran off. I had the store to mind and my son to raise, so I had to give up a lot of things."

Betsy turned and spoke from her heart. "I can't imagine the hurt his disappearance must have given you. And now this."

Martha looked up at her with wounded eyes. "Yes."

Betsy sat down. "Was he a pig before he went away?"

"A . . . pig?"

"That's the word I use to describe my ex-husband. He was a tenured professor at Merrivale, that's in San Diego, and had been cutting a swath through the undergrad women for years. I had no idea until I got a phone call from the attorney he'd hired to fight the case the university was bringing against him. Apparently, he'd dropped one student a little too abruptly in going to another, and she went to the administration. And it turned out she wasn't his first. Other women heard about it and came forward to testify—one or two actually in his favor. There were nine—nine!—willing to talk; and God knows how many weren't. I should have known, but I didn't. I mean, I met him when I was a student in one of his classes, so I really should have been more suspicious. Only I made sure he was single before I let his advances advance." Betsy looked over and saw Martha staring openmouthed at her.

"I'm sorry," Betsy said. "I came here to talk to you, not carry in the trash of my own life."

"I think perhaps you're making assumptions about Carl and me, that's what set off the confession," said Martha.

Betsy felt herself blushing. "You're right, and I shouldn't do things like that. I told Jeff and now I'll remind you, I'm an amateur. I don't know how to conduct a proper interrogation. I just ask whatever occurs to me. *Was* Carl a pig?"

Martha smiled. "He was frisky, he had a terrible reputation for it, but it was all talk. He loved to 'push the envelope,' as they call it nowadays, but he never went outside it, as far as I knew. Certainly he never ran off with anyone before."

Betsy said, "If that skeleton belongs to Trudie, then Carl didn't run away with her, either. It's even possible,

I suppose, that her murder and Carl's disappearance aren't connected. I wonder if perhaps Trudie thought he was serious, and he murdered her to shut her up.''

"I don't think Carl could commit murder," said Martha. "He was a scalawag, everyone knew that and was used to it. But he wasn't cruel or mean. He had a great many friends in Excelsior, and so did I; yet two women made it their business to tell me he was having lunch every day down at the Blue Ribbon and making time with Trudie. Jessie Turnquist was one of them—this was before we became close. I told her what Mark Twain said, that it takes two people to cut you to the heart: an enemy to slander you and a friend to tell you what the enemy said. Besides, I said, Carl would try to make time with a gorilla if he thought it was a female gorilla, he can't help himself. So you see, if I knew, and wasn't turning into a fishwife over it, why would Carl have to murder her?''

"Did Carl know you knew?"

"Indeed yes. I brought it up over supper that same day I heard about it. I said the whole town was talking, which hurt my feelings and might be bad for business. And he said something like, 'Aw, they know I don't mean anything.' But then he didn't come home the next night. It was late closing and I was tired, so I went to bed and didn't realize he hadn't come home till the next morning. I couldn't imagine where he'd got to. I went down to the store thinking someone had robbed the place and left him tied up in back, but he wasn't there. I called around and no one had seen him, so finally I called the police. It wasn't until that evening, when Trudie didn't show up for work, that people realized she was missing, too.''

"That was the evening of the day they towed the *Hopkins* out and sank her," said Betsy.

"Yes. That's why I don't have any memory of them sinking her, because it wasn't a year later, it was the same day Carl disappeared. I was so upset about Carl, I didn't notice what was happening with the *Hopkins*. But looking back, I can see that by the time they realized Trudie had disappeared, too, the boat was already sunk. And everyone was *so sure* they'd run off together it didn't occur to anyone to think one or the other's body might be on the boat."

"The big thing we have to worry about is your handkerchief. We have to figure out who got hold of one and left it on that boat. And why."

"To make it look as if I did it, of course," said Martha.

"No, that can't be right. The boat was taken out and sunk for what was supposed to be forever," said Betsy. "If someone wanted to frame you, the thing to do would be leave the body up on shore somewhere and drop your handkerchief beside it. Why hide the body and the handkerchief?"

There was a thoughtful silence. "All right, perhaps they didn't want to implicate me," said Martha at last. "Maybe whoever dropped it didn't murder Trudie, they were just there and dropped the handkerchief by accident. Certainly I did it often enough."

Betsy frowned. "But if it was just dropped casually, then it would have floated away. It was found on the bottom of the boat, after the last of the rubble was taken out. The only reason some of it was found at all was because it was tucked away under the rubble."

"What I don't understand is how it got there to begin with. I know where all my handkerchiefs are."

Betsy asked, "How many did you have to start with?"

"One," said Martha, and she smiled at her jest. "I

started making lace when I was fourteen; my grandmother showed me how. Her mother was from England
and showed her how. My mother loved to knit and crochet, she made both knitted and crocheted lace.''

"You can *knit* lace?''

"Oh, yes, on tiny, tiny needles. I used to know how,
but once I learned the techniques, I loved bobbin lace
best. My grandmother left me her bobbins. I still have
them. I've thought now and again about selling them,
but I'd rather wait and see if there's someone who would
really appreciate them, so I could make a gift of them.''

"That would be a very special gift.''

"Yes, it's a pity I couldn't have more children; I'd
have loved to teach a daughter how to make lace.'' Martha sighed, but faintly; that was an old and no longer
important sorrow. "But to answer your question, I made
bobbin lace edgings for nineteen handkerchiefs. Each
one's a little different, but they all have that butterfly.
My grandmother helped me design it. Her signature on
her lace was a bee.''

"Who else do you know who makes lace?''

Martha thought. "Alice Skoglund used to do very
nice work. But she says it gives her a headache to do it
nowadays and so she quit.''

"Did you see the design Alice made from the tangled
mess taken from the *Hopkins*?''

Martha nodded. "It's mine all right.''

"You say you know where all your handkerchiefs
are? I heard you lost two of them.''

"Well, I'm reasonably sure a pig ate one and the other
went into show business.'' She snorted genteelly and
Betsy smiled, as much in admiration as appreciation of
the joke. That Martha could jest in the face of danger
showed she was a brave woman.

"Suppose a lace maker, one who makes bobbin lace,

had gotten a really good look at one of your handkerchiefs, one you'd dropped, say. Suppose she got a
chance to really study it before she gave it back to you.
Could she then copy that design in some lace she made
herself?''

Martha thought that over. ''Maybe. She'd have to be
looking at it with that in mind.''

''Now,'' said Betsy. ''Think hard. Try to remember
back all those years ago. Did Alice Skoglund ever return
a handkerchief to you?''

''Oh, yes,'' nodded Martha. ''Several times. She was
the Reverend Skoglund's wife, you see. And I left a
hanky in church at least once a year. Sometimes the
person who found it brought it right back to me. But not
everyone knew about my butterfly, so they turned it in
to lost and found. I distinctly remember one Sunday Alice gave it back to me saying she'd heard about my
butterfly lace and so thought this was mine. We talked
about lace for a few minutes. That's when I learned she
was a lace maker.''

''So she would have had it a whole week to study, if
she wanted to make a copy,'' said Betsy.

''Well, yes. Oh, surely you don't think Alice had anything to do with this!''

But Betsy was thinking of the woman who even in
her seventies had arms and shoulders like a man.

13

Sunday afternoon Betsy went to see Alice Skoglund again, carefully choosing a time so Alice wouldn't feel obliged to feed her. "I came to talk to you about making lace," she said. "Someone told me you can't make lace anymore because you had an operation to remove cataracts and can't see well enough."

Alice grimaced angrily. "Like most gossip, that's almost sort of true. I did have early-onset cataracts. I had surgery when I was only forty-five. And it did make lace-making difficult. Not impossible, only very hard. I bought a great big magnifying glass, and ordered a lamp that sat on a stand through a catalog. But in three weeks of trying, I made four inches of lace. And it wasn't a difficult pattern or particularly fine thread, nothing like the one-twenty I used to be fond of. I can still make lace, but it's heavy gauge stuff, and I have to keep stopping and checking the pattern, and I can't see the pattern forming like I used to. When I finally realized I wasn't getting any joy out of it, I quit. I do some knitting and crocheting, but they aren't the pleasure lace-making was for me, and they aren't as easy as they once were, either. The only thing I can do real easy anymore are those darn afghan squares. I can do those practically without looking. So I make afghans and put them into fund-raisers and rummage sales and gift packages made up for people who have lost their homes to fire. That way I feel like I'm still making a contribution.''

''I'm sure there are a lot of people who feel you make a great deal of difference,'' said Betsy. Then she screwed her courage to the sticking point and said, ''You told me and Jill that you had never seen one of Martha's handkerchiefs, the kind with a butterfly on it, but Martha told me that you did, perhaps more than once. She said she left them behind in church several times, and that one time you brought it to her yourself and talked with her about lace-making.''

Alice threw herself back in her chair as if poleaxed, strong chin pointed at the ceiling, eyes closed. A sound almost like a snore escaped her throat. Betsy was about to panic, thinking the woman had had a stroke, when Alice abruptly flipped forward to say, ''Well, I guess I am a liar! Do you know, I totally forgot about that? She's right. I did handle one of her handkerchiefs that she had left in church. I told her she should enter it in the State Fair, it was so well done. I was a little afraid to talk to her, she was a superior sort of lady who simply ruled our choir, and I was a common sort of person, and my mother once told me I couldn't carry a tune in a bucket. But Martha was glad to talk lace with me. There weren't many women in town who still had that old skill.''

''Do you remember when that happened?''

''Heavens no. Probably fairly early in Martin's career, because I got less and less afraid of women like her as time went on. I guess I didn't remember it because back when people carried handkerchiefs commonly, they were the single item most often left behind. I finally set up a table in the church hall and put items people forgot on that. People will leave the oddest things behind on those pews, we once found a set of false teeth and another time a dead fish—which of course, we didn't put out to be reclaimed. There were also a lot of umbrellas and a surprising number of single overshoes." Alice chuckled. "So it appears I did have a chance to examine the butterfly she put on the corners of her handkerchiefs. I forgot all about that until just right now."

"But," said Betsy, "perhaps unconsciously you remembered seeing it, and when you were working out the pattern on the *Hopkins* fragment, your unconscious brought it out as an example."

Alice considered this, then shook her head and said slowly, "I don't think so. I do remember now looking at the lace on her handkerchiefs—she did kind of flourish them—and thinking how beautiful it was. The work was so very fine, much better than anything I could do. But I don't remember examining the lace trim on any of them with an eye to copying the pattern. I had my own patterns."

Betsy went next to see Martha Winters. She found her in her kitchen, peeling potatoes. The heavenly scent of roasting chicken filled the air. "My son and his wife are coming over," Martha said happily. "I told them how the Monday Bunch believes in me, and how you are helping, and they decided perhaps I am not so terrible after all."

Betsy hugged her even while she hoped with all her heart that Martha's faith was not misplaced.

"I suppose you have more questions?" said Martha.

Betsy didn't want to say she was floundering, throwing herself in random directions hoping for a clue, a connection, something that would help. "A few," she said.

"Have you learned anything?" Martha asked in a low voice.

"Well, it's possible that Trudie was murdered by the man who was her boyfriend at the time. They had a stormy relationship and were in the middle of a quarrel when this happened. He joined the army right about then."

Martha beamed at her. "You are *so* good at this, Betsy!" she said.

"Well," said Betsy, "the problem is, why did he murder Carl?"

"Because Carl saw him," said Martha, surprised at her. "He saw him murder Trudie and he ran for his own life. Then all these years later, he finds out I am suspected of the murder and he comes back to testify on my behalf."

"Did he say anything to you that might show this was what he was thinking?" asked Betsy.

"Ah . . . no. As I told Sergeant Malloy, I didn't want to talk to him and pretty much hung up on him."

"Did Carl and Trudie know each other long?"

"No, I don't think so. He might have met her at another restaurant or diner when she was waitressing there, but there wasn't any talk until just before it happened. Why he picked on Trudie, why he went all the way down to the Blue Ribbon, I can't imagine. Our dry cleaning store is five blocks from the lake, so Carl would have had to walk past the drugstore fountain and two perfectly nice cafés to get there. I don't know what possessed him, I really don't. It was as if he deliberately set out to do something crazy and break my heart in the bargain.''

Betsy thought about that but was even less able to make sense of it than Martha. Then she said, ''Where was the Blue Ribbon Café in relationship to the lake? Was it near the amusement park?''

''It was part of the amusement park. The two men who managed it shared Christopher Inn, which had been made into a duplex for them and their families. The amusement park ran all along the lakeshore, from City Docks down past where the little ferris wheel is. They had a roller coaster and bumper cars, and a really nice merry-go-round, a big one with beautiful horses.''

''Martha, did you know Trudie at all? Would you have known her if you'd seen her on the street?''

Martha nodded slowly. ''Probably. This habit we have of gossiping about everyone isn't new, you know. We've always pretty much kept track of one another in Excelsior. I'm sure she must have been pointed out to me. In retrospect, I wonder if she was as terrible as everyone said, because she never took any sudden little vacations or went to nurse a sick relative in another state.''

''I don't understand—oh. You mean she never went for an abortion or to have a baby. Gosh, remember when families used to do that to girls who got pregnant?''

Martha nodded. ''When the father couldn't be forced to marry her, they'd send her away till it was all over, and put her baby up for adoption.''

''Times sure have changed, haven't they?''

''Oh, they'll change back, probably. Nothing works, you know. We just keep trying one thing then another and then the first thing again.''

Betsy sighed. ''You're right, what we think of as progress is sometimes just the swing of a pendulum. But

you say Trudie either wasn't as awful as everyone
thought, or was perhaps more careful than most young
women of her type. You've known Alice Skoglund for
a very long time, haven't you? Did she have any quarrel
with Trudie?''

Martha smiled. ''I doubt if those two ever spoke more
than three words to one another—and Trudie was in
high school with Alice. That's funny, when you think
about it. If Trudie were alive today, she'd be an old
woman, like Alice.'' She made a face. ''Like me. Like
Jess.''

Betsy said, ''The older I get, the older people have to
be before I think of them as old. I don't think of you as
old at all.''

Martha smiled faintly, taking the compliment for what
it was worth. ''My grandson told me that when you
think of a policeman or your doctor as young, then
you're getting old. I reached that stage twenty years ago.
I wish I could be of more help to you.'' This last was
said with genuine pain. ''Ask me something that I can
answer, something that can really help.''

Betsy, floundering some more, said, ''That piece of
needlework Jessica made for you. Can you show it to
me?''

''Of course, if you like.'' Martha went away and came
back a minute later with a small framed object about ten
by twelve inches.

Betsy took it. The pattern was a pink heart surrounded
by little blue flowers—''forget-me-nots,'' said Martha.
Under the heart, in golden letters, was the word *Forever.*
Inside the heart was *MW & CW.* The *CW* was worked
in gold, the *MW* and ampersand in a green that matched
the tiny stems and leaves of the forget-me-nots.

''She did Carl's initials in gold because I kept insisting he must be dead. When she gave that to me, I cried

and cried, I was so touched. People had been avoiding me, not knowing what to say.'' Martha sniffed. ''They all thought he'd run off with Trudie, and I suppose they thought I was a little crazy, insisting it wasn't true. But I just couldn't believe he wouldn't write to me, explain where he was or at least try to justify what he'd done. So I was sure he was dead.''

''But he wasn't dead,'' said Betsy.

''I know, and that puzzles me,'' said Martha. ''He was always sure what he was doing was right, that he had a good reason, that he could make me understand. Up to then, I always had.'' She reached for the framed piece.

But Betsy stepped back out of reach, to take another, longer look. Her eye was becoming educated to the nuances of needlework. This piece was competently done, no fancy stitches, but no flubs or missed stitches. The piece wasn't matted; it went all the way to the frame, which was of some dark wood with a very narrow gold stripe on it. ''I suppose she framed it herself,'' said Betsy.

Martha looked at it in Betsy's hands. ''Yes, I think so. We mostly did, back then. It wasn't as if it was real art.''

Betsy smiled. ''You know, Diane Bolles came into my shop not long ago. She thinks needlework is valuable and hopes to sell some of it in Nightingale's, which as you know commands some stiff prices.''

''Wouldn't that be nice? I know some of us have far more pieces tucked away than we have on display. There just isn't enough wall space.''

Betsy smiled. ''Diane said people should rotate their displays, because otherwise it becomes invisible.'' She hid the front of Jessica's work against her chest and asked, smiling, "What color did she do your initials in?"

Martha thought. "Let's see, the heart is pink, Carl's initials are gold . . . so, uh, blue, to match the flowers."

Betsy laughed and turned the frame around. Martha laughed, too. "Diane obviously has a point," she said.

Betsy turned it back to look some more. The *MW & CW* were worked in a simplified gothic style—and, she noticed, were not quite centered. And, now she held it so the weak winter sunlight beaming through Martha's kitchen window fell on it, the area around the *MW* and the ampersand was a slightly different shade of pink than the rest of the heart. Remembering her own difficulties, Betsy could guess what had happened. Jessica had gotten it wrong, torn it out, done it again, possibly gotten it wrong again. Whether after once doing it wrong or twice—or three times—she'd run out of pink. And Betsy knew now from her own bitter experience with embroidery that dye lots can vary, so that even buying the same brand and color number didn't guarantee a perfect match. And if Jessica was like Betsy, she didn't notice the difference until she'd redone the doggone section she'd frogged. And about then she saw the initials weren't centered.

And she said to herself what Betsy would have said: *To heck with this. I have a friend in pain who needs to see this more than I need to get it done perfectly.*

Betsy felt a sudden kinship with Jessica. Betsy's bright red scarf had at least three errors in it. She had gone back and corrected others, but these three hadn't been discovered until Betsy was at least two inches away from them. And she just didn't have the heart or whatever it was that possessed "real" needleworkers, who would undo hundreds of stitches to correct one wrong stitch. And guess what? The scarf was just as warm as if it had been knit without errors.

Besides, if people like Jessica and Betsy decided to undo and redo until they got it right, the scarf and this touching tribute might *still* be unfinished, languishing in drawers somewhere, waiting for the needleworker to get over her frustration and take it up again.

She was suddenly aware that Martha was waiting for her to continue. "I'm sorry, I was standing here wool-gathering—" Betsy chuckled. "—literally, because I was thinking about knitting. Thank you for showing this to me. It's kind of an inspiration." She handed it back.

Martha looked at it doubtfully. "How can that be?"

"It tells me I should keep going toward my goal and not think so much of the process."

Martha smiled. " 'Finished is better than perfect.' You'll hear that a lot from needleworkers, though most of them take it as advice, not a rule."

"If needleworkers ruled the world, there'd be less done, but what got done would be done exceedingly well. I'll stay in touch and let you know if I find anything important or have more questions."

Monday morning there were enough customers, some with complicated questions, that noon had come and gone before Betsy and Godwin knew it. Perhaps it was because the day was sunny, a continuation of Sunday afternoon. The temperature now, at one o'clock, was forty-seven; the streets and sidewalks were wet from melting snow. "What is this, global warming?" asked Betsy.

Godwin said, "Could be. But the forecast is for much colder tomorrow." He said this with a curious sort of satisfaction. *I think he's proud of the harsh winters they have up here,* thought Betsy. *He'll actually be disap-*

*pointed if we don't have at least one blizzard before
Christmas.*

"How about I go get us some lunch?" said Betsy.

"Sandwich and salad for me," said Godwin.
"Thanks."

She went next door to the sandwich shop and bought
two chicken salad sandwiches. Instead of potato chips,
she got a double order of a "finger salad," made of baby
carrots, celery sticks, cherry tomatoes, and rings of sweet
bell peppers—no dressing, even on the side. After eating
her sandwich and enough of the crunchy stuff to feel
satisfied, she washed her hands and began working the
counted cross-stitch pattern again.

"Godwin, do you do the backstitching as you come
to it, or wait and do it all afterward?" she asked, holding
out the pattern of a raccoon, now nearly complete.

"Oh, I *hate* backstitching," he said. "So I always put
it off until the end." He reached for a carrot. "These
really *are* good for your eyes, did you know that? I used
to have *such* bad night vision, I was actually terrified to
drive after *dark.* Then I needed to lose five pounds and
started eating these things instead of candy, and one evening I was out on the road and I asked John, 'Why does
everyone have their lights on so early?' Because it didn't
seem dark at *all* to me."

He cocked his head and looked at her. "That's what
it's like for you, isn't it?"

"Oh, I suppose my night vision is about as good as
the average person's."

"No, I meant about detecting. While the rest of us
wander in darkness, it's all clear as noontime to you.
You've been going out talking to people, collecting
clues, and now you got more of them from questioning
Martha and Alice this weekend. I bet you've formulated

a theory about what really happened, haven't you?''

Betsy stared at him, then began to laugh.

Godwin sat at the library table, a blank white piece of evenweave and a heap of perle cotton floss in front of him. The Monday Bunch hadn't arrived yet, and there were no other customers in the shop. The radio was playing light jazz and big band music.

He preferred needlepoint to counted cross-stitch, but he had fallen in love with a pattern and decided to try it. He was sorting the floss, smoothing the strands through his fingers, inhaling the faint scent of the fibers, enjoying the texture. His eyes were distant. The pattern, an angel in a forest watching over a fawn, called for silks on dark green cloth, the center worked in shades of dappled sunlight. But he was going to work it on white in darker colors. Except for the angel, which he would work in cream, gold, yellow, and palest green. The forest all around would be a threat of dark green, deep blue, brown, and black. Even the edges of the fawn would be darkened. A quarter stitch of white in its eye would make it look afraid, perhaps. The subtle shimmer of perle cotton would tease the eye into finding shapes of wolves or cougars. If this worked—if!—he would enter it in the State Fair next year.

He sat dreaming of blended colors while his fingers stroked and smoothed and separated.

''Godwin?''

He came back to himself abruptly, aware this wasn't the first time his name had been called. ''Yes?'' He looked around. It was Patricia Fairland.

''Oh, is it time for the Monday Bunch meeting already?'' he asked.

''No, not yet. I came early because I wanted to talk to Betsy. Is she here?''

"No. You can ask me."

She smiled. "Are you her Watson?"

"I wish. She's playing this one very close to her chest. I know she's finding things out, she comes in excited or sad. But she won't share."

"Well, I didn't want to talk to her about this skeleton business anyway. I'm going antique hunting this weekend and I wanted to know if she could come along. She likes antiques, doesn't she?"

"I have no idea."

"I'll ask her when she comes in. Do you know where she is? The meeting starts in about fifteen minutes."

"At the nursing home out on Seven. She's starting to look for someone who would love to have a little Christmas tree."

"Oh, is she keeping up Margot's custom? How sweet! I'll ask her when she comes in. Do you know where she is? The meeting starts in about fifteen minutes."

"At the nursing home out on Seven. She's starting to look for someone who would love to have a little Christmas tree."

"Oh, is she keeping up Margot's custom? How sweet! I'll donate an ornament." Pat turned toward the tree on the checkout desk. It already had half a dozen ornaments on it. "Which one of those is hers?"

"She hasn't finished one yet. She's doing a counted cross-stitch one. Jessica was here on Saturday and says she'll do a crocheted angel for the top, and I'm going to do a kitty in a stocking on plastic canvas."

"I'll bring mine in next Monday," said Patricia, and she went to see if any new needlepoint canvases had been put up on the doors.

The nursing home was clean, and there were cheerful paintings on the walls, but it was still depressing. Patients slumped in wheelchairs or slept in easy chairs or looked with sad, haunted eyes at Betsy as she went to the window separating the receptionist from the front lounge. Betsy explained her errand and was shown to the director's office around the corner.

The director was a pleasant woman, and her office

had a real wood desk but was otherwise very modest.

"I'm Betsy Devonshire," said Betsy. "My sister Margot owned a needlework shop called Crewel World, which I have inherited. She used to offer a small Christmas tree with handmade ornaments on it as a gift to someone who didn't have anyone to remember him or her. I'd like to continue that custom."

"Unfortunately, we have a number of patients who rarely or never have visitors," said the director. "Most of them have Alzheimer's, but that doesn't mean they wouldn't like to get a present or have a visitor." She consulted a list. "But you know, we also have a patient whose mind works a little strangely, but who is quite aware and alert. She is all alone in the world. She might make an excellent candidate for your gift. Perhaps you'd like to meet her and see for yourself?"

"All right," said Betsy a little doubtfully. What could she say to someone whose mind worked a little strangely? She had no experience with this sort of person. She reminded herself not to say anything about the tree, which wouldn't be given away for weeks, and besides, she had only begun her search for a person to give it to.

She followed the director obediently and was taken to a double room. The other bed was stripped to its mattress which meant, the director said, that Dorothy didn't have a roommate at present. Betsy remembered reading somewhere that the death rate in nursing homes would give a hardened combat sergeant fits. The room was clean, with an attractive bow window, its deep shelf containing a big geranium and a plaster statue of Elvis.

"Dorothy made that in our crafts room," said the director, and left Betsy alone.

Dorothy was in bed, her blankets pulled up to her chin. She was very old and frail, exceedingly thin. She peered at Betsy fearfully. "Who are you?" she asked.

"My name is Betsy, and I've come to say hello."

"Hello. Can you take me with you when you leave?"

"Don't you like it here?"

"The food is terrible and the nurses are mean."

"I'm sorry you don't like this place. Did you really make that Elvis statue?"

"They made me make it. I wanted to make the clown, but Robert got to do that. He always gets what he wants because he's a man, and men are little tin gods. Are you the police? I think thieves work here. I can't find my glasses."

"No, I own a needlework shop. I sell knitting needles, embroidery floss, and crochet hooks."

"I used to knit."

"I'm still learning how. I made this scarf, and I'm making my first mitten."

"I made love, I made supper, I made good time with my Oldsmobile Ninety-Eight," she said.

Betsy, beginning to feel she was Alice through the looking glass, asked gamely, "Where were you born?"

"I was born at home a hundred and two years ago."

"Where's home?"

"There used to be a place in Excelsior, Minnesota, for me, a long ways from here."

"It's not so far. I live in Excelsior."

"All the people who live in Excelsior are wicked."

"Not all of them, surely," said Betsy.

"Yes, all of them. I had a son named Henry, and he got a girl drunk and scared her. I told him he was a bad boy and would come to a bad end." Her eyes filled with tears. "I didn't mean anything by it, but they played eight to the bar, Company B, and he died, a Dutchman shot him in the head in the water. Never set foot in Omaha, he was shot and drowned both together. And

Alice was married to our pastor, the naughty girl. But I never told.''

"It was good of you not to tell,'' said Betsy, trying hard to stay with the sharp curves of this discourse. ''So that makes one good person, doesn't it?''

Dorothy chuckled, the tears gone as if they had never existed. ''I guess so. But everyone else was bad. Vernon Miller hit Gertrude, broke her nose when she was only fifteen. The sheriff wouldn't arrest him, he was a bad sheriff. Vernon wanted to marry the girl, but she was too fast for him. She kissed all the bad men, and Carl, too. He was the worst. He pretended to be good, but he was in love with all the girls.''

"Didn't you like Carl Winters?''

Dorothy nodded sagely and looked at Betsy slantwise with clever, pleased eyes. ''He cheated on his mistress. He was the worst.''

"You mean he cheated on his wife.''

"He cheated on everyone who was a woman. He said he loved them, but he talked like a chicken, cluck, cluck, cluck, only he never laid that egg.''

"Trudie—Gertrude—was his mistress?''

Dorothy chuckled. ''Everyone was badly wrong. He met his mistress at the State Fair and got all greasy. They used to grease pigs and a pole at county fairs. He done her wrong with Gertrude, but he was doing Gertrude wrong, too.''

"What about his wife?''

"She didn't talk to common folk like me, proud, proud, the first deadly sin. Carl wasn't proud, but he was a bad man. They were all bad.''

"I don't understand. Who was Carl's mistress?''

Dorothy nodded several times. ''Her husband flew in airplanes way up high in the air, but they got him anyhow. She fried hot dogs and served hot food and soda pop. She thought Carl would marry her, but they had a big fight and then he ran away.''

"Who thought? Trudie?"

"Trudie thought Vern would marry her, but he joined the army, and she was mad."

"No, Vern didn't join the army until after Trudie disappeared."

"She ran away with Carl."

"No, she didn't," said Betsy. "They found her bones on a boat, the *Hopkins*."

"Ah," said Dorothy, and closed her eyes. But after awhile, she opened them again and looked sideways at Betsy. "Who are you?" she asked.

Betsy sighed. Then she remembered a simple test for brain function. "Do you know what year this is, Dorothy?"

Dorothy frowned. "It's later than nineteen ninety-seven, isn't it?"

"Yes, it is. And who is President of the United States?"

The eyes were suddenly clever and amused. "I always guess Dwight David Eisenhower, because he was my favorite."

14

It was Tuesday, late-closing night. Betsy was dead tired. There hadn't been many customers that evening, but practically every one of them had been disappointed because either the shop didn't have exactly what they were looking for or Betsy couldn't answer their how-to questions. The honeymoon, she realized, was over. She shouldn't have sent Godwin home at five; his encyclopedic knowledge and indomitable good humor would have made the evening at least endurable.

Not for the first time, Betsy wondered what on earth she thought she was doing, trying to keep the shop going. She should be working for some other company, for someone who knew his or her business, someone who would give Betsy only tasks she could actually do and not make her responsible for the welfare of the entire company. Someone who would be positively aggravated if Betsy attempted to shoulder more responsibility than she'd been hired to carry.

She could sell the shop if she wanted to, she didn't

have to wait until her sister's estate was settled. Margot
had had the wisdom to incorporate, to name Betsy as an
officer of the corporation, so that when Margot died, the
shop went directly into Betsy's hands, to do with as she
pleased. Why was she torturing herself like this?

She looked around the shop. It was quiet right now,
the darkness outside a splendid contrast to the twinkling
Christmas lights in the windows. The shop was warm
with color. The track lights picked out baskets heaped
with wine, amber, royal blue, and pine green wools,
made deeper the patterns of the sweaters. It was all so
attractive! But like all beautiful temptations, full of traps
for the unwary. One saw the beautiful yarns and the
finished sweaters or pillows or framed projects on the
wall and wanted to have done that, wanted the admiring
comments of friends when showing off a finished project. The problem came when one actually tried doing
the work, because the work was arduous and difficult.

A painted canvas in the "final discount" basket
caught her eye. The design was of a round basket full
of balls of wool. A customer had nearly bought it awhile
ago, then changed her mind, saying there was a spotted
cat asleep in that basket, and she didn't like cats. Betsy
couldn't see any cat, and neither could another customer
consulted on the matter. That's why the canvas was desperately seeking a buyer; whoever had designed it
wasn't much of an artist.

Betsy decided to put a more attractive canvas on top.
She pulled the flawed canvas out and then paused to take
another look at it. Here were black and white not-quite-
round shapes that could almost be a black and white cat,
curled tight, with some overlapping balls of yarn—was
this dark purple or more black?—well, sure, here were
the ears, and here the black tail overlay a white leg.
What you'd do, if you wanted the cat to stand out, would

be to brush the floss that you used to color the body, and maybe do a little backstitching or shading on the yarn balls, and not do that ball in dark purple but in wine or even a cherry red. Then the way the cat had snuggled itself into the basket of yarn would be more apparent. Look at how it was holding onto that green yarn, like a child with a doll.

Why, this was clever and attractive!

She'd marked the canvas down to ten dollars, which was within her own price range. Plus she got an employee discount. Let's see, how many colors would she need?

She was arranging a selection of DMC skeins on the canvas when the door went *bing* and Mayor Jamison walked in.

"Hiya, Betsy!" he said cheerily.

"Hi, Your Honor," she said, laying the DMC 321 (a rich red) next to the 821 blue—too obvious?

"How many times do I got to tell you? Just call me Odell."

"Sorry, Odell." She smiled at him. "What brings you in here? Thinking of taking up needlepoint?"

He chuckled. "Naw, I haven't got the patience for that sort of thing. I came to ask if it's true you're investigating the murder charge they've brought against Martha Winters."

"I'm trying. Jeff Winters's attorney said he needed to hire a private investigator, but he can't afford a licensed one. So he's asked me to look around and see if I can't come up with something to create reasonable doubt."

"Well, I've got kind of a weird story to tell you that may or may not help. It happened back when I was just a kid. I didn't think anything of it at the time, but now they found that skeleton on the *Hopkins*, maybe it means something."

"Odell, if you've got something you think is relevant, you should bring it to Sergeant Malloy."

"Oh, I already did that. He wrote it down and thanked me. But in the interest of fair play, I'm also telling you. What happened was, they towed the *Hopkins*—the *Minnetonka III* she was then—over to the City Docks from the dredging company, where she'd sat pulled up on the shore for years. They put a temporary patch on the hole in her bottom, which was caused by ice from a late freeze, and they were gonna take her out the next morning and sink her. I was eight years old, but I already had a notion that sinking her marked the end of an era. After all, I'd caught my first bass off her stern, y'see. So after dark I snuck out of the house and went down to see if I couldn't pry something off of her, kind of a souvenir. Now in July, dark comes after ten o'clock at night. I'd never been out that late before, except on the Fourth of July watching fireworks, and that was with my folks and about eight hundred other people.

"So here I was, all alone, sneaking from tree to tree through the park, toward the docks. There was a streetlight at the bottom of Water Street, so I could see the boat floating in the water alongside this barge, and there was this big pile of boulders and concrete chunks and old bricks heaped up on the shore. What they was gonna do was pile the rubble on the barge and tow it out with the boat, then pry off that plug on the bottom of the boat, and then pile the rubble into her to make her sink. Bein' wood, y'see, she wasn't gonna go down easy."

"So the *Hopkins* was sitting there empty."

"Oh, there was some rubble in her, maybe to test out how much they'd need, I don't know. Me an' four or five other kids had been to see her during the day, that's how I knew all that, and where she was. They'd let me climb on her, and me and some of my pals was gonna take something from her then, but they was watching too close, so we didn't.

"Well, anyhow, that night I got as far as the rubble when I heard someone on the boat. I'd talked it over with my best pal Eddie, who double-dared me to do it, so I thought maybe it was him. You know, trying to scare me so he could razz me the next day. So I come out and there's this man jumping off the boat onto the barge. I'd already said, 'Hey—' meanin' to say 'Hey, Eddie!'—and this fellow like to fell off the barge when he heard me. He spun around and came rollin' up the dock toward me in an awful hurry, but I was probably halfway home by the time he got to where I'd been standing, and I was in bed under the covers about forty-three seconds after that. I didn't go back, even to watch them tow her out, and so I never did get my souvenir."

"Who was it?" asked Betsy. "The man. Who was it?"

"I dunno. I didn't get a good look and didn't particularly want one. What I remember is, he wasn't fat or skinny, and he wasn't wearing a tie but he wasn't in overalls like a workman, either. I think I remember a coat or a jacket, though it was a hot summer night. He seemed big and dangerous coming up toward me, but that's because he about scared the pee out of me."

"Did he say anything?"

"I don't think so. And I didn't hear him running after me, but I was too scared to look over my shoulder to make sure."

"And you never told anyone?"

"Told them what? That I snuck out of my house and went down to the docks to steal something off a boat and got run off before I could accomplish my mission?"

"Oh, well, when you put it that way . . ." Betsy said and the two smiled at one another.

"Sure," Jamison said. "I kept waiting for the fellow to ring our doorbell and tell my folks what I'd been up to, but after a week went by and nothing happened, I figured I was safe. It all kind of faded into the background until they raised the boat and found that skeleton. Then I got to thinking, and finally decided I'd better tell someone. So, what do you think?"

"I think you saw the person who murdered Trudie hiding her body on the boat."

Jamison, suddenly serious, wiped his mouth with the edge of his hand. "Me, too. And it wasn't Martha Winters, was it?"

The store was closed at last. Betsy made sure the doors were locked and hastened up the dark and lonely street to make a bank deposit. The bank was barely two blocks away if she went by way of the post office.

Then she went upstairs to her apartment, took off her good clothes, and put on a thick flannel robe she'd bought at a consignment store in San Diego during her divorce proceedings. It was practically an antique and had been designed for a big man and so came nearly to the floor and overlapped comfortably in front. It had broad vertical stripes of gray and maroon and looked like something Oliver Hardy might have worn—and for all she knew, he had. Movie stars' castoffs were known to turn up in California consignment stores. She loved the robe; it was her "blankie," and generally made her feel comforted.

But it didn't tonight. Betsy heated a can of soup for supper and unbent so far as to feed half a cracker to Sophie, who actually ate it. Then, feeling a headache coming on, Betsy took her contacts out, swallowed a couple of aspirin, and lay down on her bed. She curled onto her side and tried to make her mind go blank. In a few minutes Sophie, purring loudly, came up on the bed and fell heavily beside her, tapping her hand in a request for a stroke.

Betsy complied, because stroking a cat is a soothing operation for the stroker as well; but tonight her mind remained a jumble of thoughts. Sophie was snuggled close beside her at about hip level. A fight over whether or not the cat was allowed on the bed hadn't lasted long; the night after coming home from the vet's, Sophie had cried piteously outside Betsy's bedroom only five minutes before Betsy got up and opened the door.

Sophie had slept with Margot. Obviously, the cat missed Margot. And so did Betsy. Why shouldn't they take comfort in one another's company during the long, dark hours of the night?

Now she stroked the cat's head and was rewarded with a deep, sighing purr.

She wondered what Sergeant Malloy was going to do about Mayor Jamison's story. Surely he would agree now that Martha wasn't the murderer. It was probably Carl Winters who Jamison had seen. Carl had murdered Trudie, hidden her body on the boat, and—being seen— fled town. Carl had no way of knowing the little boy would run home and not tell anyone. Doubtless as he shook the dust of Excelsior from his feet he was sure the sheriff or constable or policeman, at the excited direction of a small boy, was already making a grisly discovery in the bottom of the old *Hopkins*.

And that's why Martha never heard from him. He was afraid someone would see the letter or postcard and know where he'd run to. Or that Martha would turn him in herself.

So okay, that was solved: Carl murdered Trudie and hid her on the boat.

Well, then, who murdered Carl? If Carl was the murderer, surely no one would want to stop him from telling his story.

A glimmer of an idea began to lift its sleepy head from the back of Betsy's mind. She tried to discern something, anything about it, but felt herself growing less connected, drifting away . . . the cat purring . . . the new needlework project . . . who would want to murder Trudie?

Then she dreamed she was walking up Water Street toward Nightingale's, and ahead of her was her mother, dressed as if for church. Betsy ran and ran, calling, until she had nearly caught up. Then her mother turned, and it was her father who turned and smiled down at her from under her mother's best Sunday hat, the one with a veil.

Wednesday displayed a morning sky the color of old pewter, though the forecast did not call for rain or snow or sleet. It was supposed to be Betsy's day off, but Godwin had a doctor's appointment and they agreed he could take the rest of the day and Betsy would have Thursday off.

Betsy was ringing up a sale of a single skein of embroidery floss—and that was not by far the smallest sale she had ever made.

"Thank you, Mrs. Frazee," she said, handing over the blue Crewel World bag.

As Mrs. Frazee left the shop, she left the door open for Jill, in civvies. Jill wore a magnificent Norwegian blue patterned sweater with pewter fasteners over a white turtleneck sweater. Her mittens were white angora wool, and her cap matched them. She looked wonderful, and Betsy said so.

"Thanks," said Jill, blushing faintly. "I came to ask you to lunch—except, if it's all right, I'd like to buy something from next door and we can eat it while we chat.''

Betsy thought she read anxiety in Jill's face. ''Of course,'' she said. ''Could I have soup and a salad instead of a sandwich?''

''Oh, for that you want Antiquity Rose, not next door,'' said Jill. ''Their house salad is marvelous, and their soup comes with a homemade bread stick. My treat; I'll be right back.''

''Wait a second,'' Betsy said. ''How do you stand it out there with just that sweater?''

''This sweater is a lot warmer than it looks,'' said Jill. ''Anyhow, it's not really cold out yet. It's not even freezing today.'' She smiled a superior smile. ''Wait till January, then you'll see *weather!*''

Jill came back with a double paper sack and a friend. ''You remember Melinda Coss, don't you?'' she asked.

Betsy wasn't sure, but she smiled and said, ''Hello, Melinda.''

''Wait till you see the ornament she made for the tree!''

Melinda had a white cardboard cube in her hands, which she put on the checkout desk. She lifted out a small round ornament with a basket hanging from it.

''Oh,'' said Betsy, ''it's a hot-air balloon, how clever!''

The balloon was made of many tiny pentagons, each covered with silk gauze cross-stitched with holly, ivy, pine, a Christmas wreath, mistletoe, a bow, or a sequin snowflake held in place with a tiny bead. In the basket underneath was a mouse wearing a crown and carrying a tiny pair of binoculars.

''Do you get it?'' asked Jill, and sang, ''Good King Wencesmouse looked out . . .''

Betsy laughed so hard she nearly dropped the ornament, which alarmed her into stopping. "Where did you find the pattern?" she asked, thinking how well it would sell in the shop, especially with one already finished on display.

"I made it up. I found a papercraft book that told me how to make the ball of pentagon shapes—"

"Geodesic dome!" exclaimed Jill. "I *knew* there was a name for that shape!"

Betsy said, "You should publish the pattern, Melinda. I mean, can't you just see this on the cover of a needle-work magazine?"

Melinda smiled. "I've already submitted it."

"I'm afraid this won't go along when I give the tree away—if that's okay with you," said Betsy. "I want to keep this on permanent display."

"Of course, if you like," said Melinda, beaming with pleasure.

A few minutes later, Jill and Betsy were seated at the library table. The salad was great, with candied pecans and bits of orange; the soup a hearty ham and potato with an interesting blend of herbs.

"These bread sticks are wonderful," said Betsy. They were thick and chewy, with a thin crust of cheese on top.

Jill agreed, then asked, "Did Odell Jamison come to you with his story about seeing a man climbing around the *Hopkins* the night before it was sunk?"

"He sure did. What does Malloy say about it?"

"He thinks Odell saw Carl. He figures Carl came to meet Trudie and saw Martha getting off the boat and Trudie not there. He got suspicious and went for a look and found Trudie's body. Then he saw the boy—Odell—watching him and got scared and ran away. That would explain Martha's handkerchief on the boat and Carl's disappearance. Carl had no idea the boy wouldn't raise

the alarm, and every reason to think they'd blame him
for the murder. Then, all these years later, they find Trudie's skeleton. Carl hears about it. He's old and tired,
and back home there is a business that is rightfully his,
that he can sell or lease to take care of him in retirement.
So he comes home, phones his wife to tell her he's back,
and she, in a panic, agrees to meet him and instead she
shoots him.''

Betsy had been nodding through all this, finding it
very believable—until the end. ''Wait a second,'' she
said. ''If I thought someone was a murderer, I don't care
how many years later it got to be, I wouldn't call that
person and say come over and let's talk about it. And I
certainly wouldn't agree to meet that person all alone in
a motel room.''

''Not even if it was your wife?''

''Not even if it was Mother Teresa.''

''Hmmmm,'' said Jill.

''What does Martha say?''

''On advice of counsel, she's not talking to the police.''

''Smart lady. What else does Malloy have?''

''He says the gun used to murder Carl was a World
War II era semiautomatic pistol. Standard army officer
issue. It was in excellent condition, with original ammo
in it. Something found in an attic, maybe, tucked away
with an old uniform. Not registered.''

''Interesting,'' said Betsy. ''Was Carl in the army?''

''No. He was 4F, Malloy said.''

''Has he looked at Vern Miller?''

''Vern went down for his physical two weeks before
he got on the bus to boot camp. At that time, their quarrel was over and she was fooling around with a new
boyfriend—not Carl, someone else. Trudie was
murdered the night of July first, the boat was sunk July

second, he left town July third. He couldn't have known two weeks prior to that the sequence of those events."

"He knew the date he was leaving for boot camp. Maybe he went down to talk to Trudie, say good-bye, they quarreled, and he killed her."

"Malloy doesn't think it happened that way. How would Carl fit into that scenario?"

"He was the one Trudie was to meet in the park. He gets there in time to see Vern murder Trudie and hide her body. He runs because he knows the whole town knows he's been flirting with Trudie."

"Hmmmm." Jill nodded.

"What else does Malloy have?" asked Betsy.

"He found a picture of Trudie in an old yearbook and says the reconstructed face matches close enough."

"Well, that's not exactly news."

"No, I guess not. He says Carl was shot once in the chest from across the room. Nicked his heart, blew one lung all to pieces. He was sitting on the bed and fell back and died of internal hemorrhaging."

"Ugh," murmured Betsy, swallowing.

"And whoever murdered him waited until it was over, then walked to his side and wrapped his fingers around the gun, then let it fall on the floor beside his hand."

Betsy said, "Wait a second. Would bullets that old still fire?"

Jill said, "Malloy says some of the best ammo ever made was made during World War II. He says lots of gun enthusiasts look for it. He says there are markings on the casings that indicate it was made in Lake City in 1941. He says the gun had three bullets fired from the clip, but there was only one empty shell in the room and only one bullet in Carl."

Betsy said, "Ah."

"What, 'ah'?"

"Well, *I* didn't know ammunition could last that long, so probably whoever got the gun out didn't either. So he digs through his souvenirs of the war and finds the gun, and takes it someplace to test fire it. Who do we know who was an officer in World War II? Or a gun collector?"

"A gun collector would unload it, wouldn't he?"

"Okay, who came home from the war and put everything into a trunk in the attic?"

"Hundreds of people, probably."

"Help me out here, Jill. Who involved in this mess is a World War II veteran?"

"Vern Miller—no, he's Korea. And Vietnam. Plus he wasn't an officer."

Betsy thought that over. "Anyone else?"

"Jessica's husband was killed during World War II in a plane that got shot down over Germany." When Betsy looked exasperated, Jill shrugged. "Sorry! Those are all I know about. I suppose you can check somewhere, veterans' services or someplace; I know Malloy is doing that. Oh, I know Alice's husband didn't serve because he was a minister. Malloy's probably thinking along the same lines you are. But he also says you can go to gun shows and buy just about anything."

"Yes, but you can trace those guns, and he told you this was not traceable, right?"

"Yes."

A little silence fell, then Jill said, "Have you got anything new?"

"I was looking for someone to give the tree to, and I talked to this woman in Westwood South Nursing Home. Her name is Dorothy, and—"

"Dorothy Brown? She was my grandmother's best friend!" said Jill. "Is she still alive? How is she?"

"She's bedridden, and her mind is not as clear as it used to be."

Jill chuckled. "I don't remember her mind ever being as clear as it used to be. Of course, she was an old woman when I was a little girl." She sobered. "I should go see her someday. It's awful that I thought she was dead."

"She might not know you," said Betsy. "You know how old people get confused about modern events but remember old ones clearly? Well, Dorothy is losing old stuff, too. She said that her son never went to Omaha and was both shot and drowned by a Dutchman."

"She always says that, and she's absolutely right. Her son died in the ocean while trying to land on Omaha Beach in Normandy, shot *and* drowned, just the way she tells it."

" 'Dutchman'!" exclaimed Betsy. "That's an old word for a German. She said she is a hundred and two. Could that be right, too?"

"She was a hundred two years ago. I went to her birthday party. She knew who she was and what was going on then. They asked me as part of the entertainment to give her that little test, you know, when someone has a head injury? Do you know where you are? What year is this? Who is the President of the United States?"

Betsy said, "She told me she always guesses Dwight Eisenhower because he was her favorite."

Jill laughed. "Yes, that's what she said at the party, too. It's her favorite joke. She's not as ga-ga as people think. I really should go over there and see her."

It was Saturday. Melinda's Christmas tree ornament was as big a success as Betsy hoped it would be. She was taking the names of women who wanted to own the pattern when it was published. She would have to make sure she had enough forty-eight-count silk gauze in stock. Her own name was not on the list, of course; she was still struggling with the "easy" ornaments in the stitchery kit. Counted cross-stitch on forty-eight-count silk was not remotely within her skills at this point.

Betsy worked for awhile on the duck. Even now that she could see the picture forming on the cloth, she would still occasionally make a mistake and have to undo some stitches. And she couldn't always just unsew them, the floss would catch on something and she'd have to get out the scissors.

Finally, she just put it away and got out her knitting. She was doing another scarf, this one changing colors from blue to a blue and white mix to white and back to blue every twelve inches. She was on the seventh foot— blue—and not sure if she was going to stop there or not. If she didn't, she was going to have to do a blue/white mix, a white, and blue again so the ends would match, and a ten-foot scarf was an awful lot of scarf. Not for her to knit, for the wearer to manage. She loved knitting this; it was her favorite pattern of knit two, purl two fifty-two times with an odd stitch at either end. It made a thick, attractive pattern and she was doing it in pure wool. There were hardly any errors in it. Godwin had admired it; she hoped he had no idea it was to be his Christmas present.

Godwin was in New York with his lover, taking in a Broadway show and ice skating at Rockefeller Center. Shelly was here, consulting with a customer over some ribbon embroidery.

Betsy felt the familiar calming effect of the knitting start to take over. The customer bought her ribbon and left. Shelly came to kneel on the floor in front of Sophie and stroke her.

"When does her cast come off?"

"Monday. She's going to miss it, I think. I knew someone in California who had a dog that broke its leg, and forever after, whenever you'd scold that dog, he would start to limp."

Shelly laughed. It was very quiet in the shop; Betsy had forgotten to turn on the radio. But the silence felt good, so she didn't say anything. And Shelly didn't either, which was pleasant.

Betsy began to think about the case. "What if Odell didn't see Carl?" she asked.

She didn't realize she'd said it out loud until Shelly said, "Have you found out something new?"

"I don't know. There's just so many little things, it's hard to think of a scenario that covers all of them. You think up something that might have happened, and it seems right, but then you realize there's one little piece sticking out. Like, if Martha murdered Trudie and Carl knew it, why did he call her when he got back to town? Wasn't he afraid she'd murder him, too?"

"If he was, he wouldn't have called her, so he wasn't," said Shelly.

"But then why did he run away and not write to her or phone her? She thought he was dead."

"Maybe he did get in touch, and she was ashamed to tell anyone. Maybe he ran for some other reason than Trudie's murder. Maybe Martha was a terrible wife, jealous and mean to him, and he'd finally had enough."

"But he came back because they found the skeleton, you know. He had a newspaper clipping about the discovery of the skeleton with him."

"Oh. But what was it you were saying about Odell not seeing Carl?"

"Odell came by and told me he saw a man climbing out of the *Hopkins* the night before it was taken out and sunk. He was just a little boy, and when the man saw him, he got scared and ran home.''

Shelly stood, all excited. ''A man? Odell saw a man? Well, then, that's it, right? Carl murdered Trudie. Odell saw him after he hid the body. Wow! That's it!'' She saw the way Betsy was looking at her and said, ''Isn't it?''

''But then where did the handkerchief come from? Did Carl mean to frame his wife? Why?''

''Because . . . because he wanted to get rid of her. And in a divorce she would have gotten half his property.''

''Not in 1948. And why hide the body? If you mean to frame someone, you don't put the body where it is likely never to be found.''

''All right, that's right. What is it you're thinking of?''

''I'm not sure. This very old woman named Dorothy told me something important, but there's this other piece that's mixed in with the things I've already seen or heard. It keeps nagging me.''

''What is it?'' asked Shelly.

''That's the problem. I can't remember.''

15

Saturday evening the shop closed at five; Christmas hours didn't start until after Thanksgiving. Betsy changed to a pair of dark corduroy slacks and her old cotton sweater, had a quick supper, fed the cat, and left for Jessica Turnquist's house. She had called Jessica, who agreed to talk to her.

Jessica lived in the shortest row of townhouses Betsy had ever seen: three of them. They were white stucco with dark wood trim, located right down on the lakeshore off West Lake Street. A row of three garages lined one side of the driveway and there was a parking area beyond them. Jessica's townhouse was the middle one; she had left her porch light on.

A sharp breeze lifted Betsy's collar and rustled the brown leaves on an old oak tree that hadn't gotten the word that autumn was over. The air smelled of woodsmoke.

The fire was in Jessica's living room, in a small white-brick fireplace beside a pretty atrium door that was mere yards from the restless lake. The living room was not big but was interesting architecturally, with a canted ceiling and a loft, and the furniture was light and sophisticated.

"I have a friend who's a decorator," said Jessica when Betsy remarked on the decor. "Left to myself, I'd do everything in overstuffed blue brocade. Would you like a cup of coffee? Or some tea?"

"No, thank you, I just had supper."

"Is it too hot in here for you? Whenever I build a fire, it warms me up so much I sometimes have to open a window."

"No, I'm fine. The fire is nice."

"Sit down then," said Jessica, and when Betsy chose the couch, she took a beige leather chair. She touched her upper lip with a Kleenex and turned her slightly bulging eyes on Betsy. "What did you want to talk to me about?"

"About several things. What made you decide to make friends with Martha after Carl disappeared?"

"We already knew each other from church. Then Carl answered an ad I put in the paper and worked for me during State Fair for three or four years. I remember how a lot of people sort of drew the hems of their skirts away from her after—well, after Carl went away. She told several people she was sure he was dead, that a robber perhaps had thrown his body into a passing train. It seemed a strange thing to be sure of without any evidence, but it was then I realized she had loved him and missed him terribly, and she couldn't believe he'd just abandoned her. She was sure that even if he'd left her willingly, he'd at least write to her at some point. She was so sad and distressed, and no one would reach out to her, and well, it just made me angry. So I did that little needlework heart for her, whipped it up in kind of a hurry, and gathered my courage and went and rang her doorbell. Oh, she cried and cried when she opened the package! She was so grateful, and she needed someone to talk to so badly, and so I just kept going back. And over the next few weeks we found we had lots in common. She came over to my place for Saturday night supper—I had an apartment back then—and had me over for Sunday dinner. Soon it wasn't just pity anymore, we actually became good friends. And we've been friends ever since."

Betsy said, "It was good of you to reach out like that."

Jessica looked at the fire. "Thank you," she murmured. "But she was as good for me as I was for her."

"It must have been difficult for you, being a widow back then. But at least your husband died a hero. Did he win any medals?" Betsy, looking around, said, "I don't see his picture anywhere. Surely you were proud of him."

Her head lifted. "Of course I was proud of him! He was an officer, so handsome and so brave! We were very much in love, but we'd been married only a few months before he left for duty overseas. And then, when he didn't come home, and I went on to other things, he became just that small part of my life, less than a year, and less and less significant to what I was doing. Finally, I put all his things into storage. I should do something with them; I don't have anyone to leave them to, so I don't know why I've kept them."

"I understand the custom is, one of his friends packs his belongings up and sends them home. Was there a diary or anything like that?"

"No, just his uniforms and military records. And three medals, I remember them. But not that flag folded into a triangle, because that comes off the coffin, and Ed never had a coffin. But there was a long and kind letter full of little stories about Ed and his crew. I kept that, too.''

"Really? Any museum or historical society would be very pleased to have something like that. Historians love letters and diaries at least as much as uniforms and medals.''

"They do? Well, yes, I suppose they would. I never thought about giving Ed's things to the historical society. What a good idea. Perhaps the other families would be interested in the letter. The men were such good friends, as soldiers get to be in combat, and the stories are all about them as well. And they were all lost when the plane went down, burned to nothing. No trace was ever found, no bodies sent home to bury.''

"That's why you felt sympathy for Martha, isn't it? I mean, her not having a body to bury, either.''

Jessica showed that genuine smile that made her pretty. "You do understand, don't you? I remember dreaming that he came home and told me he'd missed the plane, he hadn't gone on that last mission. That was my favorite dream for a long time.''

"Was there a gun in the box?''

"A gun?'' Jessica looked alarmed, as if the conversation had turned an unexpected corner into unfriendly territory.

Betsy smiled her warmest. "Yes, in the box your husband's friend sent. It would have been a sidearm, a government-issue semiautomatic pistol.''

Jessica's mouth pressed into a thin, disapproving line. "Oh, no. There was a what-do-you-call-it, a holster, but they don't allow guns to go by mail, it's illegal.''

"Oh, yes, of course, I should have thought of that.''

"Oh, there's something I have for you, so before I forget—'' She got up and went to a glass-fronted cupboard whose bottom half was drawers. She opened a drawer and brought out a thin, clear-plastic bag. Inside it was a white crocheted angel made rigid with starch. "This is my donation for the tree."

"Thank you." Betsy held the bag up and twirled it very gently. "You know, my mother used to make these. I don't know what happened to the ones she gave me."

"Perhaps I can make one just for you."

"Perhaps you can show me how to make them—like showing someone how to fish versus giving him one?"

Jessica chuckled, a rich, pleasant sound. "Yes, of course, that would be better, wouldn't it? I've got a pattern somewhere. I'll bring it to the next Monday Bunch meeting."

Betsy thanked her again and left. *Oh, Jessica, you brave liar,* she thought as she got into her car. But how can I prove it? And then she remembered something Jill had told her. If it was true, then there was actual physical evidence, something more than mere words, which could be twisted to mean anything.

A few minutes later, she drove down the narrow lane that led to Martha's house. The road looked white in her headlights, which made her think it was coated with ice, but her tires clung obediently when she braked, and she realized it was dried salt. *Didn't the Romans used to sow an enemy's fields with salt to keep him from growing food?* she thought. *How can any vegetation survive alongside the streets and highways after a whole winter of this?*

But the blue spruce looked very healthy in her headlights, despite its proximity to the street. Betsy pulled into the driveway.

She rang the bell and Martha answered promptly, though she was surprised to find Betsy on her doorstep. "I thought it would be Jess," she said.

"Oh, if your friend is coming over, I'll leave and come back some other time," said Betsy.

"No, don't do that; she called to say you were coming to visit her, and I assumed she'd call or come over so we could talk about it." Martha smiled. "We do talk about you, you know. Come in, come in, we're letting all the heat out standing here with the door open."

Betsy came in and shed her coat and boots on the little tiled area. "Do you two always tell each other what's going on?"

"Pretty much," nodded Martha. "Anytime I get something new to talk about, I call her, and she lets me know what's going on with her. Did she tell you what you wanted to know tonight?"

"I think so," said Betsy.

"You sound hopeful. Are you actually making progress at last?" Martha's face was itself desperately hopeful.

"I think so," Betsy repeated. "It's been really hard, trying to figure something out just from what people say, or don't say. That's why I'm here. I think you can show me something that will speak for itself."

"I'll show you anything I have. What is it?"

"Would you be willing to take Jessica's heart out of its frame and frog some of it while I watch?"

". . . Frog?"

"Pull out some of the stitches."

"Why do you want me to do that?"

When Betsy explained, Martha, her face inexpressibly sad, went and got the needlework Jessica had given her.

Godwin came in Monday morning a few minutes late. He was positively agog with curiosity. "Tell me, tell me, tell me!" he demanded, slamming the door of the shop.

"Tell you what?" said Betsy, lifting both eyebrows and widening her eyes at him.

"That won't do, you clever wench; I heard all about it at the Waterfront Café. You went to see Sergeant Malloy Saturday night and a little later he arrested Jessica Turnquist for murder. Is that not the proper sequence of events?"

"Approximately."

"Wait a minute." He hung up his beautiful camel wool coat and went to sit at the library table. "Now," he said, "begin at the beginning, and don't stop until you reach the end."

"Don't you even want a cup of coffee?" asked someone else, and he looked toward the back of the shop, where Jill and Shelly were emerging with steaming cups.

"If you've already told them, I'm going to *die,*" said Godwin.

"No, we just got here," said Shelly.

"Why aren't you in school?" asked Godwin.

"Field trip sponsored by the parents, who are also supervising the children," said Shelly. "I'm off only until noon," she added, "so let's get started. You will not believe how pleased I am to be here." She put a cup in front of the chair at the head of the table and gestured at Betsy. "I understand you were positively brilliant," she added. "So sit and tell us everything."

Jill had turned back to the coffee urn and now reappeared with a cup for herself and another for Godwin. "I'd've stopped for cookies," she said, "but I didn't want to miss this, either."

Betsy sat down. "It was just a whole lot of little things that kept not adding up," she began. "If Vern murdered Trudie, where did the handkerchief come from? If Martha murdered Carl, where did she get that old, unregistered pistol? And why did it still have World

War II–era bullets in it? If Carl murdered Trudie and was coming home to confess, why would someone kill him? If someone wanted that handkerchief to frame Martha, why hide it and the body on the boat? If Alice Skoglund murdered Trudie to stop the blackmail, why would she also murder Carl? I just kept going in circles, trying to decide what was and what was not important.

"One thing that didn't seem important was that a very old woman said that Carl met his mistress at the State Fair and got all greasy. Another was that Jessica's husband was an army air corps officer. But that one was very important; it was practically the key to this thing. He was the only person connected with this case who was an officer in the military, and that was important because it's officers who get issued sidearms; enlisted men get rifles. When he was killed overseas, a friend packed up his belongings and shipped them to Jessica with a nice, long letter. Jessica said she got a holster but no gun. Army-issue guns are supposed to be turned in at the end of service, but that was a rule much observed in the breach. Jessica said she'd put everything into storage long ago, and that was important, because it meant it wasn't in her house, where a visitor might come across it and steal it.

"Martha said she lost two handkerchiefs with that wonderful lace trim. One she left at the Guthrie Theatre, where it ended up as a prop. The other she lost at the State Fair. Jessica had a fried-food stand at the State Fair—that's where she and Carl got all greasy. Carl worked for Jessica there, selling battered hot dogs on a stick. Martha thought she lost that handkerchief in the pig barn, but when she came to the fair, surely she would either stop by the stand to see her husband, or if Carl wasn't working they would both stop by the stand to say hello and perhaps buy something to eat and drink. And if Martha dropped that gorgeous handkerchief by the stand, someone might have picked it up and given it to Jessica, or Jessica herself found it. In either case, she kept it.''

"Why?" asked Shelly. "Didn't she know whose it was?"

"Of course she knew," said Betsy. "But she was having an affair with Carl and wasn't very fond of Carl's wife. She knew Martha was proud of those handkerchiefs, so it was a fun and spiteful thing to keep that handkerchief rather than give it back.''

"Now, just wait one second," said Godwin. "Trudie worked in a café, so she got all greasy, didn't she? You took the word of a senile old woman who doesn't know Sleep-Around-Sue from a respectable widow.''

"No, she said Carl met his mistress at the State Fair and both of them got greasy. Jessica told me she and Carl had to constantly mop the floor at her stand to keep the grease under control. Dorothy isn't senile in the ordinary sense of the word; she knows plenty. Everything else she told me was true. Her son was killed on Omaha Beach during the Normandy invasion, that same son got Alice Skoglund drunk at a private gathering and took liberties with her—''

"No!" said Godwin, much edified, and Shelly's eyes gleamed at this delicious tidbit.

"Oh, I shouldn't have said that!" said Betsy, alarmed. "So if that little fact goes beyond this gathering, I will fire both of you." And Jill looked at Shelly and Godwin with a glint in her eye that said firing might be the least of their troubles. Betsy continued, "In fact, we are going to be a whole lot nicer to Alice than we have been. She was very important to solving this case."

"Yes, ma'm," said Godwin meekly, and Shelly nodded, allowing the gleam to fade.

"Dorothy said Jessica's husband flew in airplanes and died in one, also true. Dorothy doesn't muddle her facts; she's just so tired of inquiries into her clarity of mind that she turns the tables on her questioners, making a joke or a riddle of their questions. While she spoke elliptically to me, she knew what she was saying and spoke only the truth.

"But," said Betsy, "I didn't know that until I talked to Jill. And even then, even if everything else she said was true, could it really be that Carl and *Jessica* were having an affair? It would explain a whole lot if it was. But how to prove it? And then I thought about something else Jill told me, and then I remembered that cross-stitch heart Jessica gave Martha, and I crossed my fingers in hopes I was right and went to talk to Martha."

"What did Jill tell you?" asked Shelly.

"That using metallic floss will leave a mark on fabric that only shows up after a long time. It kind of develops, like a photograph, into a gray or black mark. And when we took Martha's initials out of that fabric, there were black marks that spelled *JT*, for Jessica Turnquist. She had made that piece for Carl, not for Martha. The 'love forever' she stitched on that project was between her and Carl, not Carl and Martha. That's when I knew Jessica murdered Trudie."

"Now wait a second," said Godwin. "Odell saw a man running away from the boat. Jessica wouldn't look like a man no matter how you dressed her."

"Why was Jessica mad at Trudie?" asked Shelly.

"I'd've murdered both of them," said Jill.

Shelly and Godwin started at this odd confession from a law enforcement officer, but Jill only stared back. Then the three looked at Betsy to go on.

"Jessica told me she was surprised to learn how much Martha loved Carl. Carl bad-mouthed Martha to every-

one, especially women he was flirting with. But I think
Jessica was more surprised than average, because Carl
told her he and his wife had a sham of a marriage. It's
a favorite line of philanderers, more so back then when
divorces were rarer. Nearly as common as 'My wife
doesn't understand me.' And it's what Carl told Jessica,
along with 'She says if I try to divorce her, she'll hire
a private detective, which means it's possible your name
will be dragged through the courts.' The truth is, he
didn't want a divorce at all, because he was a businessman in a small town where his wife was highly thought
of. If he dumped her for Jessica, they'd have to leave
town and start over. Carl had a wife who, I think, he
actually loved, and he had a healthy, intelligent son, and
a successful business. I don't think he was willing to
give all that up. But he wanted the thrill of a beautiful
mistress, too.

"Jessica may have actually believed the lies Carl told
her, or at least told herself she did. She thought Martha
was a shrew who wouldn't set her unhappy husband
free. But as time went on, Jessica grew impatient; if she
wanted children, if she wanted to show her love openly,
something had to happen. So she began to press Carl,
until at last he lost his temper and they had a fight. And
to show her he was not going to be bullied, he stomped
off and flirted more seriously than he ever had before
with someone he knew wouldn't blow him off."

"Trudie Koch," said Shelly.

"That's right," said Betsy. "Everyone noticed it;
Martha scolded him about it. And Jessica was furious.
She went into a tool drawer and got out a hammer—"

"How did you deduce this?" asked Godwin, amazed.

"That's from her confession," said Jill. "We both
were there when Mike took it down."

"Go on, go on," Shelly urged Betsy.

"She went down to the Blue Ribbon Café close to the end of Trudie's shift and found that Trudie was already gone. The man at the counter said she was meeting someone at the City Docks at midnight. Jessica casually finished her coffee and left, arriving at the docks—which were just across the street—in time to see Trudie waiting alone. Trudie turned as Jessica came up and Jessica swung the hammer. She says she doesn't remember much of the next several minutes, which I understand is normal. Then she went out to the end of the dock and threw the hammer as far out as she could. On her way back, past the body, she dropped the handkerchief. Did I mention she brought the handkerchief with her? She told Sergeant Malloy this murder was an angry impulse, but that can't be true. She came prepared to frame Martha.

"Then Carl arrived for his rendezvous with Trudie. Jessica was waiting, and she told him what she'd done, pointing to the handkerchief and saying Martha was sure to be arrested for the murder and then, at last, Carl could divorce her and they could be married."

"Cold, cold, cold," murmured Godwin.

"She must have been crazy," said Shelly.

"Not within the meaning of the law," said Jill.

"And Carl just about went nuts. It made his previous rage seem like nothing. What on earth did she think she was doing? Martha was his wife; he loved her with all his heart; he wasn't about to see her framed for murder! Then he calmed down just a little bit and got as scared as he'd been furious; he could see that any attempt to tell the truth would involve him in a very unpleasant way. He told Jessica to go home, that he'd take care of everything. So she did. And Carl picked up the handkerchief and Trudie's body and hid them both on board the *Hopkins*. As he was getting off the boat, he saw a boy watching him. How much had the kid seen? If he'd seen Carl carrying the body out there, Carl was in big, big trouble. He ran after the boy, but he vanished into the night.''

"That was Odell, wasn't it?" said Shelly.

"That's right. So Carl fled. He ended up in Omaha and worked mostly at menial jobs, scared for years he'd be located. All this while, he thought the cops were looking for him. Then, at last, he sees a newspaper article, a reprint of a humorous story about a town gossip and a skeleton. All those years in hiding, and no one had been looking for him. And now his wife—same last name, so she never remarried!—is about to be charged with murdering Trudie Koch. So of course he comes home. Maybe he can still redeem himself, pick up the remaining scraps of his former life. He checks into a local motel and he calls his wife to see if things are as reported.

"But she won't talk to him, won't let him tell her what he knows. She hangs up on him. She got over Carl Winters many years ago. But then, as she does whenever she has some news to share, she calls her very best friend, Jessica Turnquist. Martha says she doesn't know what Carl had to tell her, and Jessica says she can't imagine what it might be, either.

"But Jessica does know, of course. After all—the changes she's made in herself, her good reputation, her close friendship with Martha, her comfortable life in this town—are all about to be destroyed because of a few minutes of jealous rage cooled to ashes these fifty years.

"She hurries to that storage place and digs into the box of her late husband's military gear and takes out the gun. She drives out into the country and fires it twice to make sure it works, then she goes and knocks on Carl's door. He is surprised to see her but lets her in.''

Jill said, "I wonder what they talked about? She didn't say."

Betsy said, "Maybe she tried to rekindle his old affection for her. Or did she try to scare him into promising to leave town again? But in the end she shot him. She waits until he stops breathing and then presses his still-warm fingers around the gun, lets it drop from his hand, and leaves. She thinks the police will conclude it's suicide."

Jill said, "But she doesn't know from forensics. Such as, when you shoot yourself, you leave powder residue on the wound and on your hand. Carl's body had no powder burns; he was shot from farther than the length of his arm."

"And *that's* why Jessica stopped begging you to prove Martha didn't murder Trudie," said Godwin. "Oh, my God, what a *witch*!"

Jill said, "The choice was to tell the truth and go to prison or keep silent and let Martha go to prison. Not a hard choice for her."

"What made you decide to look under Martha's initials on that heart?" asked Shelly.

"Martha had shown the needlework to me. She said it was that gift that started their friendship. Carl's and Martha's initials were in the middle of the heart, his in gold. And they weren't quite centered. And the heart was two different shades of pink, meaning it had been redone at least once. At first I thought Jessica was like me, willing to redo only so many times before deciding it was the thought that counts, not the perfection of the gift. And she was in a hurry. But after what Dorothy said, it occurred to me that maybe, originally, the heart had Carl's and Jessica's initials, both in gold. *JT* is a lot narrower than *MW*."

"Why didn't she just throw it away?" asked Godwin.

"I don't know," said Betsy. "Maybe she was afraid
someone would find it. And besides, she was trying to
think of some way to really distance herself from what
had happened, and really make sure no one suspected
she and Carl had ever had an affair. There was Martha,
so unhappy and vulnerable, and she got this idea to make
friends. Turning the needlework into a gift might have
seemed like a good idea."

Shelly said, "Maybe she had this evil notion of seeing
something that was about her and Carl's love on display.
Not in her own house, that would be dumb. So why not
in Martha's house? I can see that tickling some sick
person's fancy—"

"Ugh!" said Godwin. "You are making me not like
Jessica at *all*!"

"Anyway," said Betsy, "she picked out her initials
and cleared an area of heart around it. But she was out
of both the gold and the pink she'd used originally. She
had a pink that seemed to match perfectly and she had
some green, so she used those. The newer pink, unfortunately, faded more quickly than the old, which kind
of called attention to Martha's initials. And when Martha
and I frogged her initials, we found some gray marks
on the evenweave, just like Jill said there would be."

"Good job!" cheered Shelly, as if to a bright student.
"Sorry, force of habit."

"So now I had real evidence of a motive," said Betsy.
"I called Sergeant Malloy from Martha's house, and he
came right over, bless him. I explained what I thought
had happened and how it seemed to be the only version
of events that didn't leave little bits sticking out. I told
him that I'd talked to Jessica earlier and asked her about
a military-issue gun, so that she might be trying to de-
stroy evidence at that very moment. He drove over to

her house, and she opened the door, and he smelled leather burning. By the time he got what was left of an old holster out of the fire, she was crying and telling him some nonsense about how the historical society wouldn't want an empty holster, and then that my questions had frightened her, and she kept changing her story until she finally told the truth.''

"By which time she had been Mirandized twice," said Jill.

"Jessica Turnquist, hot mama and murderer," murmured Godwin, shaking his head. "It seems so unlikely. I mean, she's so *old*."

"Someday you'll be old," said Betsy.

"Never!" promised Godwin, hand on heart.

"She did beautiful crochet work," said Shelly.

Then silence fell, a long silence, in which many memories formed themselves into new shapes.

"I'm glad I was able to help Martha," said Betsy at last. "I'm sorry it had to be Jessica."

"She was always nice to me," said Shelly.

"I guess this confirms everyone's belief that you are a natural-born sleuth," said Jill.

"Yes, well, sleuthing doesn't put money in the cash register. Shelly, why don't you get started dusting. Goddy, bring out that shipment of wool and refill the baskets." Everyone stood, but nobody moved. They were all trying to think of a valedictory statement.

Jill said, "Betsy, Malloy said to thank you for your assistance, and to look for a summons in the mail."

Shelly said, "I guess Martha can fire that expensive lawyer and put what's left of the money toward the mortgage on her store. I'm going to bring some clothing to be dry cleaned, increase her earnings a little bit."

They looked at Godwin, who shrugged and said,

"And since it looks like Dorothy gets the tree, I'd better make a pair of ruby red slippers to put on it."

Turn the page for your free
Lacy Butterfly cross-stitch pattern.

A Lacy Butterfly
Designed by Denise Williams
After a bobbin-lace pattern
by Virginia Berringer

This pattern is worked in a combination of straight or backstitches and cross-stitches to look like bobbin lace. Use two strands of white cotton floss on 16-count, dark blue, evenweave fabric.

First, stitch around the border of the fabric to prevent fraying.

Then, find the center of the pattern and mark it. Find the center of the fabric. (If you are making a bookmark, count up seventeen rows from the bottom of the fabric to find the last row of stitching. Mark this row, count the rows across to find the middle, and begin stitching in that place.)

Cross-stitch the head and body first, then the cross-stitch portions of the wings. Do the straight stitches (backstitching) on the wings and antennas last.

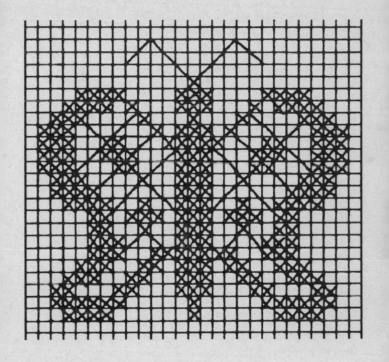

© *Design by Denise Williams*

EARLENE FOWLER

introduces Benni Harper, curator of San Celina's folk
art museum and amateur sleuth

□ **FOOL'S PUZZLE**   0-425-14545-X/$6.50

Ex-cowgirl Benni Harper moved to San Celina, California, to
begin a new career as curator of the town's folk art museum.
But when one of the museum's first quilt exhibit artists is found dead,
Benni must piece together a pattern of family secrets and small-
town lies to catch the killer.

□ **IRISH CHAIN**   0-425-15137-9/$6.50

When Brady O'Hara and his former girlfriend are murdered at the
San Celina Senior Citizen's Prom, Benni believes it's more than
mere jealousy—and she risks everything to unveil the conspiracy
O'Hara had been hiding for fifty years.

□ **KANSAS TROUBLES**   0-425-15696-6/$6.50

After their wedding, Benni and Gabe visit his hometown near
Wichita. There Benni meets Tyler Brown: aspiring country singer,
gifted quilter, and former Amish wife. But when Tyler is murdered
and the case comes between Gabe and her, Benni learns that her
marriage is much like the Kansas weather: bound to be stormy.

□ **GOOSE IN THE POND**   0-425-16239-7/$6.50
□ **DOVE IN THE WINDOW**   0-425-16894-8/$6.50
